FOR FIVE LONG YEARS, MOLLY MCINTYRE HAS BEEN LIVING EVERY MOTHER'S NIGHTMARE...

When Molly's seventeen-year-old daughter Jennifer went missing five years ago, the police concluded that Jenny had fallen victim to a sexual predator. But now a note from an anonymous "friend" offers the tiniest hope that Jenny might still be alive. The news sets Molly on a desperate quest that puts her and the young woman who might be her daughter on a collision course with a brutal killer who will stop at nothing to protect himself from being exposed and brought to justice.

Praise for James L. Thane's most recent novel Tyndall

"...Retired homicide detective Jack Oliva's heartbreaking investigation of his grandfather's death...uncovers secrets that even a detective as accustomed to skullduggery as Oliva might prefer not to know..." — *Bryan Gruley, Edgar-nominated author of the Starvation Lake and Bleak Harbor mysteries*

Previous Works

"Thane reads like Michael Connelly and his Phoenix is detailed."—*Paul French, CrimeReads*

"... *South of the Deuce* sizzles '¹'   summer...as Phoenix homicide down a sadistic killer.... James hand ..." — *Owen Laukkanen,*

"*Crossroads* is a deep dive into the kind of deadly conflict that a vast and beautiful landscape can produce. ... An engrossing read!"— *Gerry Boyle, author of Strawman and the Jack McMorrow mysteries.*

"*Fatal Blow* is a meticulous and engrossing procedural...."— *Lou Berney, Edgar Award winning author of The Long and Faraway Gone*

"*Fatal Blow* is one of the best procedurals I've read in years. Packed with twists and turns and unexpected revelations .... Thane's finest yet!" — *Christine Carbo, Award-winning author of The Wild Inside*

"*No Place to Die* is a two-in-one treat, a convincing police procedural bolted to a nail-biter suspense novel. A good novel gives you real people in a real place, and James L. Thane delivers both..." — *Sam Reaves, Author of Mean Town Blues*

"*No Place to Die* is an auspicious beginning to what I hope will become a series. Sean and Maggie make a great crime-solving team." — *Barbara D'Amato, Author of Death of a Thousand Cuts*

"An excellent debut..." — *The Poisoned Pen Booknews*

"An engaging police procedural that hooks the audience. ... Readers will relish James L. Thane's tense thriller." — *The Mystery Gazette*

"A fast action thriller" — *Suspense Magazine*

PICTURE ME GONE

James L. Thane

Moonshine Cove Publishing, LLC
Abbeville, South Carolina U.S.A.
First Moonshine Cove Edition Nov 2022

ISBN: 9781952439360

Library of Congress LCCN: 2022911767

Cover image provided by the author; cover and interior design by Moonshine Cove staff

James L. Thane was born and raised in western Montana. He has worked as a janitor, a dry cleaner, an auto parts salesman, a sawyer, an ambulance driver, and a college professor. Always an avid reader, Thane was introduced to the world of crime fiction at a tender age by his father  and mother who were fans of Erle Stanley Gardner and Agatha Christie, respectively. He began his own writing career by contributing articles on intramural basketball games to his high school newspaper. He is the author of four novels featuring Phoenix homicide detective Sean Richardson: *No Place to Die*, *Until Death*, *Fatal Blow*, and *South of the Deuce*. He has also written two stand-alone mystery novels, *Crossroads*, which is set in the Flathead Valley of northwestern Montana and *Tyndall*, which is set in South Dakota. Jim is active on Goodreads, and you may also find him on Facebook, Twitter and at his web site. He divides his time between Scottsdale, Arizona and Lakeside, Montana.

.

www.jameslthane.com

Other Works

Novels

No Place to Die

Until Death

Fatal Blow

South of the Deuce

Crossroads

Tyndall

Nonfiction

A Governor's Wife on the Mining Frontier

In memory of my father and mother,
who instilled in me at a very early age a love of crime
fiction

Part 1

The message was handwritten in black ink, carefully printed in small block letters on a piece of cheap white paper, four inches by six; it could have been torn from any notepad that the supply room had dispensed in the last twenty-five years. Molly McIntyre found the note, folded precisely in half and sealed in a plain white envelope, when she came back inside from a cigarette break just after ten o'clock on a Monday morning early in March.

Molly had first begun smoking when she was a junior in high school, a skinny, awkward kid, struggling to be cool. She'd then quit at the age of twenty, having finally blossomed into an attractive, self-confident young woman who was on the academic fast track that would ultimately lead to an M.B.A. from an excellent university. She'd also wised up and realized that smoking was a filthy and expensive addiction, and that she probably had little chance of living to a ripe old age unless she conquered it. But then, at thirty-nine, she'd surrendered to the habit once again, needing something to occupy her time and to steady her nerves, and having abruptly lost any interest in living to a ripe old age.

Molly dropped into her chair and turned to face the desk. Then she opened the envelope, noting that while her own name was printed on the outside of the envelope, there was nothing to indicate who might have left it. She took out the slip of paper, unfolded it and read:

www.FantacieLand.com
>Independent Escorts
>Brunettes

Molly looked up but saw no one hanging around outside of the office, waiting to gauge her reaction. She saw only Karen, her administrative assistant, sitting at her own desk, apparently working on the report that Molly had assigned her earlier in the morning. Molly rose from the chair, walked through the door, and waited until Karen looked up at her. "Who left this?" she asked, holding the envelope in her right hand.

Karen shook her head. "I have no idea. What is it?"

"Just a note," Molly replied, shaking her own head now, as if the matter were of no great consequence. "Who came into my office while I was outside?"

"No one, at least not that I saw. I ducked down to the Ladies' for a minute, but otherwise I was sitting here the whole time. Nobody's come by."

Molly knew damned good and well that "a minute" down at "the Ladies,'" had probably been more like ten, during which someone had slipped in and left the envelope. Standing at Karen's desk, Molly surveyed the large outer office. The seven members of her staff all appeared to be working diligently, and no one seemed to be paying the slightest bit of attention to her.

Molly was not about to log onto some blatantly obvious pornographic website, leaving a trail for the thought police in the Data Services department to follow directly back to her company computer. But she was curious to know why someone might have sent her the note, so she dug her iPad out of her bag and propped it on the desk in front of her.

While she waited for the device to waken and connect to the company's wireless network, she turned to study the photo of Alan and Jenny that sat on the corner of the desktop. Molly had taken the picture at the peak of the Syieh Pass trail in Glacier National Park, a month before Jenny had begun her senior year in high school and six months before Molly's own life had imploded. From the photo Molly's husband and daughter smiled back at her, framed by mountain peaks in the distance and a deep narrow valley below. Jenny had her right arm around her father's waist, the two of them tired and windblown, but elated at having finally reached the summit.

The iPad sprung to life and Molly tapped on the "Safari" icon. Glancing for a moment at the note lying on her desk, she typed "www.FantacieLand.com" into the web address box.

After a couple of seconds, the screen refreshed and Molly found herself looking at a photo of a young blonde with oversized breasts, wearing what Molly imagined was supposed to be a seductive smile and very little else. Next to the picture, a banner promised that FantacieLand was the home of Phoenix's "most desirable escorts." Below the banner and the photo, a warning advised that this was an adult site open only to viewers over the age of twenty-one. The warning made a number of disclaimers and offered Molly the option of entering or leaving the site.

She tapped "Enter," and the next page showed an even more scantily clad woman—a brunette this time—and offered Molly a selection of "Independent Escorts," "Agency Girls," "Massage," or "Double Delights." Checking the note again, she chose "Independent Escorts."

The page refreshed again, now offering her a choice of "Blondes," "Brunettes," "Redheads," or "All Independents." Molly selected "Brunettes," and the next page contained perhaps two dozen thumbnail-sized photos of women, all of whom were brunettes. Most of the pictures were head and shoulders shots, but in a few cases the women's faces were concealed and the photos showed little more than the women's breasts spilling out of their bras.

Molly scanned the photos, wondering what she was supposed to be looking for. The photo fourth from the last showed the left profile of a young woman named Amber, with long dark hair parted in the middle and pulled back to expose her ear. A thin red strap hung off the girl's shoulder, and the picture caught her smiling and looking back at the photographer over her shoulder.

Molly picked up the iPad and studied the photo more closely. Then she tapped the picture. The screen refreshed, now showing a larger version of the photo. Even though the girl was virtually naked, there was nothing remotely seductive about the picture. It suggested, rather, a sense of innocence and vulnerability. The girl continued to smile over

11

her shoulder, and her deep brown eyes now seemed to be looking directly into Molly's.

To the right of the photo was a message, apparently written by the young woman, which indicated that she was five feet, seven inches tall; that she weighed one hundred and twenty pounds, and that she was a "natural 36C-24-35." The text indicated that she had no piercings or tattoos and that she was "a premier, upscale companion for gentlemen 35 and over." The girl noted that she was available for incall or outcall appointments and provided a phone number.

Transfixed, Molly studied the photo for a long fifteen seconds. Slowly shaking her head, she pulled her eyes away from the photo on the iPad and looked back toward the one on the corner of her desk.

And then Molly McIntyre collapsed in a heap on the floor next to her chair.

Five Years Earlier...

2

At thirty-five degrees, the temperature was unseasonably warm for Minneapolis in the middle of February, and so Molly McIntyre and her seventeen-year-old daughter, Jenny, decided to take advantage of the opportunity to run outside for a change. Their route took them four blocks straight down the street from their home to a large city park. Several trails meandered through the park, allowing them to cobble together a three-mile course without having to run on city streets, dodging traffic and the piles of snow that were still left from the last major storm.

They ran at a reasonable pace—fast enough to give them both a workout, but slow enough so that they could talk along the way. A few other runners were out taking advantage of the break in the weather as well, and some children were sledding down a large hill in the middle of the park. For the most part, though, Molly and Jenny had the place pretty much to themselves.

Molly talked a bit about her work and Jenny filled her mother in on the events of the week at school. Otherwise, they ran in a companionable silence, which they often did, enjoying the fresh air and each other's company. As they reached the edge of the park on the return trip home, the sun was fading from the sky. They stepped into the street and Jenny tapped her mother on the arm. Pointing off to her left, she whispered, "Mom, look. A red fox!"

Molly turned, scanning the vegetation behind her, trying to pick the fox out of the darkening background. As she did, Jenny broke into a sprint, tearing down the street toward home. Molly turned back to see her daughter open a distance of a quarter-block between them. Laughing, she said to herself, "Goddammit, Molly. You're too old to fall for that stupid trick."

Molly lowered her head and raced after her daughter. With three blocks to go, the girl was now about fifty yards ahead, but Molly knew better than to try to make up the deficit too soon. Her daughter was quick off the blocks, but Molly realized that Jenny could not maintain her current pace for the entire distance between the park and the house.

Pumping her arms and breathing deeply, Molly set a quick but steady pace. By the time they were two blocks from home, she'd closed the gap to about thirty yards and Jenny was slowing visibly. One block from the house, Molly pulled alongside her daughter, turned and smiled. "You broke too soon, Babe."

Molly ran in tandem with Jenny for another half block, then tapped her arm and said, "See you at home, Jen."

With that, Molly exploded into one final burst, leaving Jenny panting in her wake. Molly raced up the driveway and slapped the back door with her palm, scoring another stupendous, record-breaking, come-from-behind victory.

Ten seconds later, Jenny tapped the back door with her right hand, then bent over and planted her hands on her knees, gasping for air. "Damn it, Mom. That is so *freaking* unfair. You're twenty years older than me."

Molly reached over, pulled the girl's stocking cap from her head and tussled her hair. Laughing, she said, "Take it up with your father, Hon. You inherited all those slow genes from his side of the family, not mine."

Molly unlocked the door and they walked into the kitchen to find the answering machine blinking and begging for attention. Jenny punched the button to play the message and heard the voice of Melinda Anderson, the next-door neighbor. "Hey, Jenny, I saw you and your mom go running down the street about thirty minutes ago, so I'm assuming you'll be home fairly soon. We just got a last-minute invitation to dinner and I was wondering if you could sit Mary Ellen. I'd need you at six, if that's okay. Give me a call when you get back, will you? Thanks, Hon."

Jenny looked to her mother and said, "What's for dinner?"

"Pork chops and fried potatoes."

"Just my luck. There's still some lasagna from last night, isn't there?"

"Yeah. Do you want me to reheat some while you shower?"

"That'd be great. Thanks."

* * *

Twenty minutes later, Jenny was back downstairs, showered and dressed in jeans and a sweater. She ate the reheated pasta sitting at the kitchen counter, talking with her mother while Molly puttered around the kitchen beginning the dinner she would now eat alone with her husband, Alan. At five minutes before six, Jenny dropped her plate into the dishwasher, gathered up her schoolwork, and hugged her mom goodbye. "I've got an early meeting tomorrow," Molly said. "So I'll probably be in bed by the time you get home. Have a good evening."

Standing at the kitchen door, Jenny turned back to her mother. "I will. Love you, Mom."

"Love you too, Sweetie."

3

Jenny McIntyre had been babysitting for the Andersons since she was thirteen years old and since Mary Ellen, the Andersons' daughter, was two. The Andersons, who lived next door, were in their middle thirties when Mary Ellen was born, and the baby had come as a complete surprise after the couple had reluctantly concluded that they would be unable to have any children.

The Andersons were elated at their good fortune and for the next couple of years they doted on the baby. However once Mary Ellen had reached the age where she could safely be entrusted to the care of a babysitter, the Andersons had resumed a fairly hectic social schedule. In consequence, Jenny's college savings account had increased rather nicely over the space of four years' time.

Mary Ellen was now six and Jenny was seventeen, an attractive high school senior with a social life of her own, which meant that she rarely had much time any more for babysitting. But the Andersons were her parents' closest friends, and Jenny was happy to help them out of a jam.

Dennis Anderson, dressed for dinner in a sport coat and tie, met Jenny at the door. Standing about five-ten, he had a round face that was somewhat at odds with the rest of his body which was thin and angular, and which reflected the strict attention he paid to his diet and exercise regimen. The first hints of silver were beginning to show at the edges of his thick dark hair, but Dennis was still at the point where the touches of gray made him look distinguished rather than old.

"Hey, Jen," he said. "Thanks for coming on such short notice. Mary Ellen is in the kitchen, finishing her dinner, and, as usual, Melinda is running late. She should be down any minute—I hope."

"That's fine," Jenny said, smiling. "I'll just go check in with Mary Ellen."

She found the little girl in the kitchen, sitting at the table, eating meatloaf and a small baked potato for dinner. Jenny dropped the backpack containing her schoolwork on the counter, and said, "Hey, M.E., how's my favorite neighbor?"

The child smiled brightly. "Fine, J.C.! Mamma said we could watch a movie if I finished all my dinner."

Jenny walked over to the table, leaned over, and hugged Mary Ellen. The little girl set her fork on the plate, twisted in her chair, and returned the hug. Jenny kissed the child on the top of the head and said, "It looks like you've got a ways to go if you think you're going to get to watch a movie."

"Don't worry, I'll finish it all."

"See that you do, young lady," said her mother with a gentle laugh.

Jenny turned to see Melinda come sweeping into the kitchen, late as always, and anxious not to further antagonize her husband, who was standing impatiently at the door looking conspicuously at his watch. Melinda gave Jenny a quick hug and said, "Sorry to be so last minute. The Taylors called an hour ago and asked if we wanted to meet them at the club for dinner. We haven't seen them in forever and I really hated to say no."

"Not a problem," Jenny said. "I can study for my history test as easily here as I can at home."

The woman gave her a smile and then turned toward the door. "Great, and thanks again, Hon. You have my cell number if you need me. Mary Ellen should be in bed by eight, and we should be home by ten."

"Got it. Have a nice evening."

"We will," Melinda replied. Then she turned and hurried to the door where her husband stood waiting. Dennis opened the door and allowed his wife to precede him into the garage. Turning back in the direction of the kitchen table, he smiled, arched his eyebrows, and said, "You girls behave yourselves." And then, without waiting for a response, he closed the door behind him and was gone.

* * *

17

For Jenny, the fact that she and Mary Ellen were both the only children in their respective families created a special bond between them. Once, when their two families were together for a picnic, Jenny had joked that Mary Ellen was the little sister that she otherwise never would have had. Jenny had made the remark somewhat in jest, but she believed that there was more than a grain of truth in the idea, and she sometimes fretted about Mary Ellen as if the little girl *were* in fact her younger sibling.

Jenny knew that she had been extremely lucky in the parent department. Her mother and father were both well-educated professionals who were devoted to each other and to her. Through the years, her parents had created a nurturing family environment, providing exactly the right measure of love, support, and freedom that had enabled Jenny to grow into a strong, intelligent and independent young woman.

Her mother, in particular, was the rock of Jenny's life and seemed to know instinctively when to move in and when to hold back. She had always understood the importance of allowing Jenny the opportunity to sometimes make her own decisions—and occasionally her own mistakes—secure in the knowledge that her mother loved her above all else and that she would always be there whenever Jenny might need her.

Jenny sometimes feared that Mary Ellen would not be so lucky. Jenny never doubted that Melinda and Dennis loved their daughter intensely. The problem, in Jenny's view, was that they expressed their love by hovering over the child's every move, and they trusted her to the care of virtually no one other than themselves, Jenny, and Jenny's parents.

When the little girl had been ready for kindergarten a few months earlier, Melinda had promptly volunteered for a teacher's aide position at the facility. Jenny feared that Melinda was determined to be a constant presence in Mary Ellen's life, in school as well as at home, and that she would effectively suffocate the girl, never allowing her the freedom and the space she would need to become a well-rounded and self-sufficient person in her own right.

In a few short months, Jenny would be leaving for college, and from that point on she would inevitably have much less direct contact with Mary Ellen. But she was determined not to lose touch completely, and she fervently hoped that, even from a distance, she might still serve as a positive role model for her "little sister" to emulate.

* * *

Fifteen minutes after the Andersons had left, Jenny rinsed Mary Ellen's plate, put it into the dishwasher and joined the little girl in the family room. For about the one hundred and forty-seventh time, they watched *The Little Mermaid*. Clutching a throw pillow, Mary Ellen snuggled up against Jenny and watched entranced, as though she'd never seen the movie before. Jenny listened to the dialogue with one arm draped around Mary Ellen. With the other hand, she flipped through the pages of the textbook for her AP American History class, reviewing the material for the test the following day.

The movie ended a little before eight o'clock, and Mary Ellen brushed her teeth and went to bed without complaint. Jenny sat on the edge of the bed for a few minutes as the child faded quickly into sleep, then she slipped out of the room and went back downstairs.

She wandered into the kitchen, helped herself to a chocolate chip cookie, and settled back onto the couch with her history book, still trying to understand the causes of the Great Depression. In particular, she was having trouble comprehending the consequences of the Hawley-Smoot Tariff, and the textbook's explanation might as well have been written in Greek.

In her haste to get over to the Andersons, Jenny had left her phone in the charger in her bedroom, which meant that she could not resort to Google in the hope of finding a clearer explanation. She knew that Dennis had a set of encyclopedias in his study and even though the room was supposed to be off-limits to everyone except Dennis, she really needed to be prepared for the test. Accordingly, she swallowed the last of the cookie, rose from the couch and headed down the hall in the direction of the study.

The thirty-two volumes of the Encyclopedia Britannica were lined up on the bottom shelf of a row of bookcases that lined the wall behind Dennis's desk. Jenny dropped to the floor and pulled out the volume for G-H but found no reference to Hawley. She returned the book to the shelf, scooted over and grabbed the volume for R-S. She pulled the book out of the shelf and as she did, she noticed a small manila envelope stuck behind the encyclopedias.

Jenny did not think of herself as a snoop, but her curiosity was naturally aroused and so she retrieved the envelope and opened it to find several photographs. She carefully pulled the first picture out of the envelope and suddenly froze in place. The image before her was simply incomprehensible, and looking at it she slowly shook her head.

She pulled the second, third and fourth pictures from the envelope and carefully studied them for several minutes, unable to believe what she was seeing. Her stomach roiling, she finally slipped one of the photos into the back pocket of her jeans. She returned the other three pictures to the envelope and put the envelope and the book back where she had found them. Then she snapped off the lights in the study and went back out to the family room to wait for the Andersons to return home.

4

Three days after Jenny discovered the photos in Dennis Anderson's study, Molly McIntyre got home from work a little after five p.m. She walked from the garage into the kitchen and dropped her keys on the counter where she usually left them, next to the small television set.

Alan's car was not in the garage and so Molly knew that he was not home from work yet. But she was surprised to see that the house was dark, which meant that Jenny had not come home yet either. Walking down the hall toward her study, Molly called out her daughter's name but received no reply.

Molly continued on down the hall to the master bedroom. She took off her suit and hung it in the closet, then slipped into her favorite jeans and pulled on a sweater. She walked back out to the kitchen and poured herself a glass of Zinfandel. She'd just begun pulling things out of the refrigerator to start dinner when she heard the sound of the garage door rolling up. Thirty seconds later, her husband walked through the door from the garage into the kitchen.

At forty-one, Alan was still fit and trim with a full head of dark wavy hair. His chiseled good looks still attracted admiring glances from lots of other women, and Molly was proud of the fact that her husband, unlike so many of his contemporaries, had refused to allow himself to begin the long, irreversible slide into the middle age wasteland of beer guts, slovenly habits, and hideous fashion choices.

Like most couples who'd been married for nearly twenty years, they'd had their occasional problems. But they'd worked through them, and Molly firmly believed that their marriage—and their love for each other—had emerged even stronger on the other side.

Like most women her age, Molly also had her guilty secrets. Thankfully, they were few in number and she kept them locked away as tightly as she could. She assumed that Alan had his own secrets, which meant nothing more than the fact that they were both fallible human beings. But Molly was secure in the fact that her husband loved her and that she loved him, now more than ever, and as only a mature and experienced woman could.

Alan walked around the large island in the middle of the room and gave his wife a quick kiss. Then he folded his suit coat over the back of a kitchen stool and poured himself a glass of the Zin. "How was your day?" he asked.

Molly set a head of Romaine out onto the counter and fluttered her hand. "Okay. How about yours?"

He shrugged. "All right. I had to endure a two-hour meeting with Mike and the other finance guys this afternoon and so needless to say, I'm glad to be home, sitting here with a drink in my hand."

She gave him a smile and began pulling apart the lettuce. "Do you know where Jen is?"

"I have no idea. Isn't she home yet?"

Molly shook her head. "She didn't say anything to you about being late for some reason?"

"Nope."

Alan turned in the direction of the phone on the counter behind him. "And, she didn't call and leave a message?"

Again, Molly shook her head.

Alan looked at his watch. "Well, we're still forty minutes short of dinner time. She'll be along."

* * *

An hour later, Molly and Alan sat facing each other across the kitchen table. Their daughter's dinner was in the oven keeping warm, but Jenny herself was still not home. Alan had called her cell phone, but he'd been answered only by voice mail. He watched his wife pick at her salmon and said, "Don't worry, Hon. I'm sure she just got hung up somewhere and forgot that she'd turned off her cell. She'll be here soon."

Molly set her fork down on the plate and shook her head. "You know as well as I do how important that phone is to her. She *never* turns it off."

"Yeah, well, maybe she just forgot to charge it again."

"That's possible. Still, it's not like her to be this late without calling. And certainly, she could have borrowed someone else's phone if hers was dead." Rising from her chair, she said, "You go ahead and finish eating. I'm going to make a couple of calls and see if I can track her down."

Alan understood that this behavior definitely *was* atypical of their daughter who was mature for her age and who was normally very responsible about things like this. Too worried now to finish his own dinner, he sat at the kitchen table and listened as Molly tried Jenny's cell phone, again without getting a response.

Molly then called four of Jenny's friends, but none of them had seen Jenny since the end of the school day, and none of them knew what plans she might have had for the rest of the afternoon. Angela Rinaldi, who had long been Jenny's closest friend, suggested that Jenny had seemed a little distant and maybe a little depressed over the last few days, "like not her usual self, you know? At lunch today I asked her if anything was wrong, but she said no, that she was fine and not to worry."

Thinking back, it struck Molly that Jenny *had* been a bit withdrawn and maybe even a little snippy on a few occasions over the last couple of days. Perhaps she was worried or preoccupied with something. But whatever the problem might have been, she had not seen fit to share it with her mother.

* * *

At ten o'clock, when Jenny still had not come home and still had not called her parents, Alan McIntyre called the police to report his daughter missing. A patrolman came out to take the report and asked if any of Jenny's things were missing as well. "What do you mean by that?" Alan said. "Are you suggesting that our daughter might have run away or something?"

23

The policeman shook his head. "Look, Mr. McIntyre, I'm a father myself. Believe me, I understand how worried you are. But when a teenager disappears, this is always a possibility that we have to consider. Have there been any family problems lately—any disagreements or maybe a disciplinary situation that caused her to be upset with you or her mother?"

Before Alan could respond, Molly said, "No, officer. None whatsoever. We've both always had a very strong and close relationship with Jenny. She's a good girl and an honor student. We've rarely ever had to discipline her for anything. The last time was nearly a year ago and we've had no problems since."

"And you say that you've talked to her girlfriends. They have no ideas to offer?"

"No, none." Alan said.

"Your daughter is seventeen; is there a boyfriend in the picture?"

"Yes," Molly said. "But I talked to his mother a couple of hours ago. I then talked to Brian himself when he came home from a basketball game. He hasn't seen or heard from Jenny since noon and he's now worried sick as well. He volunteered to go out and check some of the places where the kids usually hang out, but we haven't heard anything from him since."

The police officer made a couple of notes and jotted down the names and contact information of Jenny's closest friends. "Okay," he said. "Now if you don't mind, why don't you show me your daughter's bedroom and tell me if anything seems to be missing or out of order there."

Molly and Alan walked the patrolman up the stairs and showed him Jenny's room, which was clean and neat as a pin. The bed was made, with the pillows fluffed and resting on a comforter that had been carefully folded down, revealing a set of pale blue sheets. A mug filled with pens and pencils sat on the desk along with a photo of Molly and Alan and another of a young man that the officer assumed was Brian, the boyfriend. A couple of books sat on the desk, their spines carefully aligned with the edge of the desk.

Molly opened the closet door to reveal her daughter's wardrobe, with all the clothes hung up in perfect order. In spite of the gravity of the situation, the policeman smiled and shook his head. "This doesn't look like the room of any teenager I've ever seen before. Do you have maid service?"

"No," Molly said. "Jenny is responsible for her own room and this is the way she always keeps it."

Again, the patrolman smiled. "Well, if you don't mind, as soon as she gets home, I'd like to borrow her for a couple of days and let her teach my kids a lesson or two."

Checking the room, Jenny's parents quickly concluded that nothing unexpected appeared to be missing. "Our daughter does have a cell phone," Alan said, "and I don't see it here. But she always carries it her, so I wouldn't expect it to be here."

Pointing at the empty space in the middle of the desk, he said, "She also has a small laptop. About half the time she shoves it in her backpack and takes it to school with her. Obviously, it's not here, but that's not unusual."

Molly turned away for a moment and then turned back, wiping a tear out of her eye. She stepped over, linked her arm through her husband's, and said, "Please believe me, officer. Our daughter had absolutely no reason to run away from home, and there's nothing missing here that would suggest that she has.

"She's a very responsible girl. In her whole life, she has never failed to come home like this or to call us to let us know that she would be late. Obviously, something has happened to her. She's been in an accident or, God forbid, someone has taken her. Please, you've got to help us find her."

The patrolman nodded sympathetically. "As I said, Ma'am, I have children of my own. We'll do everything we can."

5

In the three days after Molly and Alan McIntyre reported their daughter missing, the Minneapolis police interviewed Jenny's friends, the teachers at her school, all the immediate neighbors and the people who worked at the homeless shelter where Jenny volunteered. All the people interviewed insisted that they had no idea where Jenny might have gone or what might have happened to her.

Efforts to trace the location of the girl's cell phone failed and the service provider reported that no calls had been made from or received by the phone since noon on the day that Jenny's parents had reported her missing. Her e-mail and social media accounts had also been dormant since that time.

The police also spoke quietly with the McIntyres' family doctor and with the nurse at school, wondering if perhaps the girl might have suddenly found herself pregnant and, unable to face her parents, had run away from home without confiding in any of her friends. But neither the nurse nor the doctor could offer any evidence to support such a possibility.

Jenny's boyfriend, Brian, confirmed Angela Rinaldi's impression that Jenny had been upset about something in the two or three days prior to her disappearance. He told the police that he and Jenny had studied together until ten o'clock the night before she went missing. Jenny had been unusually quiet, he said—moody and distant, and completely uninterested in the assignment that the chemistry teacher had given them.

Brian told the detectives that he initially feared that Jenny might have been angry with him for some reason. She had denied this, he said, and would tell him only that someone close to her had deeply disappointed her. Then she had dissolved into tears. The young man said that he had attempted to comfort her, but she refused to tell him anything more.

He had no idea who might have disappointed Jenny or how; he knew only that she had assured him that he was not to blame.

Brian's story left Molly thoroughly confused and she couldn't imagine who might have disappointed Jenny so bitterly. More important, she could not understand why her daughter would not have confided in her about the issue, whatever it might have been.

A week and a half after Jenny failed to come home, Molly was sitting alone in the living room, still trying to imagine why Jenny might have been so upset, when the doorbell rang. And as it had every time the phone had rung or someone had come to the door during that interminable and unbearable wait, Molly's heart leapt into her throat. Ten days after her only child had disappeared without a trace, Molly was reduced to pleading with a god she did not believe in to please let it be Jenny on the porch or at the other end of the phone call. And, at the same time, she was nearly immobilized by the prospect that instead, someone was calling or had arrived at the door, only to tell her that Jenny would never be coming home again.

Her heart pounding, Molly raced to the front door and opened it to find Marian Burns, a neighbor who lived three doors down the street. On seeing each other, both women burst into tears. Marian gathered Molly into her arms and said, "Oh Honey, I'm so sorry. We just got back from Florida and heard about Jenny. Is there any news?"

The two women finally broke their embrace and Molly shook her head. "No, Marian. Not a word. No one's seen her and we've heard nothing from her. It's as if she simply vanished into thin air."

"And none of the neighbors reported seeing anything?"

"No, why do you ask?"

As Burns hesitated, apparently struggling to find the right words, Molly reached out and gripped her friend's arm. "Marian, did *you* see something?"

Marian waited for another moment, then touched her hand to Molly's shoulder. In a halting voice, she said, "I'm sorry, Molly. I don't know if it means anything or not. But before we left ... There was a man..."

Marian Burns told detectives that on several occasions prior to leaving for Florida, she had noticed a man loitering around the neighborhood in the middle of the afternoon, which was about the time that Jenny McIntyre normally returned home from school.

Burns gave police a fairly detailed description of the man, and when detectives returned with an array of photographs, she immediately identified the picture of a man who'd been released from the state prison system several months earlier after completing his sentence for the attempted rape of a thirteen-year-old girl. He was now living with his widowed sister in a house three blocks away from the McIntyre home.

The police secured a warrant and questioned the man, whose name was William Milovich. Milovich was evasive and obviously nervous. He said that he did occasionally go out for walks in the afternoon and that his route did sometimes take him past the McIntyre house. He admitted that he "might have noticed" the missing girl as he was passing by her home, but he insisted that he had never approached her.

When the police searched Milovich's home, they removed the return air vent in his bedroom. In the ductwork behind the vent, they found several photos of Jenny McIntyre that had been taken, apparently surreptitiously, while the young woman was sunbathing in what she thought was the privacy of her back yard. The detectives also found a bra and a pair of panties in Jenny's size. DNA tests confirmed that the underwear had been worn by the missing girl.

On Milovich's computer, technicians found several additional photographs of Jenny as well as some child pornography. Milovich was then arrested and charged with violations of various laws against child pornography.

Under intense questioning, Milovich admitted that he had taken the digital photos of Jenny without her knowledge. He also confessed to having entered the McIntyre house one morning by opening a sliding glass door that had been left unlocked. He claimed that he had taken the girl's underwear from a basket in the laundry room before noticing a blinking light on the alarm panel. Milovich said he feared that he might have set off a silent alarm and that he had left the home immediately without taking anything else.

A check with the McIntyre's home security firm indicated that the company could find no record of a signal suggesting that the family's security system might have been breached during the week in question. Alan and Molly insisted that it was highly unlikely that the family had somehow neglected to lock the sliding glass door, although they did admit that they sometimes left the house without arming the alarm system.

Milovich continued to insist that he had never spoken to Jennifer McIntyre, that he had never touched the girl, and that he had absolutely nothing whatsoever to do with her disappearance. Painstaking forensic examinations of Milovich's home and of his automobile found no evidence to indicate that the missing young woman had ever been in either the home or the car. Milovich agreed to take a lie detector test, but the results were inconclusive.

In the end, police detectives were unable to develop any additional evidence linking William Milovich to Jenny McIntyre's disappearance. But they were also unable to uncover any other plausible explanation that would account for the fact that the girl had gone missing. Frustrated and exhausted, the detectives unofficially concluded that Milovich had been stalking the young woman. They surmised that he had abducted her using a vehicle other his own, that he had ultimately murdered Jenny and had then disposed of her body.

The authorities could not charge Milovich on the basis of their suppositions. But based on the evidence they had found on his computer, they did charge him with violations of the child pornography statutes.

Thoroughly drained and emotionally shattered, Molly and Alan McIntyre pleaded with the police and with the county attorney, demanding that they somehow force William Milovich to tell them what he had done with their daughter. But the authorities, sickened and distraught themselves, told the McIntyres they were sorry, but there was nothing more that they could do.

Two months after Jenny disappeared, and six weeks after Milovich had been arrested as a result of the investigation, a devastated Alan McIntyre waited in small group of onlookers as a police van delivered Milovich and several other prisoners to the courthouse where they were scheduled for various judicial procedures. The van came to a halt near the side door to the building and three police officers assisted the shackled prisoners out of the van and began herding them into the courthouse. Milovich was the third man in the procession, and as he shuffled clear of the van, Alan stepped out of the small crowd with a .38 caliber revolver. Raising the weapon, he stepped up to Milovich and said, "This is for Jennifer, you goddamned son of a bitch."

As the bystanders began screaming and ducking for cover, Alan fired three bullets into Milovich at point blank range. Two police officers returned fire, and Alan McIntyre and William Milovich were both pronounced dead at the scene.

6

During the weeks that followed Alan's death, Molly took an extended leave of absence from her job and tumbled into a state of depression and utter despair. And having lost both her daughter and her husband so abruptly and so horribly, she quickly lost any desire to continue living herself.

Molly was not a religious woman and she did not for a moment believe that she might one day be reunited with Jenny and Alan on some beautiful shore in the sweet by and by. The unbearable truth, she knew, was that both her husband and child were lost to her forever and that if nature took its course, Molly herself might easily live for another thirty or forty years in their absence.

There would be, she knew, nothing remotely "easy" about it. And the thought of awakening morning after endless morning to the pain of that loss was more than she could stand.

In the week between Alan's death and his funeral, and for two weeks after that, Molly had surrendered to the "wisdom" of her doctor and had allowed him to pump her full of pills that left her barely conscious, let alone able to function in any vaguely capable fashion. During that period, Melinda was almost constantly by her side, making sure that Molly was fed and attending to her other personal needs, while Dennis negotiated with the police department, the coroner, and the funeral home.

But all the pills and sympathy in the world could not begin to blunt the pain that seared to the core of Molly's being. In her waking hours she wandered through her empty home as if in a trance, moving from room to room, her heart breaking as her mind replayed in an endless slow-motion loop, scenes from the time she had spent there with Alan and Jenny.

The images that haunted her sleep were infinitely more excruciating. Perhaps exacerbated by the drugs she was taking, Molly's nights were dominated by the twin traumas that had been visited upon her.

Although she had not been present when Alan executed William Milovich, the event unfolded in all of its horror every night in her dreams. As clearly as if she *had* been there, she saw the small group of reporters and other observers suddenly panic and duck for cover as her husband stepped out of the crowd and raised the gun. With a grim sense of satisfaction, she watched the surprise register on Milovich's face as the bullets ripped into his chest and abdomen. And helpless, she wept as Alan twisted and slowly slumped to the ground when the police returned fire, a curious mixture of pain, regret and relief spreading over his face.

As traumatic as her visions of Alan's death might have been, her other dreams were infinitely worse. Just as Molly had not actually seen her husband execute William Milovich, she had also never seen her daughter in Milovich's company. But those images too, flooded her mind and woke her screaming from her sleep. And in the end, she blamed herself. She had not been there either for Alan or for Jenny at the times when they had needed her most.

In the immediate aftermath of Alan's death, Molly remained incapable of forming a rational reaction to what he had done. Should she hate him for abandoning her and for leaving her to grieve all alone, not just for the daughter they had lost, but now for him as well?

Should she love him for sacrificing himself in order to achieve some small measure of justice in a situation where justice seemed otherwise unattainable?

Should she envy him for being able to savor in his last moments of consciousness the knowledge that he had been able to avenge his daughter's death? Should she despise him because he had not allowed her to share in that moment?

And what of Jenny?

Molly's mind recoiled at the thought of what her daughter's final hours must have been like. She knew that she would never be able to forgive herself for bringing her daughter into a world where a horror like that could have befallen her, and Molly also knew that she could not go on living with the knowledge that she had been unable to save Jenny from it.

* * *

Three weeks after Alan's death, and two weeks after the funeral, Molly took the last of the doctor's pills from the medicine chest and flushed them down the toilet. She waited three more days to make sure that the effects of the drugs had been completely purged from her system and that she was thus as clear-headed as she could possibly be. Then she carefully set about the business of ending her own life.

At her lawyer's office, she dictated a new will, naming Melinda as her executrix. The will provided that the house, the cars and all of the remaining personal property should be sold and the proceeds combined with Molly's savings and other investments. One hundred thousand dollars of that money was to be placed in a trust to contribute to Mary Ellen Anderson's college education; the remainder was to be divided among a number of charities.

While she waited for the lawyer to draft the will, Molly methodically put her affairs in order. She burned the diary she had kept intermittently through the years, along with some letters and several other personal documents that she wanted no one else to see. She made certain that her finances were in order and that Melinda would be able to easily find a list of investments and of obligations owed.

She cleaned the house thoroughly, determined to leave it in the best condition possible. Figuring that the house should certainly sell within a few months, she signed a six-month contract with a landscaping service to mow the grass and to otherwise maintain the yard so that Melinda and Dennis would not have to worry about it.

Her job, she knew, was in capable hands. In the wake of Alan's death, Molly's boss had told her to take as much time as she needed. Jason Burke, her second in command, had stepped in to act in her absence and Molly was confident that he would do a very good job for the company when her absence became permanent.

33

Late on a Thursday afternoon, Molly slipped into the office and signed the necessary papers to designate her estate, rather than Alan, as the beneficiary of her pension and other company benefits. She had genuinely loved the job and had believed that she was doing something worthwhile with her life that went beyond simply earning a living to help support her family. But sitting alone in her office that afternoon, she wondered if her dedication to her career had somehow produced the catastrophe that had engulfed them all.

It was irrational, she knew, to think that if she had been content to be a housewife, she would have been at home and might have been able to prevent her daughter from falling into the hands of a maniac like William Milovich. But still...

Finally, on a Friday morning, the lawyer's secretary called to say that the will was ready. Molly went into the office that afternoon and signed the document with the lawyer's administrative assistant and secretary serving as the witnesses. An hour later, Molly pulled her car into the garage. At the desk in her study, she wrote a brief note in longhand, explaining that she was sober, free of the influences of any drug, and thus completely rational. "That said," she wrote, "I cannot bear to live without Alan and Jenny and so have decided to take my own life."

Molly signed her name to the end of the note, then slipped it into an envelope addressed "To the Authorities."

She addressed a second envelope to Melinda. On the note she wrote, "Please forgive me, Mel, for taking this way out and for leaving you to clean up the mess. I had no other choice. Love, Molly."

Gathering up the two notes, a copy of her will, and the photo of Alan and Jenny that she'd kept on her desk at the office, Molly made one last bittersweet tour through the house, making sure that everything was in order. Then, tears streaming down her cheeks, she closed the door to the kitchen on her way back out to the garage. In the car, she laid the two notes and the copy of the will on the passenger's seat, then cranked the ignition.

The engine sprung to life, purring softly in the confines of the closed garage. Molly lowered the two front windows and moved the driver's seat back a few inches. Then she settled back into the seat, looking at the picture of Alan and Jenny in her lap, while she waited for the carbon monoxide to work its magic.

* * *

The day had dawned cloudy and cool in northwestern Montana, and the temperature was still only in the mid-fifties when Molly, Alan and Jenny had walked across the parking lot from their motel in West Glacier to the café early that morning. Wearing tee shirts, sweatshirts, and jackets over their hiking shorts, they huddled together in a booth in the restaurant, drinking coffee and eating a hearty breakfast of pancakes, bacon, and eggs.

The temperature was even cooler at the Logan Pass visitors' center, thirty-five hundred feet in elevation above West Glacier. They'd stopped long enough to use the restrooms and then had driven over the top of the pass, down the narrow, two-lane highway to the trailhead near Siyeh Creek, six thousand feet above sea level.

Anxious to be under way, they quickly slipped out of their running shoes and into the new hiking boots that they'd broken in by walking through their neighborhood in Minneapolis. Then they shouldered the hydration backpacks containing the water and other provisions that they thought should be sufficient for a long day on the trail, and the three of them set out into the woods.

They climbed slowly through the forested northern face of Going-to-the-Sun Mountain, through thick stands of fir and spruce. An hour later, at Preston Park, the forest gave way to a magnificent field of wildflowers blowing gently in the breeze.

At seven thousand feet, the trees and the wildflowers disappeared, and the trail began switching back and forth across the rock-littered mountain slope, offering spectacular views of the surrounding mountains, the glaciers and snowfields, and the valleys below.

The slope, which had been fairly gentle initially, was much steeper by then and the climbing was significantly harder. By all appearances, Molly, Alan, and Jenny were in much better physical shape than many of the other hikers who were attempting the climb, and they passed several people who had stopped to rest along the way. Even at that, Molly found herself breathing hard and now having to stop occasionally to rest herself.

By the time they had reached seventy-five hundred feet, her thighs were screaming for mercy and the final five hundred feet of the climb seemed to take hours. Finally, though, they reached the last crest of the trail up the mountain and walked gratefully into the barren saddle of Siyeh pass.

The wind was blowing fiercely at the summit and the three of them zippered back into the jackets that they'd removed on the way up the trail. But the view around them was breathtaking and they stood for several minutes, turning in every direction, soaking it in.

Jenny, in particular, was ecstatic. When the family decided to vacation in Glacier National Park, Jenny had been the one who did the research and enthusiastically recommended that the family hike the Siyeh Pass trail. And even though they hadn't yet seen the remaining half of the hike down the other side of the mountain, they agreed unanimously that this was a once-in-a-lifetime experience.

They ate their lunch, sitting at the edge of the mountain and drinking in the view around them. Then Molly directed Alan and Jenny to stand together at the summit so that she could take the picture she now clung to in her lap. As the engine continued to pump carbon monoxide into the garage, Molly wiped at her tears and lifted the picture closer to her face. It had captured one of the happiest moments in their lives together—a moment once known only to the three of them and now known only to Molly.

In a few more minutes that moment, and all of the other private moments that the three of them had shared together, would be known to no one. It would be as if they had never happened at all, and it was that sudden realization that jolted Molly to the understanding that she could not take her own life. As long as she lived, Jenny and Alan would live also, in the memories that she alone possessed. Without Molly to nurture and preserve those memories, the two of them would die all over again. And though for the rest of her life she might blame herself for failing Alan and Jenny, she could not, in the end, allow herself to abandon them in such a fashion.

Her tears falling more freely now, Molly leaned forward and turned off the ignition. The act of doing so made her head swim, and she realized that the deadly gas had been working much more rapidly than she had thought. She leaned to her left, lifted the door handle, and used the weight of her body to force the door open.

Clinging to the door, she slowly pulled herself out of the car. Without closing the car door, she forced herself to walk the few steps to the door that led to the kitchen. Leaning against the door, she twisted the knob and fell into the kitchen as the door opened. Lying on the tile floor, she took two deep breaths and then pushed the door closed with her foot.

* * *

During the five years that followed that afternoon, Molly devoted her life to her job and she gradually lost touch with virtually all the people with whom she had socialized in her former life.

Most of her friends, even including people that she and Alan had known for years, felt awkward in Molly's presence, not knowing what they should say or how they should act. Molly did not want to make her friends uncomfortable, nor did she want to cast a pall over their gatherings. Even more than that, she no longer shared most of the interests and concerns that dominated the lives of her friends. All the endless cocktail party chatter about vacations, politics, beauty treatments, shopping and restaurants that had once been of such vital interest to Molly, now seemed trivial and unimportant.

In particular, Molly could no longer bear to listen to conversations about the problems of raising teenagers, and about their soccer games, swim meets, tennis matches and other such activities. She had once enthusiastically attended school plays, concerts, and athletic events. She had delighted in exchanging stories about the children's exploits and accomplishments. But that was another world altogether, a world from which Molly had been abruptly and tragically expelled.

A week after deciding that she could not end her own life, Molly returned to work. Four weeks after that, she sold her house and bought a condominium in a new development several miles away from her old neighborhood. And almost immediately thereafter, she lost touch with virtually everyone from her former life.

Only Melinda and Dennis had refused to let Molly slip away. They understood how awkward and emotionally difficult it would be for Molly to remain a part of their old social circle, and they did not insist that she should attempt to do so. They made it clear that Molly was always welcome at the barbecues, parties, and other such gatherings that they continued to host, but they also understood when Molly always declined.

And so, in the end, her social life narrowed down to the occasional dinner with Melinda and Dennis and to a girl's night out every once in a while, with Melinda or with one of the few other single women that Molly had met since moving into the condominium. And for Molly that was sufficient.

She spent the bulk of her evenings and weekends alone, working, reading, and watching movies and the occasional television program. In spite of the fact that she had begun smoking again, she went for long walks and otherwise exercised enough to stay in reasonably good shape, although she wasn't really sure why she bothered. She spent an occasional Saturday afternoon in a museum or gallery, sometimes eating an early dinner in a small quiet restaurant where a woman eating alone would be left to do so in peace.

And she continued to wear her wedding ring on the third finger of her left hand so as to discourage any man who might otherwise have been inclined to take an interest.

The Present Day...

7

Given that the envelope had been hand delivered, with no stamp and only her name on it, Molly assumed that the message directing her to FantacieLand.com had been left for her by someone within the company and most likely within her own department. The people within the department would have seen Jenny's pictures more often than any of the other employees, and they were much more aware of the circumstances surrounding her disappearance. It seemed logical then, that Molly begin her search for the person who had sent her the note within her own office. If she had no success there, she could broaden the scope of her inquiries.

After stewing about it most of the day, Molly picked up the phone and asked Jason Burke to step into her office. Burke, who supervised the company's training programs, was Molly's most valuable staff member and her heir apparent as Vice President for Human Resources.

Thirty-six years old, Jason was recently divorced after being married for eleven years to the woman who'd been his college sweetheart. He was a little over six feet tall with blue eyes and dark hair that he wore a bit on the longish side. In an environment where "Casual Friday" had fairly quickly conquered the rest of the workweek, Jason refused to follow the herd and instead continued to dress like a responsible adult. He appeared at Molly's door a couple of minutes later, wearing a crisp white shirt and a maroon tie with a muted pattern over a pair of dark gray dress slacks. Molly beckoned him into the office and asked him to shut the door. Given the sensitive nature of the conversations they often had, this was not an unusual request, and so Jason closed the door, dropped into the chair next to Molly's desk and said, "What's up?"

Molly waited a moment, then said, "This is kind of a delicate matter, Jason."

Burke said nothing and simply arched his eyebrows as if encouraging her to continue. Molly slid the envelope that she had received across the desk in his direction. "Someone left this envelope on my desk this morning. I'm wondering if you know anything about it."

A look of confusion spread across Jason's face. He picked up the envelope and turned it over, carefully examining both sides. Then he set it back on the desk and shook his head. "Sorry, but I've never seen it before. And I'd certainly never send you something without putting my name on it."

Molly nodded, biting her lower lip. "I understand that, Jason. It's just that this message was something out of the ordinary that had nothing to do with company business."

"I don't understand. What was in the message?"

She shook her head slightly. "Something very personal and extremely important. I believe that someone is trying to help me but feels that they must do so anonymously. Perhaps because of the nature of the message, the person might fear that I would judge them badly or something. That isn't the case at all. I'm very grateful that this matter was brought to my attention. But I desperately need to know what else this person knows about the situation, and since he or she didn't sign the note, I don't know how to contact them."

Burke shifted in his chair. "Are you asking me if I sent the message?"

"Did you? ... Please, Jason. Honestly, I'm making no judgments here. But if you did send the note, then you must know how important this is to me."

Looking directly into her eyes, Burke hesitated for a moment, then said, "I'm sorry Molly. Whatever this is about, I can see that it *is* very important to you. But I didn't send the message, and I have no idea who might have."

Molly glanced away for a moment to the photo of Jenny and Alan that sat on the desk. Then she turned back to Burke. Leaning forward, she said in a soft voice, "You were in Phoenix last month at a conference, weren't you?"

Burke shrugged. "You know I was. You signed the travel forms. But why are you asking about that?"

Molly waited a moment, then shook her head. "It's not important, I guess. You can go ahead and get back to work."

Rising from the chair, Burke gave his boss an apologetic look. "Okay. Sorry I couldn't be more help."

* * *

Molly sat for a moment, considering the situation. It was now too late in the workday to pursue the matter further and so she picked up her cell phone and called Melinda Anderson. Obviously seeing Molly's name on the caller ID, Melinda picked up the phone and said, "Hey, Molly, what's up?"

"Oh, mostly the usual crap. But thankfully, it's almost five o'clock. How are you?"

"Well, as always, I'm going ninety miles an hour in forty different directions trying to keep up with Mary Ellen's hectic schedule, but otherwise I'm fine."

"Hey, listen, Mel. I'm sorry to ask on such short notice, but I was wondering if you guys might be free to get together for a drink tonight. I have a problem I'd like to discuss with you."

"What sort of problem?"

"Well, it's something I'd really like to discuss in person and with both you and Dennis."

"This sounds serious."

"Yes, it is actually."

"Say no more, Hon. I tell you what. Why don't you come over for dinner? I'm making a beef stew and believe me, there'll be more than enough. We can have a couple glasses of wine and you can tell us what's on your mind."

"That sounds great, Mel, but I don't want to intrude into your evening."

"Oh, crap. You know full well that we'd all enjoy it if you did, and I'm not going to take no for an answer, especially since you've aroused my curiosity like this. Why don't you come over straight from work? You and I can have a drink or two and talk girl talk while we wait for Denny to get home."

"Okay, Mel, you convinced me. I am going to run by my condo and change quickly, but I can probably be there by five forty-five. Is that okay?"

"That would be perfect. See you then, Hon."

8

An hour later, Molly pulled into the Andersons' driveway, and, as she always did, she sat for a moment, looking across the narrow strip of grass that divided their house from the home that she had once shared with Alan and Jenny.

The temperature was somewhere in the middle twenties, and the gusting wind had blown a few inches of snow up against the foundation of the house. The drapes in front of the picture window were open and someone had turned on a lamp in the living room. The warm glow of the light shining through the window contrasted sharply with the frigid scene outside.

The new owners had repainted the house, changing the color that Molly felt had perfectly suited her home. They had also made some major changes to the landscaping, and looking at the house and yard, Molly was always deeply conflicted. She had loved the house and had devoted countless hours to the task of making it absolutely the perfect home for her family. It pained her to see how casually her efforts had been dismissed, and yet at the same time she realized that the pain would have been infinitely worse had the new owners left the house exactly as it was.

Looking away, Molly briefly closed her eyes and composed herself. Then she got out of the car, wrapped her coat tightly to her body, and hurried over to the Andersons' front porch. Mary Ellen, now eleven years old and favoring her father more with each passing day, answered the doorbell and said, "Hi, Aunt Molly! Mom's in the kitchen."

Molly gave the girl a quick hug, holding Mary Ellen for a couple of seconds longer and squeezing her a little tighter than she normally would have. Reluctantly letting go, she said, "You're getting prettier every day, M.E."

Mary Ellen laughed. "Right, Aunt Molly. Anyhow, thanks for pretending not to notice the brand new zit on my face."

Molly returned the laugh. "You're too much, Kiddo."

With that, the girl smiled and wandered back down the hall in the direction of her bedroom. Remembering how precocious Jenny had been at that age, Molly shook her head sadly and turned toward the kitchen. She found Melinda standing at the stove, browning some small cubes of beef. Molly gave her friend a quick hug and Melinda said, "Thank God you're finally here. I was about to start drinking without you. Why don't you open that bottle of Merlot? We can have a couple of glasses and tell Denny that most of it went into the stew."

Molly laughed, then dug an opener out of the drawer, cut the foil off the top of the bottle and pulled the cork. She grabbed two glasses from the cupboard, poured a couple ounces of wine into each of them, and handed one of the glasses to Melinda. Continuing to stir the beef with one hand, Melinda raised the glass with the other and said, "Salut!"

Molly took a sip, nodded her appreciation, and said, "This might be too good to go into a stew, even one as excellent as yours."

"Not to worry," Molly said. "Denny bought a case of this stuff a couple of weeks ago. We won't run out tonight no matter how much I pour into the stew. So, what is it that you wanted to talk to us about?"

Molly took another sip of the wine and grimaced. "I've got a major problem. But I'd really like to talk to both of you at the same time about it."

Her friend arched her eyebrows. "You won't even give me a hint?"

"It would be better if I didn't, believe me."

Melinda nodded. "Okay, Hon. But you know that, whatever the problem, we're here for you."

"I know that," Molly replied. "No one has ever had better friends. I would have never made it without you guys."

The silence built as each of the women considered the long road they had traveled together over the last five years. Melinda looked at Molly and gave a little shake of her head, as if struggling to find some new words of wisdom or comfort—some magic that could somehow erase the pain and the memories that haunted both of them still. Raising her glass, Molly shook her own head. "I know, Mel," she said.

* * *

Once dinner was over, Mary Ellen went off to her room to do her homework and the three adults settled into the family room with the remains of a second bottle of wine that Dennis had opened. He looked to his wife who was sitting in the middle of the couch and then to Molly who had taken the spot at the other end of the couch. "So, what's the problem, Molly? And how can we help"

Molly took a sip of wine and carefully set the glass on the table in front of her. Shaking her head sadly, she looked at Melinda and Dennis. "I got the shock of my life today, and I don't know what to think or do about it."

Melinda reached over and took Molly's hand. "What happened, Hon?"

"This morning someone left an anonymous note on my desk at work. The note directed me to a website that advertises Phoenix, Arizona prostitutes—or escorts, or whatever it is that they're calling themselves these days. I went to the site and I found a picture there of a young woman who looks very much like Jenny, or at least what I imagine Jenny would have looked like by now if she were still alive."

A look of shock registered on both of the Andersons' faces and for a long moment no one said anything. Then Melinda squeezed Molly's hand. In a soft voice she said, "Are you telling us you think that the girl might actually be Jenny?"

Molly shook her head and tears began rolling down her cheeks. "I don't know. It makes no sense. If it were Jenny—if she were still alive— why would she be in Phoenix? How would she have gotten there? And why would she not have contacted me?"

With that, she began crying in earnest. Melinda reached out and drew Molly into her arms while Dennis went quickly to the bathroom and returned with a box of tissues. As Molly gradually got herself under control again, Dennis said, "What are you going to do, Molly? And what would you like us to do?"

Molly sniffled and wiped her nose again. "For starters, I'd like you to look at the picture and tell me if you agree that it looks like Jenny or if you think I'm just letting my imagination run wild. I need to know if someone saw the picture, noticed a vague resemblance to Jenny, and directed me to the website in some sort of sick vicious joke. Or did someone genuinely think that the woman might be Jenny and wanted to alert me to what they had found?"

Nodding, Dennis got up from the couch and said, "Let's take a look at it."

They walked down the hall and Dennis flipped on the lights in his study. The computer was already running, and on the monitor was a photo of an Old English sheepdog that Dennis had owned as a child. Dennis sat in the desk chair and the two women stood on either side of him.

Molly directed Dennis to the website and then to the photos of the brunette escorts. She pointed to the picture of "Amber" and Dennis clicked on the photo. When it enlarged, Melinda brought her hand to her mouth, drew a sharp breath, and said, "Omigod!"

Looking at the photo rather than at her friend, Molly said, "Do you think it's her?"

Melinda shook her head. "I don't know, Hon. I don't want to get your hopes up unrealistically, but it sure looks like her to me. Obviously, this girl is several years older, and her hair is longer. But her eyes look the same, and so does her facial structure. And that smile..."

Tearing up again, Molly nodded. "I know. It was the eyes and the smile that convinced me too. What do you think, Dennis?"

Leaning in and studying the photo carefully, he said, "I agree that there are some similarities. But people change a lot between seventeen and twenty-two and, to be honest, I'm not sure this is the way I would have imagined Jenny looking at this age. In particular, Jenny was always very lean. This woman is not overweight, but she's certainly not as thin as Jenny was."

The two women shrugged, and Dennis said, "Hell, Molly, I don't know. Maybe I'm being too cautious here. But if I am, I hope you know that it's only because I'd hate to see you get your hopes up only to have them dashed."

Molly squeezed his shoulder. "I know that Denny, and I appreciate the thought. But I'm afraid my hopes are already raised. Could you please print a copy of the page for me?"

Dennis hit the appropriate keys and the page with the young woman's picture and the text of her ad spooled out of the printer. He handed the page to Molly then exited the website and the three of them returned to the family room. Once there, Melinda looked at Molly and said, "So what are you planning to do next? Are you going to call the police?"

Molly shook her head. "No, at least not yet. What would I tell them? And what could I ask them to do? I'm not sure that the authorities in Phoenix would even talk to this girl simply on the basis of my suspicions, and I certainly wouldn't want them to.

"If, by some miracle, it is Jenny in the picture, then I have to face the fact that for some reason she left home and has chosen not to come back or to contact me in any way for the past five years. The last thing I would want is to have the police spook her into running away again before I even had a chance to see her in person."

"So, what *are* you going to do? Dennis asked.

"Well, I'm hoping that I can discover who sent me the message. I'd like to know if the person simply saw the girl's photo on the web, or if he—at least I'm assuming it's a he—actually saw the girl in person. So, for starters, I'll continue to make some discreet inquiries around the company hoping that the person will come forward. But even if they don't, I'm going to go to Phoenix fairly soon and try to see the girl myself."

Melinda nodded. "Do you want me to go with you?"

Molly reached over and touched her best friend's hand. "Thanks Mel. I really appreciate the offer. Let me see if I can first find the person who sent me the message and then we can talk about it."

9

Her heart pounding against her ribcage, Jenny McIntyre held her breath as the trunk lid slowly opened above her. She assumed that she would get only one chance to save herself, if even that, and she would have to make the most of it.

A light rain pinged steadily against the car and fortunately, as a result of the dense cloud cover, the night sky was nearly as dark as the interior of the trunk had been. Jenny's eyes adjusted quickly to the little additional light as it seeped into the cramped space, and she watched as the dark shape of the man slowly came into view. She guessed that about an hour had elapsed since she had passed him on the way home from her run, just long enough for the dusk of the late afternoon to morph into the darkness of the early evening.

The park had been deserted on a cold, rainy afternoon and Jenny had opted to run along a gravel service road that looped through the park. A hundred yards from the park's boundary, the road curved around a stand of trees before straightening to merge with a broad residential street that would take Jenny directly back to her home. She saw the man standing next to an older beat-up sedan, which was parked off to the side of the narrow road just ahead of the curve. The trunk of the car was open, and the man was leaning into it, fiddling with something that Jenny couldn't see.

The man was apparently too engrossed in his problems to pay any attention to Jenny as she approached, her footsteps crunching the gravel behind him. Just the same, she moved to the far side of the road, intent on placing as much room between the man and herself as possible.

As Jenny drew abreast of the car, the man finally popped his head out of the trunk and apparently noticed her for the first time. She gave him a slight nod and picked up her pace a bit as she passed. But in just that instant, the man somehow closed the short gap between them and grabbed her from behind.

Panicked, Jenny kicked back at the man and tried to scream, but he clamped a rough dirty hand over her mouth and dragged her back toward the rear of the car. Once there, he bent the girl forward from the waist and shoved her upper body into the trunk, slamming her forehead into the cheap carpet that lined the bottom of the space. Pinning her there with his own body and with his left hand still over her mouth, the man used his right hand to grab a piece of duct tape that had been torn from a roll and set off to the side of the trunk. He removed his left hand and slapped the tape over Jenny's mouth, muffling her cries for help. He then used a second, longer piece of tape to bind her hands behind her. That done, the man had grabbed her by the ankles, flipped her into the trunk, and slammed it closed.

Jenny had no idea how far the car might have traveled. For maybe fifteen minutes, they had obviously been in traffic, moving slowly and stopping frequently for stop signs or traffic signals. They had then driven at a steady speed without interruption until a few minutes earlier when the driver slowed and turned onto a rough gravel road. The car moved gingerly down the bumpy road for another couple of minutes before finally coming to a stop.

Though thoroughly terrified, Jenny fought to control herself and to think as clearly as she could. For the first few minutes, she struggled fiercely to loosen the tape that bound her hands behind her back. When that proved futile, she tried crabbing her way around inside the tight confines of the trunk in the vain hope of latching onto something sharp with which she might somehow manage to cut the tape. That failed as well and so Jenny began planning for the moment when the trunk would inevitably open, finally twisting around so that she was curled up in a fetal position with her head at the rear of the trunk and her legs drawn up at the front of the space.

As the trunk lid now opened slowly into the night sky, Jenny saw her captor gradually revealed, facing squarely toward her, his right hand rising with the trunk lid. In his left hand he held a flashlight, which he

49

had not turned on. As the trunk lid reached its apex, Jenny flexed her knees and drew her calves tightly to her thighs for the briefest instant. Then, with as much force as she could possibly muster, she kicked forward, slamming both of her feet into the man's crotch.

Screaming in agony, the man dropped the flashlight and doubled over, cursing and gasping for breath. As he fell to his knees in the road, Jenny hooked her ankles over the car's rear bumper, pulled herself forward and hit the ground running.

Twenty yards from the car, she broke into the woods on her right, intending to circle around the front of the car and then race back up the road in the direction from which they had come, in the hope of finding the highway and help. But as she moved to turn right again, she saw that the man was back on his feet, flashlight in hand, and moving to block her escape. Having no other choice, Jenny turned to her left instead and ran deeper into the woods.

Her snap impression, upon seeing the man for the first time, was that he was older and overweight. She assumed that, in any fair contest, she would be easily able to outrun him. But this was no fair contest. She was attempting to run in the dark through a heavily wooded forest with her hands taped behind her back. She was also unable to breathe except through her nose, and the two conditions together constituted a huge handicap. Even the first thirty yards of the effort proved much more difficult than Jenny could have ever imagined.

Behind her the man was slowly gaining ground, tracking Jenny's every movement with the flashlight, cursing her, screaming that she should stop running, and threatening to inflict the most horrible and degrading punishments upon her if she did not.

The rain was falling harder now and with the temperature somewhere in the low thirties, Jenny was soaked to the skin and freezing. She chanced a quick look behind her and saw that the man was still closing the gap. As she turned to face forward again, a branch slapped her hard in the face and opened a cut in her cheek.

Crying now, and hoping desperately for some sort of miracle, Jenny looked to her left and suddenly saw a light, perhaps two hundred yards down a hill in front of her. She veered off in that direction and managed to pick up her pace just a bit, spurred on by the adrenaline rush of glimpsing her first real hope of escape.

A few yards later, Jenny realized that she was seeing the light of a house in a clearing at the edge of the woods. A pickup truck was parked in front of the house and Jenny could now smell the faint aroma of wood smoke drifting on the night air, mingled with the fresh scent of the cold rain. Gasping for breath, she willed herself forward, calling on every last ounce of strength that she could muster.

Behind her the man came thrashing through the woods, still demanding that she stop in her tracks, but threatening her more quietly now, perhaps for fear of alerting the people in the house below.

Seventy-five yards from the edge of the woods, Jenny chanced another glance back at her assailant, and as she did, her left foot slipped on a pile of wet leaves and she went down in a heap. In desperation she pushed hard against the wet, slippery earth, using her feet in an effort to propel herself down the hill and slide on her back to safety. But only fifty yards from the clearing the man was suddenly on top of her.

He transferred the flashlight to his left hand and with his right he slapped Jenny hard across the face. Sobbing harder now, she attempted to scream through the tape that covered her mouth.

Shaking his head, the man laughed quietly as he slowly unzipped the front of Jenny's running suit. And as he did, Molly snapped awake, drenched with perspiration as she was every time she awoke from one of these nightmares.

The dreams were never exactly the same, but rather variations on a theme. Though the circumstances varied, they always began with Jenny somehow falling into the clutches of William Milovich. In some manner, she always managed to escape from the man, but only briefly— just long enough to taunt her, and by extension, her mother, with the faint hope of a rescue that would never materialize. And in the end, Milovich always ran Jenny down just short of safety.

Molly swung her legs out from under the covers, planted her feet on the floor, and dropped her face into her hands. She assumed that this evening's nightmare had been triggered by the photo of the young woman on the FantacieLand website. Could the woman possibly be Jenny? And if so, was there any way Molly could find her?

Molly slowly rose from the bed and went out to the kitchen to get a glass of water, wondering as she walked through the darkened condominium if the abrupt and unexpected appearance of "Amber" would eventually rid her of her old nightmares or if instead, it might ultimately create new and even more terrifying ones.

10

Just after seven o'clock the next morning, Molly walked down the stairs to the condo complex's underground parking garage. She dropped her brief bag on the passenger's seat of her 1974 BMW 2002Tii and headed off to work. Two blocks from home, she tapped the brakes and slowed to a stop at a four-way intersection, noting that the brakes seemed a little mushy. The car was due for service in a couple of weeks, and Molly made a mental note to be sure to ask Andrew, the mechanical genius who kept the classic car in peak condition, to check the level of the brake fluid.

The early portion of Molly's commute took her through a heavily wooded residential area with relatively little traffic and only the single stop sign to interrupt the flow of the drive. Just short of a mile beyond the stop sign, Molly was mentally mapping out the rest of her day when she came to a steep hill that that descended to a major intersection, marking the transition to heavier traffic and a much slower commute.

Molly reached the top of the hill driving a couple of miles per hour over the posted limit of 40. As she crested the hill, she downshifted and tapped the brake pedal but felt no resistance at all until the pedal was depressed about halfway to the firewall that separated the passenger compartment from the engine. She gripped the steering wheel tightly with both hands and began furiously pumping the brake pedal, but after three or four attempts, the pedal sank all the way to the firewall with absolutely no effect on the car's forward momentum.

Molly was now a third of the way down the hill and the needle on the speedometer was slipping past 45 MPH. In the crosswalk at the bottom of the hill, a school crossing guard had taken up her position, holding a stop sign in front of the traffic coming down the hill, and seven or eight children had begun making their way across the street.

Beyond the crosswalk, vehicles moving as quickly as the morning traffic would allow jammed all four lanes of the major thoroughfare.

Still pumping the brakes to no effect, Molly laid on the horn. The crossing guard and several of the children looked up but stood frozen in place, as though incapable of believing that Molly's car was bearing down on them and gaining speed. After a second or two, the crossing guard snapped out of her trance and began frantically trying to herd the children back in the direction of the curb. But in their confusion, some of the children began racing toward the far side of the street instead, and two small girls stood rooted in the middle of the street, seemingly unable to move.

Cars were parked along both sides of the road, in most places bumper-to-bumper, leaving Molly no possible escape route to either side of the street until a point nearly two-thirds of the way down the hill where she saw a gap on her left between a small compact car and a pickup truck that was parked perhaps ten feet farther down the hill.

As the needle on the speedometer passed through 50 MPH, Molly reached for the gearshift and slammed it into second. The engine screamed in response, but Molly felt the car begin to slow, almost imperceptibly. In the next split second, she grabbed the emergency brake and pulled with all her might as she turned her front wheels in the direction of the gap on her left ahead of the pickup.

In response, the rear end of the car began slewing around to the right and Molly held her breath as the BMW skidded through the gap in the parked cars and up over the curb, clipping the right front fender of the pickup in the process. As it drifted across the lawn in front of someone's house, the car continued to rotate slowly in a counterclockwise direction until Molly was looking through the windshield back up the hill in the direction from which she had come.

Molly braced herself again, gripping the steering wheel with both hands as hard as she possibly could as the Bimmer took out a split-rail fence in front of the house, further slowing her momentum. And then, fifteen seconds after Molly had first applied the brakes at the top of the hill, the passenger's side of the car slammed into a giant Oak.

As the right side of the car crumpled into the tree, Molly was pitched violently to her right but was restrained by her seat belt. Twenty-five seconds after she had first applied the brakes, the car finally rocked to a stop, leaving Molly in tears, shaking violently and gasping for breath.

A few moments later, the driver's door jerked open. A man leaned into the car and said, "Jesus, Lady, are you okay?"

Molly dropped her head into her hands, gathered herself for a couple of moments, and then stuttered, "I think so.... I don't know...."

"Can you move?" the man demanded.

"Yes, I think so."

"Then we need to get you out the hell of here in case you ruptured the fuel tank. We don't want this damned thing to explode with you still in it."

The man leaned into the car, reached across Molly and released her seat belt. Taking both of her hands in his, he said, "Okay, can you get up and out of there?"

Molly turned in the seat and set her feet out onto the grass. The man gently pulled her forward and she rose to her feet. He led her slowly away from the wrecked car through a ring of people that had gathered around the crash, including the panic-stricken crossing guard who was now on her cell phone, talking frantically to the 911 operator.

Back out at the street, Molly slumped against the fender of the pickup truck she'd grazed. She was still trembling badly and her right hip felt like it was on fire at the point where the seatbelt had restrained her and prevented her from being thrown across the front seats in the direction of the tree that had brought the car to a grinding halt. But otherwise she did not feel like she might have been seriously injured, and only then did she begin to think about what might have happened had she slammed through the children in the crosswalk and head-on into one of the vehicles passing on the street below.

* * *

Two hours later, Molly sat on the edge of an examining table in the emergency room as the doctor summarized her apparent condition. "You're an extremely lucky woman," the doctor said. "You're going to have a nasty bruise on your hip, and the skin is pretty badly chafed where the seatbelt grabbed you. But otherwise, you check out fine. You didn't hit your head; and you don't appear to have suffered any other injuries of any consequence. You're going to be pretty sore for a while, but as I said, all things considered, you're lucky to be walking out of here in one piece."

"I know," Molly said. "I can't begin to tell you how terrified I was when I saw those children ahead of me and realized that I had no brakes. I thought I was dead, and infinitely worse, that I was going to kill several of those children as well."

"Well, happily you didn't. And in spite of what you've been through this morning, that's something you can be grateful for. I'd strongly recommend that you call a cab or a friend and have them drive you very slowly home. Take the rest of the day off and start all over again tomorrow."

"Thanks, Doctor, but I don't think that will be necessary. I'd be just as stiff and sore at home as I would be at work, and I think I'd be better off in my office, concentrating on other things, rather than sitting at home all afternoon, thinking about sliding helplessly down that hill."

The doctor nodded. "As you wish, but at least let me give you a prescription for some mild pain medication in the event that the abrasion on your hip gets to hurting too much."

* * *

Molly thanked the doctor and walked gingerly out to the reception desk where she filled out the paperwork for her insurance company and called for a cab to take her to her office so that she could finish preparing for a three o'clock meeting. She was in the middle of making some notes for the meeting when Jason Burke knocked tentatively on her door. Molly looked up from her notes and waved him into the office. Burke shut the door behind him and took one of the three chairs that faced Molly's desk.

"How are you feeling?" he asked. "And are you really sure you should be here this afternoon?"

56

"I'm okay, Jason, and I appreciate the concern. But while my car is pretty much totaled, I'm in reasonably good shape. I wouldn't be doing myself any good at home, and I really can't miss this meeting."

"So, what in the world happened?"

"I have no idea. The brakes were working fine yesterday, but they felt a little soft when I left for work this morning. If I had half a brain, I would have checked to make sure they were okay before going any farther, but I assumed that the fluid level was simply a bit low and that otherwise things were fine. Big mistake.

"Anyhow, I had the car towed to my mechanic and he's going over it, trying to figure out what might have gone wrong. Needless to say, I'm more than a little anxious to see what he might find. So, what's on your mind?"

For a moment, the man said nothing. Then he swallowed hard and shook his head. "I'm sorry, this is difficult."

Molly waited him out until finally Burke raised his eyes to meet hers and said, "I put the note on your desk.... I'm sorry I lied about it yesterday. I was hoping that I could help you by giving you the information without exposing myself as a world-class jerk. But I understand that your need to know what might be going on here is way more important than me covering my pathetic ass."

Molly got up, walked around the desk, and took the chair next to Burke's. Leaning forward, she said, "Please believe me, Jason, I'm not remotely interested in passing any sort of judgment here. I'm not asking you to explain anything about your personal life, but I'm desperate to know whatever you can tell me about the girl in the photo."

Burke nodded. Looking at the floor rather than at Molly, he said, "I know. I've hardly slept a wink in the last couple of weeks trying to figure out what to do about this. I finally decided that I had to let you know what I'd found, no matter what it might do to me personally."

Molly nodded. "I appreciate that more than you can ever know,."

She gave him a moment, then said, "Did you actually see the woman in the picture?"

"Yes, when I was in Phoenix last month."

57

Burke hesitated a moment, still unable to meet Molly's eyes. "Since Andrea and I divorced..."

He shook his head and finally looked up. "Well, you really don't want to hear about that.... Anyhow, while I was in Phoenix last month, I found the website that I sent to you. I saw the photo of the girl, Amber, and thought that she looked attractive. She did look vaguely familiar to me, but I couldn't figure out how I could possibly know her.

"I made an appointment to see her and she came to my hotel room. As soon as she walked through the door, I realized why she looked so familiar. It's been a long time since I've seen your daughter of course, but the resemblance was uncanny. I couldn't be sure that it was her, but I was stunned nevertheless.

"Obviously, I couldn't go through with it. I apologized to the girl and told her that I'd just been called to an urgent meeting with my boss and that I wouldn't be able to see her. Ever since, I've been wrestling with myself trying to figure out what to do. I can't be sure that the woman was Jenny, but on the chance that it was, I couldn't in good conscience avoid telling you. That's why I decided to send you the note, so that you could at least see the picture and decide for yourself."

Molly nodded. "Do you think that the woman recognized you?"

Burke shook his head. "No, I don't think so. I gave her the fee and thanked her for coming. She told me that she understood and said that she would just take a hundred dollars for the inconvenience. She tried to give the rest of the money back to me, suggesting that we could reschedule for some time later. But I told her that I was leaving town the next day and that I wouldn't be able to do that. I told her to take the money—that it was my fault, and that the money was no problem. In the end, she did, but she told me to call her the next time I was in town and she'd give me a break on the fee."

"Did you give her your real name?"

"Only my real last name. I used my cell phone to make the appointment because I didn't want the record of the call to show up on my hotel bill. But she asked what name I was registered under. I'd registered as J. E. Burke and so I told her I was Jeff Burke."

"Did you tell her that you would be back in Phoenix any time soon?"

"No, but when I talked to her initially, she asked what brought me to town. I told her that I came to Phoenix on business occasionally, and so she assumed that I would be coming back."

Molly sat quietly, looking into her lap while she processed the information. Finally, Jason broke the silence. "What are you going to do?"

Molly leaned back in her chair. "I'm not sure. I want to get to Phoenix and try to see this woman for myself as quickly as I possibly can, but I'm not sure how I'll manage it. The last thing I want to do is put her on guard or scare her off before I even have a chance to talk to her."

"Well, you know I'll do anything I can to help."

Molly leaned forward again. "Would you go to Phoenix with me?"

Burke said nothing, contemplating the situation, and Molly reached out and touched his arm. "You've been there, Jason. You know how to contact the woman. And from what you've told me, she'd readily consent to seeing you again. For obvious reasons, it would be difficult for me to make an appointment with her without explaining why I wanted to see her, and that might scare her off. You could make the appointment and she wouldn't expect anything out of the ordinary. I could be in the room when she arrived and that would at least give me the opportunity to see her and to talk to her."

"How would we explain going to Phoenix?"

"We'd call it a business trip—a follow up to your meeting with the people at the Trinka Company last month. Like always, I'd charge the expenses to my personal credit card, but then I wouldn't submit them for reimbursement."

Molly smiled, finally breaking the tension that had permeated the room since Burke first sat down. "You know damned good and well that by the time the bills come in, Dan will have forgotten that we ever made the trip. And he's certainly *never* going to remind me to file a reimbursement request for expenses that he thinks I might have forgotten."

Jason returned the smile. "No, that's one thing you'd probably never have to worry about, and I'm willing to do it."

"Okay," Molly nodded. "I'll set up the trip right away and let you know as soon as the details are in place."

11

On the Monday afternoon following her accident, Molly was working at her desk when Andrew, her mechanic, called to report that he had finished the examination of her wrecked car. "The problem," he said, "was that all the brake fluid had leaked away somewhere. The reservoir was virtually bone dry."

"I don't understand," Molly said. "How could that have happened?"

At the other end of the phone, the mechanic said, "Unfortunately, there are a number of points in the system where the fluid might have gradually leaked out. It was all fine when I redid the brakes a couple of years ago, but you must have developed a problem in the interim. When was the last time you checked the level of the brake fluid?"

Although he couldn't see her, Molly shook her head. "To be honest, Andrew, I don't know. It's been a while, I'm afraid."

"Well, I don't want to add to your misery, Molly, but as I've told you, when you're driving a car that's over forty years old, you need to pay pretty close attention to it."

"I know, and I feel awful. I loved that car, but after this experience, I think I'm going to be buying something brand new with a lot more built-in safety features."

"I don't blame you, of course. Once you've had a chance to think it over and discuss the matter with your insurance company, let me know what you want to do with what's left of this one."

* * *

At ten o'clock the following morning, Molly was still thinking about the conversation as the American Airlines flight from Minneapolis banked over Phoenix and descended slowly toward Sky Harbor Airport. Sitting in a window seat, she watched the city rise into view. Far below, sunlight out of a delft blue sky sparkled off the downtown buildings, and traffic appeared to be flowing smoothly along the network of freeways that looped around and through the metro area. The roof of Chase Field was open to the sun, and although the season was still a month away, Molly could see workmen, who looked like ants from this distance, moving slowly around the baseball diamond.

In Minneapolis four hours earlier, the day had begun cold, gray and gloomy. But after collecting their bags, Molly and Jason stepped out of the terminal into a bright sunny morning with the temperature already hovering somewhere in the low seventies. Walking toward the bus that would take them to the rental car facility, Molly could easily understand why several thousand people a year would happily abandon their lives in the Midwest for southern and central Arizona.

Molly had booked two connecting rooms in the same resort hotel where Jason had stayed for his meetings a month earlier, and thirty minutes after leaving the airport, they reached the hotel. Too anxious to even think about unpacking, Molly waited until the bellman had brought up her luggage and then she knocked on the connecting door to Jason's room. He answered immediately and Molly stepped into the room, holding the copy of the web page that Dennis had printed out for her.

Jason glanced at the page and punched "Amber's" phone number into his cell phone. Waiting anxiously, Molly curled her fingers into her hands and pressed her fingernails into the flesh of her palms. Perhaps fifteen seconds passed and then, in a bright voice, Jason said, "Hi Amber. This is Jeff Burke. You may remember that we had an appointment a few weeks ago and unfortunately, I had to cancel at the last minute. Anyhow, I'm back in town a bit sooner than I expected, and I was hoping to make another appointment to see you."

Jason recited his number into the phone and said, "Please give me a call when you get this message. I'm really looking forward to seeing you again." With that, he disconnected and set the phone down on the desk. "Let's give her a few minutes to see if she calls back right away. If not, we might as well unpack and get some lunch while we wait to hear from her."

Molly nodded and dropped into the chair next to the desk, folding her hands together in her lap. Jason retreated to the bed and sat down, and for the next ten minutes, the two of them stared at the cell phone, as if willing it to ring. Finally, Jason looked up at Molly and said, "Well, it doesn't look like she's monitoring her phone. Why don't we get our things put away, go downstairs, and find some lunch?"

Reluctantly, Molly stood, still looking at the phone. "Okay, but let's leave the connecting door open if you don't mind. I want to be able to hear the phone when she does call."

"Sure, no problem. It will only take me a couple of minutes to get organized and then I'll be ready to go."

* * *

The hotel restaurant had a nicely landscaped patio with a view of the Phoenix Mountains. About half of the tables were occupied, and Jason requested one that was off to the side, which would allow them a bit of privacy. The hostess left them with menus and Jason set the cell phone on the table between them. They took a couple of minutes to look over the menu and Molly settled on a grilled chicken salad and an iced tea. Jason handed his menu to the waitress and said, "I'll also have an iced tea please, and the tuna sandwich on whole wheat."

The waitress pronounced their choices "excellent," and promised to be right back with the drinks. As the young woman headed in the direction of the kitchen, Molly looked at the cell phone and said, "How long do you suppose this might take?"

Jason hesitated a moment. Then, looking off at the mountains in the distance, he said, "Well, I'd hardly expect you to believe me, but the truth of the matter is that I have very little experience with this and so I don't know what to expect. I would imagine that some of these women are fairly responsible about these matters and that others aren't.

"All I can say is that when I called this girl last month, she was monitoring her phone and returned my call immediately. Obviously, she's not doing that today. But my impression from talking to her on the phone then and from briefly meeting her in person was that she was

63

very professional in her approach to this business, and so I would assume that she'd call back fairly soon."

Molly waited until he finally looked back to meet her eyes. "Why would you think that I wouldn't believe you, Jason?"

Coloring a bit, he shook his head and looked down at the table. "I don't know... First, I tell you that I didn't leave the note on your desk, then I confess that I did. Now I tell you that I've only done this sort of thing a couple of times before and yet somehow, the third time I do it I wind up making an appointment with a woman who might be your daughter. I mean, what are the odds of that? If I were you, I'd sure as hell be skeptical."

Molly leaned across the table and waited until he looked up at her again. Speaking softly, she said, "Well, I'm not skeptical. As I told you before, I'm making no judgments here. I understand that since your divorce you're going through a complicated period in your life. I can also certainly understand why you initially denied leaving the note on my desk, and I respect the fact that you had the courage—and the decency—to come in and tell me that you were the one who left it. I know that wasn't an easy thing to do."

Jason remained quiet for a moment, toying with his silverware, and then said, "Yeah, well ... as you said, it can get very complicated...."

A few minutes later, the server appeared with their lunch orders and refilled their drinks. Molly and Jason ate methodically, saying little, both of them acutely aware of the cell phone sitting on the table between them. Forty minutes after they entered the restaurant, the waitress collected their plates and left the check. Through it all, the cell phone remained silent.

12

A little after three o'clock, Jason called "Amber's" cell phone again, got her recorded greeting and left another message asking her to call him. Listening, Molly paced the floor, growing increasingly nervous. Strangely, she hadn't felt the need for a cigarette since the morning she'd discovered the photo on the website. But now she dug a pack of Winstons out of her purse, shook out a cigarette, and lit it. Exhaling a plume of smoke, she turned to Jason and asked again, "Why do you suppose it's taking her so long to call back?"

"I'm sorry, Molly, but I have no idea. I know it seems like it's taking forever, but it's only been a few hours since we left the first message. When I called her a few weeks ago, it was in the evening. Maybe she has a day job and the other is something that she does on the side. In that case, she may not even check these messages during the day."

Molly took another drag on her cigarette and exhaled. "Do you suppose it's possible that she could be upset about the fact that you cancelled your first appointment and now she's refusing to respond to a call from you?"

Jason shrugged. "It's possible, but I can't imagine why she'd do that. I paid her in full for that appointment, even though we didn't do anything. I can't see why she would've been upset about that."

"No, I suppose not. And I'm sorry to be so impatient. It's just so hard, waiting like this."

"I understand; please don't apologize. I know you must be going through hell right now." Looking at the web page that was sitting on the desk, Jason said, "Have you been back to the website since you printed this out?"

Molly shook her head.

"Well, why don't we log on again and see if there's another way to contact her?"

Jason turned on his laptop, typed "www.FantacieLand.com" into the web browser and navigated to the page for brunettes. When it appeared, Molly inhaled sharply. Turning to look over his shoulder, Jason said, "What?"

Her voice breaking, Molly pointed at the screen. "The picture's gone."

Jason turned back to look for himself. There were photos of twenty-two women on the screen. None of the women was named Amber and none of them even remotely resembled the girl that had Jason had seen.

After checking and double-checking the photos, Jason navigated back to the home page and chose the "All Escorts" option. The screen refreshed, now showing photos of perhaps sixty women, including blondes and redheads as well as brunettes. One of the blondes was using the name Amber, but she was easily in her early thirties and she looked nothing like Jenny. Neither did any of the other women.

Molly stepped back and slumped down on the bed. Holding her head in her hands, she said, "What do you suppose happened?"

Jason turned in the chair and said, "It could mean anything. Maybe she's just not advertising on this website anymore. Apparently, she hasn't given up her cell phone number, and that's a good sign, I would think. If we check some other sites, we might find her that way."

Molly nodded and Jason turned back to the computer, He typed "escort Amber Phoenix" into the Google search box and pressed "Enter."

The first hit was for "Amber, Upscale Phoenix Playmate." As Molly pulled a second chair up to the desk beside him, Jason clicked on the link which took him to an ad on Adultsearch.com. The woman in the photo was an overweight blonde who was advertising a daily special through three o'clock in the afternoon of "complete service" for $200.00.

Jason clicked on the page's "escorts" link which took them to a list of perhaps seventy-five women offering sexual services of one kind or the other. He and Molly worked their way through the ads, looking at the photos and carefully checking the descriptions of those women who had not included photos in their ads.

Failing to find the girl they were seeking on Adultsearch.com, they then spent another ninety minutes searching unsuccessfully through several other sites. As Jason exited the last of them, Molly exhaled and shook her head. "She's gone, isn't she?"

Sounding equally dispirited, Jason said, "Maybe. ... I really don't know what to think at this point."

He waited a moment, then said softly, "I'm so sorry, Molly. If I had come to you with this immediately..."

They sat quietly for a couple of long minutes, the only sound in the room coming from the quiet hum of the air conditioning unit. Then Jason slowly turned away from Molly and looked back at the computer. After a moment, he lifted his fingers to the keyboard and returned to FantacieLand.com.

When the home page appeared, he clicked on "Double Delights." The screen refreshed, showing six photos, each of which featured two women posed together. The fifth of the six photos was of "Candee and Amber," and smiling into the camera with her arm around her blonde companion was the girl who had set Molly's search into motion.

Molly's eyes widened and she squeezed Jason's shoulder as she leaned in for a closer look. "It's her," was all she could manage to say.

Jason nodded slowly. "Yeah, it's her. Definitely."

Without any further discussion, Jason reached for his cell phone and punched in "Candee's" contact number. After a few seconds, he said into the phone, "Hi, Candee. My name is Jeff Burke. I'm in town on business and I saw your ad on the web. I was hoping that I could make an appointment to see you and your friend Amber." He recited his number into the phone, expressed the hope that he would hear from her soon, and then disconnected.

Molly walked over to the window and stood looking out at the mountains in the distance. For six and a half minutes the room remained perfectly silent and then Jason's cell phone rang.

As Molly moved quickly to his side, Jason snatched the phone from the desk and connected to the call. After a couple of seconds, he said, "Hi, Candee. Thanks for getting back to me so quickly.... Right. I was hoping to see you and Amber together."

Several seconds passed, then Molly watched as Jason squeezed his eyes tightly shut. Into the phone, he said, "Oh, I see.... Well, that sounds nice, but to be honest, I really had my hopes set on seeing both of you. I met Amber when I was here in town a few weeks ago and she seemed like a really nice girl. Then I saw the ad of the two of you together and thought it would be a lot of fun to see you both."

Again, Jason paused for a few moments, listening to whatever the woman was telling him. Then he said, "Look, Candee, if Amber isn't available, I don't think I'd like to do a threesome. But you sound really interesting. Would you be free to see me, just the two of us? ... Well, whatever works for you would be fine, but as far as I'm concerned, the sooner the better."

Looking at his watch, Jason said, "Six o'clock would be great." He recited the name of the hotel into the phone and said, "Okay, Candee. I'm really looking forward to meeting you. See you then."

Jason disconnected from the call, set the phone on the desk, and turned to Molly. "She says that Amber is out of town and offered to bring another girl in her place. I wasn't sure what to do, but I thought we'd want to talk to this woman and see what she might know about Amber. If you think it's a bad idea, I can call back and cancel."

"Did she say why Amber was out of town or how long she might be gone?"

"No. And I really didn't think I should press the issue and maybe scare her off."

Molly nodded. "I agree. The risk we run is that Candee will tell Amber that we're trying to find her and that will scare Amber off. God knows, I don't want that to happen. But I don't know how else we're going to get a line on her. I think we have to take the chance and see this Candee woman."

13

Over the next ninety minutes, Molly and Jason discussed the various ways that they might approach the woman once she arrived. They finally agreed that Jason should see her alone and try to get what information he could about Amber before they tried anything else. By ten to six, they were both pacing the small room. They watched anxiously as the clock ticked past five fifty-five, then six o'clock and then five minutes after six. Shaking her head, Molly looked to Jason. "Do you think she's not coming?"

Trying to contain his own nervous anxiety, Jason said, "It's okay, Molly. She's only five minutes late. I'm sure she'll be here."

At eleven minutes after six, Jason's cell phone rang. He connected to the call, listened for a few seconds and then said, "Great! I'll see you in a couple of minutes."

He gave the woman the room number, disconnected from the call, and turned to Molly. "She's on her way up."

Jason tapped the phone again and dialed Molly's number. When her phone rang, she connected to the call and nodded at Jason who set his phone on the back of the dresser without breaking the connection. Holding her own phone to her ear, Molly retreated into her room and closed the connecting door behind her. A few minutes passed at a glacial pace and then, standing next to the connecting door with the phone to her ear, Molly heard Jason say, "Hi, Candee. Come on in."

Molly heard the door close and the sound of Jason engaging the security chain. A few moments later a woman's voice said, "So what brings you to town, Sweetie? Are you here on business?"

"Yeah," Jason said. "I come here a couple of times a year. I really like Phoenix a lot, especially in the winter. I envy you people who get to live here year-round."

The woman laughed. "Well, why don't you come back and see me in the middle of next August and tell me how you like it then."

Molly imagined Jason smiling as she heard him say, "You might have a point there. Have you always lived here?"

"No, I'm from Iowa originally. I've been here for a little over three years."

Molly listened as the two made small talk, and then the woman said, "Well, Honey, why don't we get the business out of the way and then we can get down to the fun part."

For a few moments no sound came through the phone and then Molly heard Jason say, "Why don't you hang on there for a couple of minutes, Candee? We don't need to rush, do we? I'd like to get to know you a little better first."

"Sure, Honey, whatever. But I have a really nice idea of how we could get to know each other better in a hurry."

Jason's voice came faintly through the phone. "Yeah, me too.... I was really disappointed that I couldn't see you and Amber together. You say that she went out of town?"

"No, I just said that she wasn't available right now. Actually, I haven't seen her in the last couple of weeks.

"Is that unusual?"

"No, not really. It's not like all of us girls are living together in a big sorority house or something. Amber and I work together occasionally, but we can sometimes go two or three weeks between gigs. I didn't even know she was gone until yesterday. I got a call from another guy who was hoping to book us together, but when I called her, she never got back to me."

"That seems odd. I only met her the one time, but she didn't seem like the sort of person who'd neglect to return a call like that."

"No, it's not really like her. She usually calls me right back, even if she can't make the appointment. But trust me, Honey, I can give you all the action you can handle all by myself. Why don't we get a bit more comfortable here?"

Leaning against the door, Molly heard Jason say through the phone, "Hang on, Candee. Let's not go there yet." Then the woman's voice saying, "What's the matter, Baby, are you nervous?"

"A little, I guess."

"Well, don't worry, Honey, it's going to be fine. I'm gonna to take real good care of you. You don't have to be nervous at all."

"Candee, please.... Slow down a bit."

In a voice that now sounded both bewildered and a bit exasperated, the woman said, "Baby, you're starting to hurt my feelings here. I've never had a man before who wasn't in a huge hurry to get his hands all over me. If you didn't want to get it on, why did you call me?"

"Well, to be honest, I was hoping you could tell me how to get a hold of Amber. I was really looking forward to seeing her again, and I hate to think I'm not going to be able to have the two of you together. That was really my fantasy. That's why I called."

"Well, I'm sorry, Baby. But Amber isn't here." The woman lowered her voice and through the cell phone, Molly could barely hear her say, "If you want, Sugar, while we're doing it, I can tell you what Amber would be doing if she was here with us."

"No. Thanks, Candee, that's not what I want."

"Well then Honey, you need to tell me what it is you *do* want. I'm here; you paid me the money, and I'm all yours. But the clock is ticking, Baby. If we're gonna do it, you need to get naked. Otherwise you're going to wind up spending your money just for a little conversation and the chance to check out my tits."

For the next few seconds, Molly heard nothing through the cell phone, as Jason apparently struggled, trying to decide what he should do or say next.

Molly was torn herself. She didn't want to scare the woman off, and she certainly didn't want her to alert Amber/Jennifer to the fact that her mother was in town looking for her. But this was the only very tentative link to Jenny that she and Jason had found. He was obviously uncomfortable with whatever was going on in the room next door, and it didn't seem likely that he was going to be able to extract any additional information from the woman. Reluctantly, Molly turned off her phone and set it down on a table. Then she took a deep breath and opened the door that connected the two rooms.

14

Molly stepped through the door and saw Jason sitting on the bed next to a petite blonde who appeared to be somewhere in her early twenties. The girl was naked from the waist up, and when she saw Molly, she jumped up from the bed and crossed her arms in front of her oversized breasts. She looked from Molly to Jason and said in a sharp voice, "Whoa! What the fuck is going on here?"

Staying in place by the door, Molly raised her arms and showed the woman the palms of her hands. "It's okay. Please, Miss, we just want to talk to you."

The girl reached out and snatched her tee shirt from the bed. Holding the shirt in front of her protectively, she said, "I don't know what the two of you are into here, but I don't do couples, and I'm leaving right now. If either one of you so much as touches me, I'll scream so fuckin' loud that hotel security will be on your asses in a nanosecond."

Jason shook his head. "Please, Candee, just listen for a minute. We're not going to hurt you. We're not going to touch you. We just want to talk to you."

Shaking her head, Candee backed toward the door, still holding the tee shirt in front of her. Molly remained rooted to the spot just inside the connecting door. "Please, Miss. It's not what you think. This isn't anything sexual.... Look, you have the four hundred dollars that Jason gave you; I'll give you another two hundred if you'll just stay and talk to us for a few minutes."

"About what?"

"About my daughter."

A look of panic had been pasted on the young woman's face from the moment Molly had walked through the door. Now it gave way to

73

one of puzzlement. "Your daughter? What in the hell makes you think I'd know anything about your daughter?"

A tear rolled slowly down Molly's cheek. Making no effort to wipe it away, she looked at the woman and said, "My daughter disappeared five years ago. The police concluded that she'd been murdered, but her body was never found." Gesturing toward Jason, she continued. "Jason knew Jenny—my daughter. A few weeks ago, he made an appointment to see your friend, Amber. When the girl came to the room, he recognized her as Jenny."

Standing at the door to the hallway, the young woman shook her head and looked from Molly to Jason and back to Molly again.

Crying harder now, Molly pleaded softly. "Please, Miss. We mean you no harm, but my husband died because of this. If Jenny is still alive, she's all that I have left. I just want to know that she's all right... I just want to know why she left and why she never came home again...."

The girl hesitated, watching Molly cry. Finally, she nodded and said, "Okay, I'll talk to you, but I really don't know that I can help you much." She slipped her arms into the tee shirt and pulled it over her head. Without moving from her place near the door, she looked to Molly. "What do you want to ask me?"

Molly wiped her tears with the back of her hand. "I have a couple of pictures. Would you please look at them and tell me what you think?"

Candee nodded tentatively and Molly stepped back into her own room for a moment. Returning, Molly handed her the photo that Dennis had printed from the web site. "Is this what Amber looks like now?"

Looking at the picture, the girl shrugged. "Yeah. I mean, this picture is about a year old. The one of the two of us together is a bit more current and her hair is a little longer now than it is in this picture, but that's her."

Molly pulled her billfold from her purse, opened it and pointed to a photo. "This picture was taken when Jenny was seventeen. It's the last one I had of her. Do you think this is the woman who's now calling herself Amber?"

The woman who was now calling herself "Candee" took the billfold and turned a bit, holding the picture directly under the ceiling light. She studied the picture for several seconds, then handed the billfold back to Molly. "I don't really know. It could be, but this girl is a lot younger, you know?"

"Has she ever talked about her past—where she's from, that sort of thing?"

Candee shook her head. "Not really. Some girls in the business become pretty close friends and tell each other all their secrets, but I don't think Amber has any friends like that. She keeps her working life and her straight life totally separate, and she never talks about the other. For all I know, she could be married and have a couple of kids—some girls do.

"I've known her for a little over a year, which is how long we've been working as a twosome. We rent a place together that we use for incalls, and I know that she lives in an apartment. But I've never been there, and I don't even know where it is except that it's in north Phoenix someplace.

"Sometimes, me and her will go out to eat or for a drink or something, but we always just talk about general things—movies, music, clothes—stuff like that. She told me that she's been in the business for three years, and when I asked her once where she was from originally, she told me L.A. But she never talked at all about her family or anything like that, and she made it pretty clear that she didn't want to."

Molly gestured toward the printout from the web site. "Do you know why she took her ad off this site?"

The younger woman shook her head. Looking in Jason's direction, she said, "No. Like I told him, I didn't even realize that Amber wasn't answering her phone until yesterday. I called her and left a message, but she never called me back. I tried her a couple of times after that, but she still hasn't called."

"When was the last time you saw her?"

The girl scrunched her face as if in deep thought. Finally, she said, "It was a Thursday—a week ago from last Thursday. We did a gig together that evening and after we went to P. F. Chang's for dinner. I haven't seen or heard from her since."

Still sitting on the bed, Jason asked, "Has Amber ever disappeared like this before?"

"No. Some of us girls occasionally go out of town to work for a week or two at a time in Vegas and places like that. But Amber stays pretty close to home, and in the time we've been working together she's never gone out of town that I know of."

Molly nodded. "You said that the two of you shared an apartment. Are her things still there?"

"Yeah. And now that you mention it, even though I didn't see her, I know that she used the incall at least a couple of times after the night I saw her last."

"Could we see it."

Candee shook her head. "No. And it wouldn't do you any good anyhow. All we keep there are the clothes that we use for appointments. There's no personal stuff that would help you find her."

"Can you tell us the names of any of her other friends we might talk to?" Jason asked.

"Not really. Amber knows a few of the other girls working in town, but I'm the only one she works with. I don't think the other girls would be able to tell you anything more than me."

The room fell silent for a few moments, then in a tentative voice, Candee said, "About the ad.... The guy who runs the website is named Ron. If you go there and click on the place where it tells you how to put an ad on the page, there's a phone number. Maybe he can tell you why she took the ad off and where she went."

Molly looked to Jason who shook his head as if to suggest that he couldn't think of anything else to ask. Molly reached into her billfold, took out a card, and handed it to the girl. "Thank you very much for talking to us Candee, and again, I'm sorry if we alarmed you. My cell phone number is on this card. If you think of anything else that might help us find Amber, or if you see her, I'd be very grateful if you'd call me. I promise you that I don't want to cause any problems for her. I just want to talk to her."

Nodding, the young woman took the card and slipped it into the pocket of her jeans. Reaching back into her billfold, Molly took out two hundred-dollar bills and held them out to the girl.

The young woman shook her head and reached out to open the door. She looked up at Molly for a moment. Then, in a sad, soft voice, she said, "It's okay. You don't have to do that. I just wish my own mother would've cared enough to come after me like this."

And with that, she stepped through the door and closed it behind her.

15

As soon as Candee left the room, Jason went back to his computer, called up the FantacieLand website and found the "Technical Support" page. Turning to Molly, he said, "How do you want to handle this?"

Molly leaned over his shoulder and looked closely at the page for a minute or two. Then she said, "I'm thinking I might call, posing as a woman who wants to put an ad on the site. They indicate that they have a photographer available. I could tell them that I need photos and ask about making an appointment to have them take some. That should at least get me through the door."

Jason nodded. Molly picked up her cell phone and dialed the number. The phone rang twice and then a man who sounded younger than Molly would have expected said, "Hello?"

"Hello," she said. "Is the Technical Support for the FantacieLand website?"

"Yes, it is."

"My name is Carolyn. I'm new in town and I'd like to put an ad on your site."

"Have you been to the site?"

"Yes."

"Well, Carolyn, all of the information you need is on the site. It's really very simple. You write your ad, attach your photo, and email the message to me along with the number of the credit card you want me to bill. You'll need to print out the model's release form and either fax it to the number on the form or mail it to the P.O. box. If you're paying by money order instead of a credit card, you'll need to mail that as well. As soon as I have all the info, I'll get the ad up and running immediately."

"Well, the problem is that I don't have any good pictures—nothing that compares to ones on your site. Could I make an appointment to have you take my picture? Then I could give you the release and the other information at the same time."

"Well, I don't actually take the pictures myself, but I can refer you to someone."

"I see. Well, if I got the pictures taken and dropped them off to you, could you post the ad for me? I'm not good with computers and I wouldn't know how to send the pictures to you."

"Oh, that's not a problem, the photographer can email them to me for you, and you can send the rest to the P.O. box."

Molly looked at Jason and shook her head slightly. Into the phone, she said, "Well I guess that would work okay. Can you put me in touch with your photographer? I'd really like to get my ad up as soon as possible."

With her free hand Molly jotted the name and address of the photographer's studio onto a notepad next to the phone. "Okay, thanks very much. Tell Ron that I'll be there right at eleven thirty tomorrow."

Disconnecting from the call, she looked at Jason. "He claims that he doesn't take the pictures himself but that he could make an appointment for me with the photographer, a guy named Ron, for tomorrow morning."

"You don't believe him?"

"No. Remember, Candee told us that they guy who runs the website is named Ron. It would just be too much of a coincidence if the photographer were also named Ron. I'm guessing that what we have here is a guy who's running this website as a sideline. His public face is Ron, the straight-up professional photographer, while the webmaster stays hidden behind the scenes. If that's not the case, we'll just have to play it by ear, but I'm sure we'll get a better feel for the situation tomorrow morning."

"Sounds good. So, what do you want to do now?"

Looking at her watch, Molly said, "I'm not sure there's much else that we can do tonight, Jason. It's now after nine, Minneapolis time, and I've been up since four o'clock this morning. I think I'm going to order a salad from room service and then I'm going to crawl into bed and try to get some sleep. Tomorrow could be a pretty full day."

16

The photography studio was located in a strip mall just off of Thunderbird Road in the northwest corner of the city. Promptly at eleven thirty on their second morning in Phoenix, Molly and Jason stepped through the front door of the studio and into a small anteroom.

The room was bright, with white walls and a gray tiled floor. A contemporary desk and chair were positioned to the right of the door, and a slim laptop computer sat on the desk. Classical music played softly through speakers hanging from the corners of the room.

A number of photos decorated the walls, apparently intended to illustrate the variety of work done by the studio. Virtually all of the pictures were posed shots of weddings, baptisms, graduations, family photos and the like. There were a few individual portraits, including three or four that might have been described as "glamour shots," but none of the photos was nearly as risqué as those of the women on the escort website.

Molly stepped over to the desk and picked one of the photographer's business card out of a tray. As she did, a man stepped through a door in the wall directly in front of them. Early thirties, maybe. Tall and rangy with short, reddish-brown hair and bright hazel eyes. He was dressed in tan chinos, a light blue long-sleeved shirt that appeared soft and comfortable, and Top Siders on his otherwise bare feet. He looked from Jason to Molly, flashed a warm smile and said, "May I help you?"

Molly glanced at the card, then looked up at the man and said, "Are you Ron Newton?"

The man smiled. "Guilty. And you are... ?"

"My name is Molly McIntyre, and this is my friend, Jason Burke. I spoke with you on the phone last evening and made an appointment for eleven thirty this morning."

Looking confused, Newton slowly shook his head. "No, I don't think so."

Maintaining eye contact, Molly said, "Yes, in fact, I did. Using the name 'Carolyn,' I made an appointment to have you take some pictures of me for your website."

Newton shook his head more vigorously. "No, I'm sorry, you didn't. You talked to the man who operates the website and he called me and made an appointment for a woman named Carolyn. But I have nothing to do with the website, save for the fact that I occasionally take pictures for women who want to advertise on it."

Molly gave him a moment, then said, "Look, Mr. Newton, I'm really not at all concerned about what you do with your website. I'd simply like to talk to you for a few minutes."

"Talk to me about what?"

"My daughter. She disappeared five years ago, and then last month a friend stumbled across her photo on your site."

Molly reached into her purse, pulled out the printout of the ad from the web page, and handed it to Newton. The man studied the page for a few seconds, then looked up at Molly. "All I want is an opportunity to talk to her," she said.

Newton handed the picture back to her and shook his head. "I'm sorry, ma'am, but I can't help you. I don't know this girl and, as I've tried to tell you, I don't own the website."

Pointing to the ad, Molly said, "Did you take this picture?"

Looking at Molly, rather than at the picture, the man said, "No, I didn't."

Molly set the printout down on the desk and then looked up at Newton. In a distinctly cooler voice, she said, "Mr. Newton, there are a number of ways we can handle this. I have no desire to cause any problems for you. But if you refuse to help me, then I am perfectly willing to cause you all kinds of problems.

"You insist that we did not talk on the phone last night, but I have an excellent ear for voices, and there's no doubt in my mind that you are the man I talked to. So far, I have not involved the police in the search for my daughter. But if I have no other alternative, I will go to see them, and I will point them straight at you. Beyond that, I have lots of money and very good attorneys, and I will tie you up in knots in ways you can't even begin to imagine."

Newton drew himself up to his full height and crossed his arms over his chest. "And what in the hell makes you think you could do that?"

"For openers, I could do it because you signed my daughter up for your escort service when she was not of legal age. I know that she must have signed your model's release form claiming that she was of age, but she wasn't. And obviously you must not have verified her age before you put her photo on the site. You might be able to wriggle your way out of criminal charges, but I'll sue your ass off in civil court and at a very minimum, the connection between this studio and your website will receive a lot of public exposure. And win or lose, you'll wind up paying a fortune in attorney's fees. Believe me, it would be a lot simpler and a lot less expensive to just quietly help me out here."

Newton gave her a hard stare. "Just say, hypothetically, that I did run the website. Why should I believe you? You waltz in here claiming to be somebody's mother. How do I know if you are or not?" Nodding in Jason's direction, he said, "How do I know that you and your buddy here aren't running a scam of some sort?"

Molly nodded, opened her purse again, and dug out her wallet. She opened the wallet, found a picture of Jenny, and set it next to the printout on the desk. "This is a picture of my daughter. As you can easily see, it's the same girl."

Newton picked up the printout and spent several seconds looking back and forth between the two photos. "Well, lady, maybe you can easily see it, but it's not all that obvious to me." Pointing to the picture in Molly's wallet, he said, "This girl is clearly a lot younger than the one in the ad. She could be a different girl altogether."

"But she isn't, Mr. Newton. I'm her mother. Believe me, I know."

"Again, assuming hypothetically that I did run the website, what is it you think I'd be able to tell you?"

"I printed the page from the website last week. When I went back to the site last night, my daughter's ad was gone. Why?"

The photographer threw up his hands. "Even if I did run the site, how would you expect me to know that? Lots of women in this business come and go fairly quickly, and when they decide to move on, they just stop paying and their ad stops running."

Molly nodded. "You told me that you didn't take the photo of this girl, but I couldn't help noticing that there was a striking similarity between her picture and those of several of the other women on the site. I also notice that many of these pictures, including my daughter's, have an imprint indicating that the photo has been verified. Certainly, you must have had some direct contact with these women if only so that you could verify the photos..."

Molly waited for a moment, but Newton said nothing. In a softer voice, she said, "Please, Mr. Newton, Jenny is all I have left.... Did you take the picture?"

Newton waited a moment, watching her, as if weighing some important decision. Then he said, "Okay, yes, I took the picture."

"How long ago?"

Newton pointed at the printout. "I took this a year or so ago. It replaced one that I'd taken a year or so before that."

"What name did the girl give you on the model release form?"

"She said her name was Jennifer Douglas."

Molly swallowed hard. "You must still have the form on file."

The photographer just shook his head. "Wait here."

Newton turned and walked through the door that led to the back of the studio. Molly turned to Jason who had remained near the front door of the studio, following the conversation carefully. Saying nothing, he gave her a nod of encouragement. A couple of minutes later, Newton returned, carrying a manila file folder.

He pulled a sheet of paper from the folder, glanced at it and then handed it to Molly. She looked at the form then let out a small gasp and brought her hand to her mouth. Tears glistened in her eyes and she looked up at the photographer. "Even though she signed her name as Jennifer Douglas, that's her handwriting. I'd recognize it anywhere."

On the release form, the woman had sworn under penalty of perjury that her true name was Jennifer Douglas and that she was twenty-two years old. She listed her stage name as "Amber," and promised to hold the website harmless for any actions or damages that might result should she have misrepresented either her name or her age.

A notation on the bottom of the sheet indicated that the young woman had paid fifty-five dollars to post an ad for sixty days and that the ad had begun running on the fourteenth of April, two years earlier.

Reading the release form over Molly's shoulder, Jason asked, "How did she make her payments, Mr. Newton? Did she use a credit card?"

"No. She always paid by money order.

"Once she began advertising on your site, did she do so continuously?"

"Yes."

"Then I don't understand. Women buy their space on the site in one-month blocks. According to this form, Jenny's ad first appeared on the site on April fourteenth. If she advertised continuously as you say, then her ad should have expired either on the fourteenth of last month or the fourteenth of this month. Why would it have suddenly disappeared from the website when I went to look for it yesterday?

Newton looked away, then shook his head and turned back to Molly. "Because she sent me an e-mail Monday evening asking me to take down the ad."

"Why did she do that?"

"I have absolutely no idea. All she said in the message was that she'd decided to stop booking appointments for a while and that she was thinking of taking a trip. She said that when she got back to town and was ready to start working again, she'd let me know. And no, before you even ask, she didn't say where she was going, and I didn't keep a copy of the message. I deleted it and took down the ad as she requested."

"And you didn't think that was unusual?" Jason asked.

Newton shrugged. "It was none of my business. I sent her a message telling her to have a good time and that I'd be here when she got back and was ready to run the ad again."

The three stood silently in the small room for several seconds and then Molly pointed back at the form. "And you're sure that you have no address for her?"

The photographer shook his head. "I don't need one. The women who advertise on this site have to pay in advance. I'm not sending them statements, and I don't go out collecting. The only contact information I ever had for her is the phone number that she posted in her ad."

Molly nodded and looked to Jason who shrugged as if to suggest that he had no other questions. Turning back to the photographer, she said, "Look, Mr. Newton. I don't know if you have children yourself, or if you can even begin to imagine the nightmare that I've been living since the day Jenny went missing. I don't know how or why she disappeared from home in the first place. And if she wasn't ... If she really has been alive all this time, I can't begin to understand why she has never made any attempt to contact me.... I love her very much. I just want a chance to talk to her. I just want to know that she's all right."

Molly pulled out a card, wrote the name of the hotel where she and Jason were staying, and handed it to Newton. "I'm not sure what I'm going to do next, but I'll be here for at least a few more days, trying to contact my daughter. My cell phone number is on the card. If she contacts you, and if you could somehow arrange for me to meet her without telling her who I am, I'd pay a substantial reward for your help."

Taking the card, Newton said, "Look, Ms. McIntyre. I know you must think I'm a major sleezeball, and I'm not going to waste my time or yours attempting to justify what it is that I do for a living. But I have an obligation to the women who advertise on this site. They trust me to respect their privacy, and I've already told you a lot more than I should have, simply because I don't need the grief and because I can see that you really are concerned about this girl.

"But you need to understand that most of the women who get into this business have their own very practical and personal reasons for doing so. They're not living in some fantasy world. They aren't expecting Richard Gere to come riding to the rescue and believe me when I say that most of them wouldn't want their mothers to be doing so either.

"Forgive me for being so blunt, but if your daughter did just up and run away from home, and if she hasn't tried to get in touch with you since, then she must've had a reason. Believe me when I say that no one is holding her here against her will. If she wanted to go home, or if she wanted to get in touch with you, she could've done so at any time. I know you don't want to hear it, but my advice to you is just to go back home. I assume that your daughter knows how to find you, and that if she wants to, she will."

Blinking back tears, Molly shook her head. "I can't do that, Mr. Newton. One way or another, I am going to see my daughter. If *she* tells me to go back home and leave her alone, I will. But irrespective of who else might be hurt in the process, I *will* see this through."

17

Molly stared numbly out the window as Jason steered the Nissan back in the direction of their hotel. After several minutes of silence, he chanced a glance in her direction and saw that she was crying quietly. Instinctively, he reached across the console and took her hand. "Molly, what's wrong?"

She shook her head and swiped at her tears with the back of her free hand. Without looking at him she said, "I'm sorry. It's just that seeing Jenny's signature on that model's release form...

"Up until that moment, I couldn't bring myself to believe that that she might possibly be alive. I was absolutely certain that we would get here and find 'Amber,' only to discover that she was not Jenny and that the resemblance was just another of the horrible little jokes that the gods have been enjoying at my expense these last five years.

"But now, to know that she really *is* still alive—to know that she's out there somewhere, perhaps only a few miles away from me, and to know at the same time that for the last five years she's allowed me to think that she was dead..."

Sobbing harder, she said, "Why would she do it, Jason? How could she simply leave like that, saying nothing, breaking my heart and destroying all our lives so heedlessly? She was my daughter—my only child. I thought I knew her better than anyone on earth, and now it turns out that I apparently didn't know her at all."

Jason squeezed her hand. "I'm sorry. I barely knew Jenny and so I can't begin to speculate about why she might have done any of the things that she apparently has done. But for whatever it might be worth, I *do* know you, and I don't believe for a moment that whatever might have happened could possibly have been any fault of yours. Obviously, something way off norm must have occurred. As corny as it sounds, maybe she was in an accident and came away from it not knowing who she was or where she belonged."

"That hardly seems very likely. The police checked every hospital for miles around the Twin Cities. They would have found Jenny even if she hadn't known her own identity."

"Well, perhaps she *was* abducted, but not by the man the police suspected. She could have been taken directly here or perhaps to some other city first and had an accident there. She could have been drugged or hypnotized and have no recollection of her life before she was kidnapped. I know that it sounds impossible, but it doesn't sound nearly as improbable as the idea that she would deliberately run away and cause you such pain."

Molly gave a sad smile, squeezed his hand and then released it. "I appreciate the effort, Jason, but there's no getting around the ugly truth of it. The fact that Jenny is still alive is forcing me to confront some pretty harsh realities."

She sat quietly for a few moments, then finally turned to face Jason and said, "Tell me about her."

"What do you mean?"

"You're the last person I know who's actually seen Jenny, more than five years after I last saw her myself. What was she like? How did she look? What were your impressions of her?"

Without taking his eyes off the road, Jason said, "She looked good, Molly. I mean, she looked healthy and appeared to be in good physical condition. As you could tell from the photograph on the website, she's a very attractive woman. There's certainly no outward sign that she's being abused—at least not physically."

"What were your impressions of her mental state?"

"She was sharp—logical and clear headed, not like someone who was doing drugs or who might have any sort of mental problem.... She seemed happy.

"Admittedly her attitude could have all been part of an act, but if so, it was a good one. She appeared genuinely upbeat and positive, in spite of what she was proposing to do. I didn't get any sense that there was someone waiting for her outside the door or perhaps somewhere else that she would have to report to when she was done. And the fact that she tried to give back most of the money when I told her that I couldn't keep the appointment suggests pretty clearly that she wasn't under the control of some pimp who would punish her for not coming back with all of the cash."

Molly turned to look back out the window again. "That certainly doesn't sound like a woman who wouldn't know where she was from. And it certainly doesn't sound like a woman who wouldn't realize that she had a mother who must have died a thousand deaths in the last five years."

"I know, Molly, but I still insist that there has to be some logical explanation for all of this. And once we've found Jenny, I'll be looking forward to hearing it."

* * *

Just after one o'clock Molly and Jason stepped off the hotel elevator and turned in the direction of their rooms. A tall, thin man in a tan suit was leaning against the wall next to the door to Jason's room. He appeared to be in his middle thirties with longish dark hair.

As Molly and Jason closed the distance between them, the man straightened and reached into the inside pocket of his suit coat, even the casual movement suggesting the fluid grace of a natural athlete. He produced a brown leather wallet and flipped it open, revealing a badge and an identification card. Looking to Jason, he said, "Are you Mr. Burke?"

Jason nodded and the man said, "I'm Detective Sean Richardson of the Phoenix P.D. If you don't mind, sir, I've got a couple of questions for you."

"About what?"

The detective glanced at Molly, then turned back to Jason. "About matters that you'd probably rather discuss in private, sir."

Jason shook his head. "Anything you want to ask me you can certainly ask me in front of Ms. McIntyre."

Richardson nodded. "That's fine, but you'd probably rather not do it out here in the hall. Why don't we step into your room where we can have at least a bit of privacy?"

Jason unlocked the door and they all stepped into the room and took seats around the table next to the window. Turning to the detective, Jason asked, "Why do you want to see me?"

From his coat pocket, Richardson produced a pen and a small notebook. "Mr. Burke, are you acquainted with a woman named Susan Taylor?"

Jason hesitated for a moment as if thinking about it, and then shook his head. "No, Detective, I'm not."

Richardson glanced briefly at Molly, then turned back to Jason. "Ms. Taylor is a petite blonde, twenty-four years old, with shoulder-length hair. You may know her as "Candee.""

Jason looked quickly to Molly who drew a sharp breath and said, "Detective Richardson, are you talking about a young woman who's working as an escort and using that name?"

"Yes, Ma'am, I am."

Without looking back at Jason, Molly said, "Jason and I both met Candee for the first time last night."

The detective looked from Molly to Jason and cleared his throat. Before he could say anything else, Molly gave a nervous laugh. "Oh, you're thinking ..." She waited a moment, then shook her head. "No, Detective, it's not that. We were not seeing Candee in her professional capacity. We were trying to get information about my daughter."

"I'm sorry, Ms. McIntyre, but I don't understand."

Molly nodded. "My daughter, whose name is Jennifer McIntyre, disappeared from our home in Minnesota five years ago. The police determined that she had been abducted and murdered, but her body was never found. Then a few weeks ago, Jason was here in Phoenix and saw a woman that he thought might be Jenny. She was working as an escort and using the name 'Amber.' We flew down and attempted to contact her, but she's not returning our phone messages and she's taken her ad off the website she was using.

"We discovered that she was working with a woman named Candee and so we made an appointment with Candee last evening. She came to the room here; Jason and I talked to her together, and she gave us what little information she had about Amber."

The detective nodded. "And what time was this?"

Molly looked to Jason and said, "She got here a little after six o'clock and left around six thirty."

"Did either of you see or talk to her again after that?"

Molly and Jason both shook their heads, and Molly said, "No, we didn't."

"And may I ask how the two of you spent the rest of the evening after Ms. Taylor left?"

"I was very tired," Molly said. "It had been a long day and I haven't been sleeping very well since I learned that my daughter might still be alive." Nodding in the direction of the connecting door, she continued, "I went back to my room, ordered room service, and went to sleep."

"You didn't leave your room the rest of the night?"

"No, not until I met Jason this morning."

"And you, Mr. Burke?" Richardson asked.

"I was pretty tired too, but I was too keyed up to sleep. I went out for a long walk and then stopped into a restaurant down the street. I had dinner and a couple of drinks, then I walked back here and went to bed."

"What time did you leave the hotel?"

"Around seven, I guess."

"And you got back to your room at ..."

"About nine or nine-thirty, I think. I'm not really sure."

The detective made a couple of notes. Toying with the pen, he looked to Jason and said, "At the restaurant, did you pay cash or did you use a credit card?"

"Cash. But why are you asking?"

Ignoring the question, Richardson said, "Is there anyone who can corroborate your whereabouts during this walk and while you were having dinner?"

"I don't know. I suppose the waitress might remember me, but then again, she might not. She was pretty busy."

Molly leaned across the table. "Why are you asking these questions, Detective. What's going on here?"

Finally returning his pen to the table, Richardson looked from Molly to Jason. "I'm asking, Ms. McIntyre, because Susan Taylor—"Candee"—was murdered last night almost certainly sometime while Mr. Burke here was out taking his walk."

Molly gasped. Reaching across the table, she laid her hand on Jason's arm. "Murdered? How? Where?"

"She was killed about three miles from here in an apartment that she used for appointments."

"But why are you asking Jason to account for his whereabouts? Certainly, you can't think that he had anything to do with her death."

Richardson picked up his pen again. "The two of you have a rental car?"

"Yes," Molly answered.

"And who had the keys last night?"

"I did," Jason said.

"And you called Ms. Taylor to set up the appointment so that the two of you could interview her regarding Ms. McIntyre's daughter?"

"Yes."

"And you did this using your cell phone?"

"Yes."

"And you're certain that you didn't talk to Ms. Taylor again once she left this room around six-thirty last night?"

"No, Detective Richardson, I didn't."

Richardson steeled his eyes on Jason. "Well then, Mr. Burke, can you explain why Ms. Taylor's cell phone records show a call received from your phone at seven-thirty last night while you were allegedly out for your walk?"

Jason shook his head and looked down at the table. After a moment, he looked back up to the detective. "I didn't say that I hadn't called her, Detective Richardson. I said that I hadn't *talked* to her. I *did* call her cell phone at about seven-thirty, but she didn't answer and I didn't leave a message."

"And you called her why?"

"Because I'd thought of another question I wanted to ask her about Ms. McIntyre's daughter."

"So, when Ms. Taylor didn't answer, why didn't you leave a message asking her to call you back?"

"I don't know; I just didn't. I intended to call her back today to ask the question, but then Ms. McIntyre and I learned the answer from another source this morning and so I didn't need to call Candee—Ms. Taylor—back."

Richardson nodded and gave Jason a long look as if attempting to gauge the honesty of his reply. Then, holding Jason's eyes with his own, he said, "You're sure that, after you and Ms. McIntyre interviewed Ms. Taylor, you didn't decide that you'd like to see Ms. Taylor in her 'professional capacity', as Ms. McIntyre describes it?"

Jason shook his head vigorously. "No. Absolutely not."

"You didn't call and make an appointment to see her at the apartment she used for appointments?"

"No, I did not."

"And you did not go to the apartment and visit her there, maybe just to ask the question you'd forgotten?"

"No."

The detective nodded. "Well, in that case then, would you mind accompanying me down to police headquarters so that one of our technicians can take your fingerprints and swab you for a DNA sample?"

"Why should he do that?" Molly asked.

Still looking at Jason rather than at Molly, Richardson said, "He should do that so that we can check his fingerprints and DNA against those that we found at the scene. If, as Mr. Burke insists, he was never in the apartment that will allow us to eliminate him from suspicion."

"And if he refuses your request?"

Before the detective could respond, Jason leaned forward. "It's not a problem at all, Detective. As I said, I was never anywhere near Ms. Taylor's apartment and I'll be happy to do whatever I can to help."

Molly looked from Jason to Richardson. "You said that Ms. Taylor was killed in an apartment that she used for appointments?"

The detective nodded.

Molly drew a sharp breath. "Last night Ms. Taylor told us that she and the woman that I believe might be my daughter shared an apartment for that purpose. There wasn't ... was Ms. Taylor the only victim?"

Richardson nodded. "Yes, she was. It's apparent that two women were using the apartment, although it does not appear that either of them was living there full-time. We're trying to identify and locate the second woman, but we haven't been able to do so yet. What did Ms. Taylor tell you about the woman who was sharing the apartment?"

Molly recounted in detail the conversation with Candee the previous evening and then described the meeting with Ron Newton, the photographer, earlier in the morning. The detective made a few notes, then looked up to Molly. "Naturally, we'll be following up with the guy who runs the website. And of course, we have ways of bringing pressure to bear on him that you wouldn't have. Hopefully, he'll be more cooperative with us than he was with you."

Richardson dug into his pocket, extracted a business card, and passed it over to Molly. "Meanwhile, should you hear from the woman—'Amber' or whoever she is—it's very important that you call us immediately. We need to know what she might be able to tell us about what went on in that apartment last night. But beyond that, it's at least possible that this 'Amber' could be in some danger herself."

Molly swallowed hard. "You're not suggesting that she might have been in the apartment at the time and that something might have happened to her as well?"

Richardson shook his head. "At the moment, there's nothing to suggest that anything like that might have happened. But until we have a motive for the crime that was committed against Ms. Taylor, and/or a suspect, there's no way of knowing for certain that Ms. Taylor's roommate isn't also at risk."

Molly nodded her understanding. Richardson stood up from the table and looked to Jason. "Are you ready to go, Mr. Burke?"

Jason and Molly rose to their feet and Molly said, "Should we be asking a lawyer to accompany us?"

The detective shook his head. "If you'd like to do so, that's your right, of course. But we're not arresting you, Mr. Burke, and we will not be formally questioning you. All we need is for you to let us take your fingerprints and a DNA sample. It's a very quick and painless process; you'll be in and out in a matter of minutes. There's really no need for you to have a lawyer at this point."

Jason rose from his chair and nodded at the detective. "Okay, then. Let's get this done."

Part II

18

Any lingering childish illusions that Jenny McIntyre might once have harbored about life and love were abruptly and irreparably shattered the night she accidentally discovered the pictures of her mother, naked and having sex with Dennis Anderson. And even five years later, she still got a knot in her stomach every time the images rose unbidden into her consciousness.

In the two days and nights after she found the pictures, Jenny had wandered around in a total daze. Looking back, she realized that she must have been in shock, protected perhaps by some sort of psychological circuit breaker that was shutting down neurological connections and shielding her from the incomprehensible horror.

Fortunately, when the Andersons came home that night, Dennis had gone directly to his study, saying that he had to make an urgent phone call and sparing Jenny the difficulty of having to speak to him. She'd walked across the lawn to her own home and discovered that, thankfully, her mother had gone to bed early and so Jenny would not have to face her immediately either. She had called "Goodnight" to her father who was watching television in the family room and had gone directly up to her own room.

Over the next two days, she'd barely been able to face her mother, and she had no idea when or how she would ever be able to do so again. Until that moment in Dennis' study, Jenny had loved her mother unconditionally and had simply assumed that she always would. In the abstract, she could never have imagined any scenario that would have caused her to feel differently. But in the moment when she saw the first of the photos, the earth had shifted on its axis and nothing would ever be the same again. Her mother had betrayed her father; even more so, she had betrayed Jennifer as well, and Jenny suddenly felt nothing but contempt for the woman who had given her life.

And what of her father? Jenny couldn't imagine that he knew about her mother's betrayal, but what did that say about him? His next-door neighbor—one of his best friends—was having sex with his wife right under his nose. And her father was so pathetic that he didn't even realize what was going on?

At breakfast the next morning, Jenny sat at her usual place between her parents. She ate her fruit and Cheerios, saying nothing, astounded that the two of them could carry on as if it were just another normal day. But sitting in class two hours later, tuning out her history teacher who was droning on about Franklin D. Roosevelt and the New Deal, it struck Jenny that, for her parents, maybe it *was* just another normal day in which Mom sneaks out of the office in the middle of the afternoon to screw the next door neighbor while Dad sits in his office totally clueless, like Ward Fucking Cleaver on the Nickelodeon channel.

Her parents' marriage and their whole life together as a family were a total sham. All that bullshit about love, honor and fidelity—all that crap they had fed her through her entire life—was a total crock. She was furious, of course, but more important, she was totally adrift. In the blink of an eye, she had found herself completely unmoored from the bedrock principles upon which she had based her entire life. What now could she believe in? Who now could she ever trust again?

* * *

There was no one with whom she could share this awful burden, not even Brian or Angela. Even if her mother felt no apparent shame, Jenny felt more than enough for both of them. She could never reveal this horrible secret to her friends, and she knew she would die of embarrassment should they ever somehow discover the truth. More than that, she realized that she no longer had any interest in living the lie that had once been life with her family.

On the Friday afternoon after she found the pictures, Jenny came home from school while her parents were still at work. She stuffed a polo shirt and a change of underwear into her backpack along with her passport, cell phone, and computer. She retrieved the five hundred and fifty-seven dollars that she'd held out of her college savings account and hidden in a copy of *The Scarlet Letter* and slipped the money into the pocket of her jeans.

Standing in the door, she took one last look around the room she had grown up in. Then she slung the backpack over her shoulder, hurried down the stairs and out of the house.

At the bus station, Jenny went into the rest room and filled a sink with water. She turned on her cell phone, set it into the sink, and watched for a couple of minutes until the lights on the phone finally blinked out. She retrieved the phone and checked to make sure that she could no longer get a dial tone. She dropped the phone into a trash basket, then she pulled up the hood of her winter coat and tied it tightly, concealing her hair and a good portion of her face. Still shivering from the cold outside, she stepped up to the counter and paid cash for a one-way ticket to Phoenix, Arizona.

19

When Jenny stepped off of the bus in Phoenix after two days on the road, she had a little over three hundred and fifty dollars left in her pocket and needed nothing so much as a hot shower and the chance to sleep in a real bed.

Perhaps thirty people were scattered around the small waiting room. Some sat slumped into seats apparently attempting to sleep while a few others watched the two television monitors that hung from the ceiling. But most of those in the room sat or stood quietly, wearing the resigned expressions of people who were used to waiting. All the signage in the terminal was in both English and Spanish, and a little more than half of the patrons appeared to be Hispanic.

As Jenny walked through the waiting room, she saw to her left a counter designated as "Tickets/Information." She turned in that direction and took her place in line behind seven other people who were waiting for attention. Two clerks stood behind the counter, one a man who appeared to be in his early fifties, and the other a woman who was perhaps ten years older than that.

Jenny waited for several minutes and finally the male clerk waved her ahead. She hesitated for a second and then stepped aside to allow a woman with a small child who'd been waiting in line behind her to step up to the counter. A minute later, the female clerk beckoned Jenny forward and said, "How may I help you, Miss?"

Without trying to disguise the nervousness she was feeling, Jenny pointed back toward the door. "I just came in on the bus out there. I was here on vacation with my family several years ago, but I really don't know Phoenix at all. I came here to take a job, but I need some place to stay until I can get settled. I was wondering if you might be able to recommend a hotel or a boarding house or something like that that would be safe but not too expensive."

The woman looked Jenny over carefully. Then, in a sympathetic voice she asked, "How old are you, Honey?"

"Eighteen."

"And no one is meeting you? You don't have any relatives or friends here?"

Jenny shook her head.

The clerk leaned across the counter, looked at the backpack hanging off of Jenny's shoulder and then scanned the floor around Jenny, apparently checking to see if she had any other luggage. Quietly, the woman said, "Do you have any money at all, Sweetheart?"

"Yes," Jenny assured her. "It's just that I need to make it last as long as I can until I get my first paycheck. Then I'll be able to get an apartment and get settled in. I'm just looking for somewhere to stay until then."

The woman straightened up and gave Jenny a look that suggested that she wasn't quite sure whether she believed her or not. Then she opened a drawer in the counter in front of her and pulled out a sheet of paper. Reading upside down, Jenny saw that the paper was titled "Emergency Numbers."

The clerk grabbed a pen and a notepad. Looking at the list in front of her, she wrote an address and phone number on the pad. Then she tore the sheet from the pad and slid it across the counter to Jenny. "This is the phone number and the address for Haven House. It's a shelter for abused women and children that's run by the YWCA. If you call them, they can probably recommend someplace safe for you to stay."

The clerk pointed Jenny in the direction of a group of pay phones back in the waiting room. Leaning against the wall near the phones was a tall man who looked to be in his late twenties, wearing a pair of tan slacks over brightly shined cordovan shoes. A bulky gold watch dangled off his left wrist, just below the cuff of a dark blue shirt. The top two buttons of the shirt were undone, and the man had a well-toned body. He wore his hair closely cropped and sported a neatly trimmed moustache above a pair of relatively thin lips.

Jenny felt the man's eyes on her every step of the way from the ticket counter to the phones. She walked at a deliberate pace to a phone as far away from the man as possible. Turning her back toward him, she leaned into the small enclosure, dropped two coins into the phone, and dialed the number from the slip of paper in front of her.

A woman answered the phone at Haven House and Jenny explained her situation as succinctly as possible. The woman at the other end of the phone asked a couple of questions, gently probing to see if Jenny was being abused or if she was otherwise in any trouble or danger. Jenny assured her that she was not, and the woman recommended a boarding house near the downtown area that accepted only female tenants. "It's not luxurious," the woman said, "and you'll have to share a bath. But it is safe, and the rent is not unreasonable."

Jenny dug a pen out of her backpack and wrote the address and phone number on the paper that the clerk had given her. She thanked the woman and broke the connection. Then she dropped two more coins into the phone and dialed the number of the rooming house.

A woman answered the phone and Jenny again described her situation. The woman indicated that she had one small room available with a shared bath down the hall. Meals were available for an additional fee, although the fee would be reduced if Jenny were willing to assist in the kitchen. Jenny asked the woman to hold the room and promised to be there as quickly as she could.

As Jenny stepped away from the phones, the man who'd been leaning against the wall straightened and walked up beside her. Jenny quickened her pace toward the exit that led from the waiting room to the front door of the terminal. Matching his own pace to hers, the man leaned over, touched his hand to Jenny's arm and said, "Excuse me, Miss. My name's Eric. I saw you get off the bus just now, and so I know you must be new in town. I see that nobody's here to meet you and I was wondering if I could be of some assistance?"

Jenny kept her eyes tightly focused on the door ahead of her. "No, I don't need any assistance."

The man touched his hand to her arm. "Look, Miss. I just want to help. This is a hard city to find your way around in and I'd be happy to drop you wherever you might want to go."

Ten feet short of the exit, Jenny stopped and turned to look at him. In as firm a voice as she could manage, she said, "The only place I'm going is to that cab stand outside. And if you don't turn around right now and go back to leaning on your wall over there, I'm going to tell the security guard that you're propositioning me and that I want him to call the police."

For a few moments the man just stood, staring at her. Then his lips twisted into a leering smile and again he reached out to touch Jenny's arm. "Okay, you just run along there, Little Missy. But the next time we meet up, you might be a lot happier to see me."

Turning away, Jenny walked quickly toward the exit. She hesitated briefly near the security guard's station and turned back to see the man still standing in the middle of the room, watching her. Then she pushed through the front door and hurried outside into a waiting cab. Shaking, she looked at the note and recited the address of the rooming house for the driver. As the cab pulled away, Jenny turned and looked through the back window, then breathed a sigh of relief when she saw that the man had not followed her out of the bus station.

At the rooming house, she signed the register as Jennifer Douglas, which was the name on the fake driver's license she'd bought for a hundred dollars from a kid at school. Using his computer, the boy had copied the photo from Jenny's real license onto the new one and the finished product looked exactly like the real thing, save, of course, for the fact that Jennifer Douglas was three months past her twenty-first birthday. Jenny had bought the fake license so that she could go clubbing with her friends in downtown Minneapolis and never imagined that she'd ever have any other use for it. But as Jennifer Douglas slowly walked up the stairs and stepped into her new room, she said a sad and quiet goodbye to Jenny McIntyre.

20

For two months in the summer between her junior and senior years in high school, Jenny McIntyre had worked as a waitress in a hotel dining room. The day after she moved into the rooming house in Phoenix, Jennifer Douglas filled out a job application claiming eight months experience and landed a job as a waitress in an upscale steakhouse on Camelback Road in downtown Phoenix.

Technically it was a part-time job, which enabled her employer to avoid giving her health insurance or any other significant benefits. But by working both the lunch and dinner shifts five or six days a week, Jenny cobbled together a significant number of hours. The restaurant catered to a high-end clientele and Jenny learned quickly. She was an attractive, outgoing young woman, and she rapidly became an excellent waitress, popular with the customers and with her fellow employees.

While her base pay was minimal, Jenny's tips were very good. After working at the restaurant for two months, she was able to move out of the rooming house and into a small apartment. It was nothing fancy, but it was clean and in a relatively safe neighborhood. After another two months, she'd saved enough money to make a down payment on a used Volkswagen Bug, which freed her from the tyranny of living by the bus schedule and allowed her the opportunity to finally begin exploring the larger metro area.

The day after she bought the Volkswagen, Jenny went down to the Motor Vehicles Department on 51st Avenue, timing her arrival for the noon hour when she figured the office would be busiest. She told the woman at the reception desk that she was new in town and needed to exchange her Minnesota driver's license for an Arizona license. The clerk gave her a number and told her to take a seat.

As Jenny had hoped, the place was jammed. She sat for thirty-five minutes before being called to the camera station to have her photo taken. That done, she waited another forty-five minutes before being called to a window to complete the process.

Jenny had filled out the application online and her biggest fear was that the clerk might keep her old license and that the MVD in Arizona might report back to Minnesota that the license had been surrendered. That would be very bad news because the Minnesota Department of Public Safety would quickly discover that "Jennifer Douglas" had never had a valid driver's license in the first place.

The second hurdle was that she had to provide two valid forms of ID to get the Arizona license, one of which had to have her photo on it. She hoped that the fake Minnesota license would serve that purpose and that her passport would serve as the second necessary document. Of course the passport was in the name of Jennifer McIntyre, but if the clerk happened to notice that, Jenny planned to say that she had recently been married and had not yet applied for a new passport. She didn't know if the clerk would buy the story, but she assumed that the worst that could happen was that the clerk would send her home for her marriage license as proof of the name change. She also desperately hoped, of course, that the clerk would not notice that the birthdate on the passport did not match the one on her driver's license. In either event, Jenny would have to come up with another plan.

She reached the desk and smiled at the clerk who appeared to be in his middle fifties and more than a little put out at the fact that his afternoon was so busy. He examined the application that Jenny had made online and asked for her Minnesota license. She handed over the license and at the same time set her passport on the desktop, facing in her direction.

The clerk examined the license, looking back and forth from Jenny to the photo on the license. Apparently satisfied, he set down the license, picked up the passport and flipped it open. He glanced quickly at the photo and then at Jenny, aiming, she thought, at her breasts rather than her face. Saying nothing, he snapped the passport closed and handed it back to her. Then, to her amazement, he picked up the Minnesota license, used a paper punch to put a hole in the middle of it, and handed that back to her as well. "You can destroy this as you see fit," he said. "It's no longer valid. If you step back to the camera window and wait for a moment, they'll call your name and give you your new license."

Twenty minutes later, Jenny walked back out into the sunny afternoon with a valid Arizona license, and on a Wednesday afternoon two weeks later, she left work following the lunch shift and drove over to the Haven House Transitional Shelter on East Willetta Street. She asked to see a counselor, and the receptionist led her down a hallway and introduced her to a woman named Cathy Nickles.

Nickles was somewhere in her middle forties, a small lithe woman with the body of a gymnast. She was dressed in blue jeans, athletic shoes, and a black tee shirt. Her hair, dark with a few strands of gray, was pulled back into a ponytail that fell just past her shoulders. Large dark eyes highlighted a face that seemed immediately sympathetic, as if designed to invite confidences. Nickles smiled warmly, offered Jenny a chair in front of her desk, and asked how she might be of help.

Jenny had been rehearsing her story for weeks, but now that the moment was finally at hand, she was still more nervous than she would have expected. She didn't want to lie to the woman; even worse, she didn't want to waste her time, especially when Nickles doubtless had many more important things to do. But she needed the help, and she didn't know where else to turn. Swallowing hard, she looked at the older woman and said in a soft voice, "I understand that you help battered and abused women and children."

"Yes, we do," Nickles replied. Then she waited quietly for Jenny to continue.

The girl folded her hands in her lap. Looking into her lap, rather than at Nickles, she said, "I was in a bad situation at home in another state far from here. I ran away and came to Phoenix. That was some time ago. I'm not in any danger at the moment. I have a job and an apartment...."

"But..."

"But, when I ran away from home, I was only a couple of months short of my high school graduation." A tear dropped onto her cheek, and she said in a soft voice, "I was a good student. I expected to go to college and make something of myself, and I don't want to lose that chance. I don't want to spend the rest of my life working as a waitress."

With that, she began crying earnestly. Nickles picked a box of tissues off the desk, walked around the desk and took the chair next to Jenny's. Jenny pulled a couple of tissues from the box, wiped at her eyes and then blew her nose. Nickles gently touched her arm. "How old are you now, Jenny?"

"Eighteen."

"Well, legally that's old enough for you to be out on your own and to resume your education."

Jenny, who suddenly appeared younger and much more vulnerable than an eighteen-year-old woman, sniffled, wiped her nose again, and said, "I can't."

"I don't understand."

"If I go back to school, I'll have to send for my high school records. My family will find out where I am. It doesn't matter that I'm eighteen. I can't let them find me, even if I never get to go back to school."

The silence built for a few moments as Nickles allowed the girl to sort through her thoughts. Then Jenny looked at her and said, "I saw on your website that you can help people get their GED degrees. I was wondering ... if I applied to take the GED under my new name, would they have to see my high school records or would the fact that I knew enough to pass the test be enough for them to give me the degree? And could I then use the GED to get into one of the community colleges here without them having to have my high school transcripts?"

"You're using your new name at your job and to rent an apartment?"

The girl nodded.

"You have an ID of some sort?"

Again, Jenny nodded.

Nickles studied the girl for a moment. Then, without asking how Jenny might have obtained such an ID, she said, "Well, to answer your question, yes, you can take the GED without providing your high school transcripts. And with the GED in hand, you can enroll in the Maricopa Community College system as well, without having to send for your high school records."

A wave of relief washed over Jenny, and she gave Nickles a small but grateful smile. "Could you tell me what I need to do to take the GED?"

The woman referred her to an office downtown where she could sign up to take the exam. Given that Jenny had enjoyed an excellent high school education, the test itself posed no challenge whatsoever, and three weeks later she passed the exam with flying colors. With the GED in hand, seven months after arriving in Arizona, Jenny enrolled at Scottsdale Community College, indicating that her goal was to complete an Associate in Arts degree so that she could transfer to a four-year university.

21

On leaving Minneapolis, Jenny had cut herself off completely both from the city and from everyone that she had known there, including Brian and all of her other friends. It had pained her especially to lose her relationship with Angela Rinaldi, who had been her best friend since kindergarten. But she knew that if she made any effort to somehow maintain ties with Brian, Angela, or anyone else, it would only be a matter of time before her parents found her and dragged her back to Minneapolis.

She assumed, of course, that her parents would be frantic when she failed to return home. She'd thought about leaving a note, explaining why she was running away, but in the end, she'd abandoned the idea. There was no way she could have begun to explain the depth of her hurt and disappointment. And, angry as she was at the time, she decided that her parents deserved to share some of her pain.

She never could have imagined the chain of events that her disappearance would set into motion. She realized, of course, that her parents would report her missing. But she naively assumed that, absent any evidence that something tragic had befallen her, the police would do little more than file a report before concluding that Jenny was simply another of the scores of teenage runaways who disappeared from Minnesota every year.

Given that there were so many such runaways, Jenny's disappearance had been barely newsworthy and had attracted very little attention in the media. Then, when William Milovich was arrested in connection with her disappearance, the story made a splash in the metro sections of the local papers and was naturally exploited for every possible ratings point by the "news" departments of the local television stations.

When Alan McIntyre shot and killed Milovich and was then shot and killed himself by the Minneapolis police, the story exploded into prominence and for the next several days the local media rode it for all it was worth. The cable news networks also devoted some coverage to the tragic story of Jenny's presumed death at Milovich's hand and of the carnage that had followed. But for the most part, it remained a local story, and after a few days, even the media in Minneapolis had abandoned it for The Next Big Thing.

None of which had made the slightest impact on Jenny.

In the days and weeks after she arrived in Phoenix, she kept her head down and was completely preoccupied with the urgent task of finding a place to live and some way of supporting herself while at the same time trying not to do something stupid that would get her shipped back home to her parents. During that period, she had no time for or interest in the news from Minnesota, or from anywhere else for that matter.

She did not own a television set that she could have been watching even casually and which might have allowed her to chance upon some coverage of the story that had unfolded in Minneapolis. And since she had, at least for the moment, dyed her hair blonde and cut it very close to her head, no one watching the coverage in Phoenix would have ever recognized Jenny as the girl who had caused such a commotion up north.

Four months after her father's death, Jenny bought a small television set, and she was also reading the Internet edition of the *Arizona Republic*. But by then, at least as far as the media were concerned, the events in Minnesota had been filed under the category of ancient history. Finally, seven months after arriving in Phoenix, Jenny was working online late one night and, on an impulse, typed her former name and the words "Minneapolis Minnesota" into a Google search box.

When the screen refreshed, she was stunned to see that the first reference listed was to a newspaper article about "Alan McIntyre, father of **JENNIFER MCINTYRE** of **MINNEAPOLIS MINNESOTA,** missing and presumed dead."

Her hand trembling, Jenny clicked on the link and began sobbing quietly as she read the account of how her father had been shot to death by Minneapolis police after he himself had shot and killed someone named William Milovich. Minneapolis police had identified Milovich, a convicted sex offender, as their principal suspect in the disappearance and presumed death of McIntyre's seventeen-year-old daughter, Jenny.

She read a number of the other articles that the search had produced, and only then did she begin to realize the havoc that she had unintentionally released by running away from home. And she felt more desolated, more alone, and more ashamed than at any other moment in her life.

Jenny had once loved her father with all her heart, but then overnight she had come to despise him for being so clueless and so pathetically unaware of the way in which her mother had combined with Dennis Anderson to make a mockery out of their life as a family. But her father had then given his own life to avenge what he thought was her death at the hands of William Milovich.

The photographs of Milovich that ran with the news articles kindled no recollection at all. She had never seen the man, she was sure. The articles detailed the evidence against Milovich, but again, Jenny was mystified. How could Milovich have taken the pictures? And how could he have possibly had had her underwear?

Totally perplexed and sick to her core, Jenny logged off the computer and spent the next two days sitting in her darkened apartment, eating virtually nothing, cutting her classes, calling in sick to work, and ignoring the phone.

22

Once enrolled at Scottsdale Community College, Jenny kept her nose to the grindstone. She was determined to progress toward her AA degree as quickly as possible and to compile along the way an excellent GPA that would allow her to transfer to a good university.

As a full-time student who was also employed virtually full-time, she had very little social life. She dated only rarely, and she refused to allow herself to get seriously involved with anyone. The brutal shock of simultaneously discovering both her mother's infidelity and her father's naive passivity had left her emotionally detached and resolutely determined to maintain a distance that would prevent anyone from ever again disappointing her that severely. Beyond that, Jenny well understood the theory of delayed gratification. And at this point in her life her main objective—indeed her *only* objective—was to invest in herself and in her future.

Jenny soon discovered that the real problem with being a full-time student and a nearly full-time waitress was the fact that she was almost constantly broke, and complicating matters was the fact that she was on a strictly pay-as-you-go basis. Even though she now had a legitimate ID, and even though she was paying taxes and had begun to develop a credit history, there was no way that she could apply for financial aid or for a student loan. Either would require a financial history that Jenny could not afford to divulge. Thus she lived from paycheck to paycheck, paying for school, groceries and utilities and making the rent and her car payments, with very little left over for clothes, personal expenses, entertainment, or even the smallest occasional luxury.

As Jenny knew, most of her fellow servers were basically in the same boat, surviving from one paycheck to the next, an illness, an accident, or a layoff away from financial catastrophe. The exception was Traci, a stunning brunette who had joined the wait staff about three months after Jenny. Like Jenny, Traci's good looks allowed her to garner excellent tips, even though the level of service she provided was no faster or better than anyone else's.

Unlike Jenny, Traci usually worked only one shift a day. Nonetheless she appeared to be very comfortable financially. While most of her fellow employees lived in apartments, often with one or more roommates, Traci lived by herself in a rented luxury condominium. She drove a nearly new Audi convertible and spent what must have been a sizeable amount of money every month on clothes, on her hair, and for other personal expenses.

Some of her fellow employees speculated that Traci had been fortunate enough to come from a family that was well heeled financially. Behind her back, some of the cattier members of the staff suggested that Traci might have found a generous sugar daddy. But Traci never addressed this speculation and rarely ever discussed the details of her personal life.

Jenny had little interest in and even less time for this sort of idle gossip, but she was, understandably, a bit envious of Traci's good fortune. She was also more than a little curious about how Traci had come to enjoy it, but she figured that it was really none of her business.

Traci was twenty-two—three years older than Jennifer McIntyre, but the same age as "Jennifer Douglas," and in the course of working together over the space of several months, the two women gradually got to know each other in a casual sort of way. They discovered that they had some similar interests, and, in particular, that they liked some of the same music. Which was why, at the end of the shift one Friday night, Traci asked Jenny what her plans were for the rest of the evening.

Jenny looked up from the stack of tickets she was totaling, pushed a stray hair back into place, and said, "I'm going to go home, pour myself a beer, and spend some time working on a paper I have due in my American Lit class on Monday morning."

Standing in front of Jenny, clutching her own stack of tickets, Traci said, "So what's your paper about?"

"Arthur Miller's play, *The Crucible*."

"Oh, Jesus, that sounds like an exciting Friday night."

Jenny shrugged and shook her head. "Yeah, well, what can I say?"

"What you can say is that you'll blow off your paper, at least for tonight, and come out with me to hear Chris Clouse who's playing at Sol y Sambra."

"Who's Chris Clouse? I've never heard of him."

"No, but you will. And you'll like him—I promise. Come on, Jenny. You know what they say about all work and no play. When was the last time you had a night out?"

Jenny sighed. "Longer ago than I'd like to remember, that's for sure."

"Well, that settles it." Traci laughed. "Let's finish up these tickets and get the hell out of here. With any luck, we can still get to the club in time to catch at least a part of the first set."

* * *

Forty minutes later, Jenny parked her Volkswagen next to Traci's Audi in the parking lot behind Sol y Sambra. Traci was still wearing the short black skirt that was part of her waitress uniform, but she'd changed into a teal-colored top that accented the swell of her breasts.

She swung her feet out of the car, kicked off the sensible flats she'd been wearing for work, and slipped into a pair of high heels that looked particularly wicked. Jennifer, still dressed in the white blouse and low heels that she'd been wearing with her own short black skirt, arched her eyebrows and said, "I'm probably not dressed for this place."

Traci shook her head. "Don't even think about it. You'd look fantastic no matter what you're wearing. Believe me, none of the guys in here are going to look at you and be anything less than totally impressed."

The two women walked up the stairs at the back of the building and entered the restaurant, which was on the second floor. The club was decorated in a contemporary motif, mostly in shades of brown and ivory. Comfortable upholstered chairs and couches were scattered around the room which was dimly lit, creating a very intimate, almost sensual environment.

The bar was jammed with people, most of who appeared to be in their twenties and early thirties with fashionable clothes and haircuts. Interspersed among the younger clientele were a few older couples and several single men in their late thirties or beyond who obviously had their eyes out for the younger women.

Traci and Jenny squeezed into a small opening at the bar, and following Traci's lead, Jenny ordered a Cosmopolitan. Traci insisted on paying for the drinks, and as the sexy young bartender handed her the change, a tall, thin man, who looked to be somewhere in his mid-twenties, stepped up to the small stage and began tuning an electric guitar. Once satisfied, he launched in to the first song of what was apparently his second set.

Jenny listened for a couple of minutes, then leaned in Traci's direction. Trying to make herself heard over the music and general rumble of the conversations around them, she said, "You're right; he really *is* good."

"Told you. So, are you happy you came?"

"Yeah, but you're going to have to come over and do my laundry tomorrow while I'm working on the paper that I should be doing now."

Traci laughed and they turned to watch the few couples who were attempting to dance in the small space between the stage and the bar. Four songs into the set, a man stepped up behind Traci and put his hand on her right shoulder. "Hey, Maria! How're you?"

The guy looked to be about forty-five, a little overweight with a square face, dark eyes, and short brown hair. His free hand held the remains of some drink with a lime in it, and his flushed complexion and slurred voice suggested that the drink hadn't been his first of the evening.

Traci turned to face the guy and lifted his hand from her shoulder. "Sorry, pal," she said. "You've made a mistake."

The man returned his hand to her shoulder, squeezing it gently. "Whad'ya mean?" he said. "It's me, Jerry!"

Again, Traci removed the guy's hand from her shoulder. Giving him a long, hard look, she said, "Listen, Jerry, or whoever the hell you are.

I'm telling you that you're making a huge mistake here. Now please just leave me alone."

"Oh, what?" the guy practically yelled over the music. "In your apartment, you're more than happy to take my money and fuck my brains out. But out here in public, I'm just shit under your heel or something? Gimmie a break, Baby."

With his free hand, the drunk grabbed Traci's arm just above her elbow and turned toward her, placing himself between Traci and Jenny. "Listen, Sweetheart...," was all he managed to say before Jenny poured the remaining two-thirds of her Cosmo down the back of the guy's neck. Without releasing Traci's arm, the man turned to Jenny. "What the fuck? You little bitch!"

The guy pulled his right arm back, apparently intending to pitch the remains of his own drink into Jenny's face. But before he could do so, a bouncer who easily outweighed the drunk, moved in and grabbed the guy's arm. A second bouncer moved in from the other side and deftly removed the glass from the guy's hand, then together the bouncers maneuvered him through the crowd and out the door. A manager materialized in front of Traci and Jenny. "I'm very sorry about that, ladies." Looking to Traci, he said, "Are you okay, Miss?"

Traci nodded. "Yeah, I'm okay. Thanks for helping out."

The manager insisted on buying the women fresh drinks, and they retreated to a free table near the back of the restaurant. Traci took a sip, then looked at Jenny and gave her a rueful smile. "Thanks for coming to the rescue. If you haven't figured it out already, that asshole was Jerry."

"I don't understand," Jenny said. "Who in the hell is Jerry, and why was he calling you Maria?"

Traci took a deep breath and then exhaled. "I'm 'Maria' in my other life, although I'd really prefer that the rest of the world didn't know it. Jerry, the dumb shit, is a client—or rather an ex-client as of five minutes ago."

Jenny shook her head, still not comprehending.

Traci shrugged. "I have fairly expensive tastes, and there's no way I could make ends meet simply by working at the restaurant. So, I'm also working as an escort. I take four or five dates a week and that brings in enough money to let me drive a nice car and otherwise live fairly comfortably."

"You're a hooker?" Jenny asked incredulously.

Traci gave a small laugh. "Well, I really don't think of myself as a 'hooker,' or even a 'prostitute,' for that matter. I don't have a pimp running my life; I don't stand out on street corners soliciting business, and I'm not sitting in hotel bars trying to seduce the occasional conventioneer.

"I work independently, only for myself. I have an ad on a website that features upscale escorts, and I work only if and when I want to. I make my own dates and screen the guys very carefully." Inclining her head toward the bar, she continued, "And in spite of what you might think after seeing Jerry over there, I don't take dates with guys that are repulsive physically or that might cause me problems."

Jenny arched her eyebrows. "Well, you could have fooled me."

"Yeah." Traci laughed. "That was definitely an unpleasant surprise. But that's the first time I've ever seen Jerry anywhere outside of our appointments, and it's the first time I've ever seen him when he's been drinking. Sober, he's actually a pretty nice guy. But apparently, nobody ever told him that the first major rule in this game is that if a working girl and a client ever see each other in a social setting like this, they never let on that they know each other. Drunk or sober, for him to approach me in public like that was inexcusable."

Jenny took a sip of her drink. "Please forgive me for prying, and just tell me to shut up if you don't want to talk about it, but why did you decide to start doing this?"

"Having sex with guys for money, you mean?"

Jenny nodded.

"Well, I was never Snow White, that's for sure. From the time I was in high school, I've always had a pretty strong sex drive, and I've never been particularly monogamous. I *like* sex, and I like some variety.

"Anyhow, I did a year of college, but decided that I just wasn't cut out for it. I took a number of shitty jobs that didn't pay very much, but I finally learned how to be a reasonably decent waitress and I landed a job at a nice restaurant in Scottsdale. I'd been working there for a few weeks, and then one night I got a party of four guys who were out for dinner after a business meeting or something. They were all well dressed, obviously very affluent.

"At the end of the dinner, I brought them the check. They guy who took it was in his late thirties and very good looking. When I went back to the register to run his credit card, I saw that, along with his platinum AmEx, he'd slipped his business card into the check folder. His name was David, and he was the vice president of an investment group. On the back of the card, he'd written a note, asking if he could have my number.

"Well, like I said, he was very cute and obviously well-off, and so I figured, why not? I wrote my name and number on the card and slipped it under his credit card when I put it back in the folder."

"So, what happened?"

Traci shrugged. "A couple days later, he called and asked me out to dinner. I accepted and called in sick to work that night. David picked me up in his Porsche and we had a very nice dinner at a quiet little restaurant. We danced, had a couple of drinks, and I had a great time—

he was a really nice guy. We went back to my place and we ultimately wound up in bed. He was very good, and it was the perfect end to the evening. Then, after a couple of hours, he said that he had to go, that he couldn't stay the night—like they ever do, right?"

Jenny smiled, and Traci continued. "So anyhow, he got dressed and let himself out. And when I got up the next morning, I discovered that he'd left an envelope on my dresser with four hundred dollars in it."

"You're kidding!"

"No, I'm not, and at first I was really pissed. He called me that afternoon and told me that he'd had a really nice evening and that he hoped we could do it again. I told him that I didn't know about that and that I thought he had gotten the wrong impression about me."

"What did he say to that?"

"There was this long pause, and then he said, 'Are you talking about the envelope I left?' I said that I was, and he said that he hoped I hadn't taken it the wrong way. He didn't mean to imply anything by it, he said. But he knew that I'd taken the night off from work to go out with him, that I'd missed out on the money I would have made, and that he was just trying to make it up to me.

"I told him that wasn't necessary, and he said he was sorry if he had hurt my feelings or insulted me. He said he really had a great time and wanted to know if he could see me again, maybe some afternoon before I had to go to work.

"I said okay, and a couple of days later, he came over to my apartment. To make a long story short, it turns out that the guy was married and looking for something on the side. He said that he was very attracted to me and that he'd like to see me occasionally. He said that he thought that I'd enjoyed myself the night we went out, including the time we spent in bed. I admitted that I had but told him that I wouldn't have gone out with him if I had known he was married and that I was still uncomfortable about the money he'd left."

She paused to take a sip of her drink, and Jenny said, "So?"

Traci set her glass back on the table and said, "So ... He gave me the usual song and dance about how his wife 'didn't understand his needs.'

He said that he really liked me a lot and that he was sorry he couldn't have an open relationship with me. As for the money, he said that he had a lot of it and that he knew I had to be struggling to make ends meet as a waitress. He wasn't paying me for the sex, he said. He just wanted to help me out.

"Well, I *was* struggling. And I figured, 'What's the harm?' I enjoyed having sex with the guy. What would it hurt if he gave me a little money from time to time? So, we went out a couple of times after that, but before long, we weren't going out hardly at all. He'd come by my apartment once or twice a week; we'd spend an hour or so in bed, and on the way out the door, he'd leave me another four hundred.

"Of course, I knew that he *was* paying me for the sex; obviously, if there wasn't any sex, there wouldn't have been any 'helping me out.' But the sex was still good, and I figured that no one was being hurt, so I kept doing it."

"But how did you get from that to..."

Traci shrugged. "I'd been seeing David for about three months, and then one afternoon, he said that he was going to be out of town for a couple of weeks and wouldn't be able to see me. He asked me if I'd like to meet a friend of his in the meantime. He told me that his friend was very nice, that he was sure I would like him, and that the money would be the same.

"I knew that if I said yes, I'd definitely be crossing the line. I mean it was one thing to take money for having sex with a guy that I'd dated and who was 'just helping me out.' It would be something altogether different to take money for screwing a guy that I'd never even met before. There'd be no way of sugarcoating that."

"So, what'd you do?"

"I told him that I needed to think about it. But the truth is that the extra money was a huge help. For the first time in forever, I'd been able to buy some good clothes and get a decent haircut. And it wasn't like it was hard work; I was enjoying the sex with David and even though he was paying for it, he always made sure that I was satisfied as well.

"In the end, I decided that if I wanted to have sex with the guy, and if he wanted to pay me for it, that was nobody's business but our own. And I figured that even if the sex wasn't all that great the money would make it worthwhile. So, I saw the guy, and he was okay—not nearly as cute as David, and not nearly as good in bed—but he was nice, and when we were finished, he asked if he could see me again. I said that he could. As a result, I then had two clients, and my little business was off and running."

"But isn't it dangerous? And what do you do when some fat, ugly gross guy sees your ad on the web and shows up at your door?"

Traci laughed. "That's not the way it works, Hon. Every new client has to be vouched for, either by another client or by another provider that I know and trust. That gives me the chance to screen out the guys I'd rather not deal with. I've never really had a problem with any of my clients, unless you count old Jerry tonight."

For a few moments, Jenny toyed with her empty glass, saying nothing. Finally, Traci leaned across the table and said in a quiet voice, "So now you think I'm a total slut and you wish you'd never met me?"

Jenny shook her head. "No, not at all. In fact, I like you a lot. Personally, I don't think that anyone but a complete moron would ever buy into the idea of 'True Love,' and I think that who people have sex with and why should be nobody's business but their own, even if they are paying for it or being paid for it. But I just don't think that it's something I ever could do myself."

"I know," Traci said, signaling the waitress for another round of drinks. "There was a time when I would have said exactly the same thing myself."

24

Molly and Jason walked out of the police headquarters building on Washington Street in downtown Phoenix into another gorgeous afternoon. While they waited for the patrol officer who was assigned to give them a ride back to their hotel, Jason put on his sunglasses and said, "You don't suppose that you could convince the Powers That Be that it would be a good idea to move the company headquarters from Minneapolis to Phoenix?"

"Probably not," Molly laughed. "But it sure would be nice, at least at this time of the year."

As Richardson had promised, taking Jason's fingerprints and swabbing his mouth for the DNA sample had been a fairly quick and painless process. On the ride downtown, Molly had asked the detective how "Candee" had died. But Richardson had remained fairly tight-lipped on the subject. He would say only that the young woman's death had been drawn out and doubtless very painful. "It was not a pretty sight," he said.

Waiting for their ride, Molly looked to Jason. "I'm surprised you didn't say anything to me about calling Candee again last night. What did you want to ask her?"

"I wanted to know how much personal information a woman had to give the webmaster to post an ad on the site. In particular, would he have the girl's real name and address? But since I hadn't been able to get in touch with her, I didn't think it was important to mention it. I was going to suggest that you try calling her after we talked to the photographer this morning, but then he answered the question himself and it became irrelevant."

Molly gave a slight nod.

Changing the subject, Jason said, "Doesn't it seems more than a little odd that Candee—or Susan—would be murdered within a couple of hours of talking to us?

"It is strange, but you're not thinking that her murder had anything to do with her talking to us, are you?"

"No, I can't imagine how that could be. But I can't stop thinking about her. She seemed like a nice girl, and more than a bit vulnerable."

"That was my impression too, and I feel awful for her. But it strikes me that, doing what she did for a living, a woman is almost certain to run into the occasional maniac, which makes me all that much more determined to find Jenny as quickly as we can."

"Agreed. But there's something else about all of this that strikes me as a pretty amazing coincidence."

"What's that."

"I'm wondering why Jenny would take her ad off the website only a few hours before we got to town looking for her. I mean, she's had the ad on the site for over two years, and she suddenly decides *now* to take it down and take a break from the business?"

"Yes, I've been thinking that that was a pretty amazing coincidence too. But I can't see how it could have been anything more than that. Certainly, she couldn't have known that we were on our way to Phoenix to look for her."

"That's true, but the timing still seems awfully curious. And coupled with Candee's murder, that's two pretty amazing coincidences within a very short amount of time." He paused for a moment, then said, "So what do you propose we do next?"

On the street in front of them, a woman in an SUV who was yammering on a cell phone and paying no attention whatsoever to her driving, abruptly changed lanes and nearly creamed a small Toyota convertible. The girl driving the Toyota laid on the horn and flipped off the woman in the SUV, who remained totally oblivious to anything that was happening behind her.

Watching, Molly shook her head, then turned to Jason, "I've been thinking about our conversation with Candee. She said that many of the

123

women on the website were acquainted with each other, even if they didn't work together. It's probably a long shot, but I was thinking that you might call some of the other women on the website and tell them that you're looking for a double date, or whatever they call it, with the woman and Amber. You could say that you saw Amber when you were here a few weeks ago, but that you'd somehow misplaced her contact information and can't find it on the web. Tell her that you'd be willing to pay very well if she could contact Amber and set up the date."

As the patrolman finally pulled up to the curb to ferry them back to the hotel, Jason said, "You're right—it *does* sound like a long shot, but I don't have a better idea. Let's go give it a try."

The squad car came to a halt in front of them and Jason opened the back door of the car, holding the door for Molly. She'd just started to slip into the back seat when her cell phone began vibrating in her purse. She excused herself for a moment, straightened and turned away from the car. Checking the phone, she saw that the caller was "unknown." She connected to the call and said, "Hello, this is Molly."

From the other end of the call a voice that sounded like it belonged to a relatively young woman asked, "Are you the woman who's running around town claiming to be Amber's mother?"

Molly shot Jason a glance and said into the phone, "Yes, I am. Do you know Amber?"

"I *am* Amber, lady," the voice shot back. "And whoever the hell you are, you're for damn sure not my mother."

Gathering herself and attempting to overcome the shock, Molly said, "You're the woman who had the ad on the website? A brunette with long hair? You were wearing a red slip and bra and looking back over your shoulder?"

"Yes."

"Can I ask why you suddenly took your ad off the website?"

"That's none of your concern, lady. I'm just calling to tell you that I'm not the girl you're looking for. My mother is dead and thankfully won't be coming back to life to look for me. I want you to stop butting into my business."

"But how do I know that you are the woman whose ad I saw? You're just a voice on the phone. You could be anyone."

"Well, I'm not just anyone," the voice insisted. "It was my ad."

"Will you see me in person, so that I can know for sure? I'll gladly pay you your regular hourly rate just to meet me for a few minutes. You can name the time and place, and whether you are my daughter or not, you certainly have nothing to fear from me."

"Look lady, I have no idea who you are or what you think you're doing. But I don't need your money and there's no way I'm going to meet with you. So, you might just as well go back to wherever in the hell you came from because you're wasting your time and money here."

Before Molly could respond, the caller disconnected. Molly looked at Jason who remained standing beside her. "The woman claims to be Amber. She insists that her mother is dead, that she is not my daughter and that she will not see me. She wants me to go home and stop trying to find her."

"Do you believe her?"

"I don't know. She didn't sound like Jenny to me. Of course, if she really isn't Jenny, then she wouldn't sound like her. But without seeing her in person, I have no way of knowing whether she's the woman in the ad or not, let alone whether she might be Jenny."

"So, what are you going to do?"

Molly shrugged. "I'm going to stay right here and keep on looking. This woman says that she doesn't want me poking around in her life. I can only hope that if I keep on doing it, she'll finally break down and agree to see me. Then I'll know if she's really Jenny or not."

25

The patrol officer dropped Molly and Jason at the door of their hotel, and they walked through the lobby to the bank of elevators. As they were waiting for an elevator to arrive, Molly said, "I'm thinking about the phone call that I got as we were leaving the police station."

"And?"

"And I'm wondering where the woman got my number. *You've* been making the calls to the other women we've been contacting, and you've been giving them *your* phone number, not mine. We've only given my number to two people, Candee and Ron Newton. The woman who called me claiming to be Amber could only have gotten the number from one of them.

"It seems hard to imagine that in the short period between the time we saw Candee and the time she was killed, Amber would have suddenly decided to finally contact her and that Candee gave her the number. So, I'm thinking that the only way the woman could have gotten it would have been from Newton."

Jason nodded. "There is, of course, one other possibility."

"What's that?"

"That the person who killed Candee found the card and either called you or had someone else do it."

Molly nodded. "You're right. Detective Richardson said that the police didn't find my card in Candee's things. It's certainly possible that the killer found it and took it with him."

As she stood there, quietly contemplating the matter, an elevator finally appeared and the doors slid open. Turning away from the open car, Molly touched Jason's arm and said, "Let's go have another chat with Ron Newton."

* * *

They found the photographer still at his studio and obviously not at all happy to see them again. As they walked through the door and into the reception area, Newton looked up from his computer. Without rising to his feet, he looked to Molly and said, "Haven't you two caused me enough trouble for one day? What in the hell do you want now?"

Molly stepped up to the desk and looked down at Newton. "Exactly what sort of trouble do you think we've caused for you?"

"I've had the police here most of the afternoon, thanks to you."

Molly shook her head. "The fact that the police were here had nothing to do with Jason and me. It had *everything* to do with the fact that you allowed that poor girl to advertise on your sleazy website, and in the end, it got her killed. And believe me when I say that if anything happens to my daughter, the police will be the least of your problems."

Finally rising to his feet, the photographer stabbed his finger in Molly's direction. "Bullshit, lady. I did not twist the woman's arm and force her to sell herself; that was a choice she made on her own. And I sure as hell did not tell her to avoid common sense procedures and let some sick fuck into her incall so that he could butcher her. That was her decision as well. And her stupidity—and yours—has put me in a world of hurt."

"And just how have I behaved stupidly, Mr. Newton?"

"By refusing to accept the obvious fact that's right in front of your damned eyes! If Amber really is your daughter, she doesn't want to see you. And you're blundering around looking for her is simply roiling the waters and causing problems for her and for me."

Yielding no ground, Molly said, "Mr. Newton, I couldn't care less about causing problems for you, and I'll happily continue to do so if that's what it takes to find my daughter. You'd be a lot better off helping me do that rather than standing in the way."

The photographer paused for a moment, then leaned forward, placing his hands on the desk and steeling his eyes on Molly's. "Well, lady, that's not what Amber says."

Startled, Molly said, "What do you mean? You've talked to her?"

Newton gave her a hard smile. "Not fifteen minutes after you left this morning. She'd forgotten to ask me to take down the photo of her and Candee together. After seeing the news, she called to make sure that I had."

"Did you tell her that I had talked to you?"

"Yes, I did. I even gave her your number."

"And what did she say?"

"She told me that she had no mother, that the bitch was dead. And she said that even if her mother had somehow managed to rise from the grave, she wouldn't waste five seconds of her life talking with her."

"I don't believe you."

Newton threw up his hands. "Lady, I don't give a shit if you believe me or not. I just want you out of my studio and out of my life. Go back to Bumfuck, Minnesota or wherever you're from and leave me the hell alone!"

* * *

Back at the hotel two hours later, Jason hung up the phone and shook his head. By seven o'clock that evening, he'd managed to contact eight of the other women who advertised on the same website that "Amber" had used. Three of the women claimed that they knew Amber and two of the three promised that they would try to contact her and set up a date as Jason had requested.

The third woman told Jason that she didn't do threesomes, but that she'd be happy to see him by himself if he wanted. Jason thanked the woman and told her that he'd keep the offer in mind. Turning in his chair, he looked to Molly and said, "Well, let's hope that one of these women can get through to Jenny and that she'll be willing to take the date. Otherwise, I'm not sure what else we might do"

"Me either."

"There is something else that I hate to bring up," Jason said.

"What's that?"

"I'm supposed to be leading a training session on Monday morning. I could call Anna and have her reschedule it, but we've retained Denis

Patrick to come in and do a session on the legal aspects of the new sexual harassment policy. Rescheduling him could be a problem."

Molly dropped her head into her hands and massaged her eyes. After a couple of moments, she looked up again. "No, Jason, we really can't do that. I've already taken you away from the office for what will be four days now for something that has absolutely nothing whatsoever to do with the business. You need to fly home on Saturday morning so that you're ready to get back to work on Monday."

"You're going to stay?"

"I'm going to call Karen and tell her that I'm taking a few days of vacation."

"But what will you do?"

Molly shook her head. "I'm hoping that one of these women will call back and say that she's made an appointment for you to see her and Jenny. If that doesn't work, then I guess I'll wait to see if the police are able to find her."

Jason got up from the small desk, walked over to the bed and sat down beside her. "Are you sure you don't want me to stay? I could certainly take a couple of days of vacation myself."

"No. Thank you, Jason. You've been a tremendous help, and I wouldn't have gotten anywhere here without you. But I'm not sure what more the two of us can do, and I really can't ask you to stay any longer. It wouldn't be fair either to you or to the company."

As Jason reluctantly nodded his agreement, Molly's cell phone began buzzing. She connected to the call and Melinda Anderson said, "Hi, Hon. I just wanted to check in to see how things were going today. Are you having any better luck?"

"No, not really, I'm sorry to say. And in fact, things took a very unsettling turn this morning."

Molly described the events of the day, including the interview with Detective Richardson and the subsequent visit to police headquarters, ending with the decision that Jason should return to Minneapolis on Saturday.

"Jesus, Molly, I'm really worried about you. No way should you be in the middle of this all by yourself."

"Not to worry, Mel. I'm a big girl, and certainly what happened to that poor woman has nothing to do with me. It's just an awful coincidence."

"Well, I still don't like it and I especially don't like the idea that you would be down there all by yourself. Are you really sure that Jason has to go back?"

Molly looked briefly in Jason's direction and said, Yeah, I'm sure."

"Okay," Melinda said. "But I talked to Denny just before I called you. He says that he's nearly finished with his business in Dallas and that he's about to come home. I'm going to call him back and tell him to go to Phoenix instead. He can take over for Jason."

"No, really, Mel. There's no need, and I really don't know what he could do. I'll be fine by myself."

"Well then, think of it as a favor to me," her friend said. "I'll sleep a lot better knowing that Denny is there to help out. This is not a time when you should be alone."

Part III

26

In spite of what he'd told Molly and Melinda, Dennis Anderson was virtually certain that "Amber" was, in fact, Molly's long-lost daughter, and he'd nearly stroked out when her picture popped onto his computer screen. The resemblance was simply too striking to be a coincidence and the sight of the girl staring back at him from the monitor struck Dennis like a bolt of lightning. From out of nowhere, little Jenny was suddenly and inexplicably back, threatening by her very existence to wreak havoc on the life that he had so carefully created and which was already teetering on the brink of disaster.

Hoping to delay Molly from rushing off to Phoenix immediately, Dennis tried to raise at least some doubt in her mind. He also insisted that Molly should wait to go to Arizona until Melinda could accompany her. And, risky as it might have been, he had also slipped into the parking garage at Molly's condominium building in the dead of night, popped the top off the brake fluid reservoir on her BMW, and, using Melinda's turkey baster, had drawn virtually all of the fluid out of the reservoir.

He hoped that, at a minimum, even a minor accident would prevent Molly from leaving for Phoenix immediately, giving him time to get there ahead of her by at least a few days. He realized, of course, that Molly could be seriously injured or perhaps even killed when the brakes failed, and while he might regret that at one level, at another, he would be tremendously relieved.

But then Molly had walked away from the accident with only minor injuries, and if that weren't bad enough, Jason Burke had then admitted directing Molly to the website. Burke had agreed to accompany her to Phoenix in an effort to contact "Amber." Thankfully, though, they would not be able to leave Minneapolis until the following Tuesday.

Grateful for even a small head start, Dennis told Melinda that he had to make a last-minute business trip to Dallas. He then stepped off the plane in Phoenix two days ahead of Molly, in a frantic effort to find Jenny before her mother could.

Dennis was not by nature a violent man. But caught in the trap where he suddenly found himself, he was ready and willing to embrace any tactic, no matter how extreme, in an effort to stave off the disaster that would surely result should Molly and Jennifer somehow find each other again. It was a simple matter of self-defense, and Dennis reasoned that if anyone were to blame for the repellant actions he might now be forced to take, it was Jennifer and certainly not Dennis himself.

He had no idea whether Jenny might still have the picture that had gone missing that fateful night or if she had destroyed it. Dennis figured that he could bluff his way through the situation if the girl should now surface again, claiming that she'd seen such a picture but without actually having the photo to support her contention. He would deny ever having had such a photo, and he knew that Molly would certainly support him in his denial. They would both insist that Jenny was obviously confused about what she had seen. Naturally, Jenny would refuse to believe their denials, but absent the proof of the picture itself, it would be her word against theirs.

But, of course, if Jenny still had the picture, it would be another story altogether. And that was a chance that Dennis simply could not afford to take.

Dennis would have described himself as a very astute investor. And he would have insisted that the fact that he was now in such serious financial difficulty was due only to a remarkable run of bad luck that no one could have possibly anticipated.

As a senior trust officer in a large Minneapolis bank, Dennis guided the investments and oversaw the finances of several very wealthy clients. And in those cases, he had handled the monies entrusted to him very astutely. He always very carefully balanced risk and reward, and he never exposed a client to an unacceptable level of financial jeopardy. As a result, over the long term his clients had enjoyed returns significantly larger than those produced by most of the bank's other trust officers and, for that matter, by many other financial advisors.

Unfortunately, his own investments were another matter altogether.

On the one hand, Dennis *had* followed conventional wisdom and diversified his investments. But he did not possess the patience or the mindset to accept for himself the slow and steady gains he recommended to his clients. In consequence, while he had invested in a variety of financial instruments, in too many cases he had gone chasing after the promise of a quick and large return. And unfortunately, several of his investments had gone south in recent months, virtually all at the same time.

In particular, Dennis had poured a significant amount of money into a real estate investment trust that was building three condominium projects in Miami, Florida. At the time the trust was formed, the Miami real estate market was exploding, along with that of the rest of southern Florida. Buyers were lining up, cash in hand, and paying huge premiums for the privilege of being allowed to buy condos in buildings that wouldn't even be constructed for another two or three years.

While Dennis had not gotten in on the ground floor of the boom, he'd bought in early enough to feel certain that he'd enjoy a huge return on his investment. But then, while the projects were still under construction, Miami real estate had suddenly gone into the tank, thanks to a perfect storm created by a saturated condo market, a sudden and unexpected rise in interest rates and an ill-timed category four hurricane that drove insurance rates through the roof and made many prospective buyers wonder if they wouldn't be a lot happier sunning themselves in Nevada or Arizona where they wouldn't have to worry about their homes flooding or blowing away.

The dismal performance of the REIT in particular, had left Dennis in a world of hurt financially, and the fact that he was the family's sole breadwinner complicated matters even more. While Melinda whiled away her days doing god-knows-what and spending money about as fast as Dennis could make it, the burden of maintaining the lifestyle that he and the rest of his family had come to enjoy fell squarely upon his shoulders alone.

It was a difficult job even under the best of circumstances, especially as Mary Ellen got older and seemed to be constantly in need of newer and ever more expensive clothes, gadgets, and lessons in everything from dance to piano to tennis—all in addition, of course, to the tuition at the private school that Melinda insisted would ultimately give their daughter her best shot at a college scholarship.

His back to the wall, Dennis had performed a complicated juggling act and "borrowed" seventy-five thousand dollars from the account of one of his wealthiest clients, an eighty-seven- year-old widow whose husband had left his entire fortune in Dennis's hands to manage on behalf of the widow who knew absolutely nothing about money or investments.

Dennis assumed that he would be able to slip the money back into the account relatively quickly once a couple of his own investments turned around. But that hadn't happened yet, and now his best hope—and, indeed, perhaps his *only* hope of avoiding disgrace and a possible prison sentence—lay with his dying father-in-law.

Although Dennis had dropped any number of not-so-subtle hints through the years that the old man might consider allowing Dennis to do some estate planning on his behalf, Melinda's father, a self-made industrialist, had insisted on controlling his own money right to the bitter end. And unfortunately for Dennis, the end, although certainly bitter, was not coming nearly quickly enough.

Melinda's father had smoked since the age of thirteen. And in spite of all the health warnings, and without regard for Melinda's constant nagging, he had continued to do so until four months earlier, when he'd been hospitalized with a particularly aggressive form of throat cancer. The doctors had given him three months to live, and he'd now lasted an additional five weeks beyond the deadline. He was weakening steadily, but in defiance of all the odds, he gave every appearance of hanging on indefinitely.

When there was finally no way of avoiding it, the old man had at last written a very simple will, and once he went to his just reward, his fortune would be settled on Melinda, his only child. Given that Melinda knew barely more about money and investments than did Dennis's client, the elderly widow, Dennis expected to step in and manage the money. At that point, he could perform another slight-of-hand in which the seventy-five thousand dollars would be returned to the client's account, leaving Dennis to breathe a huge sigh of relief.

Which assumed, of course, that Jenny McIntyre did not suddenly come back to life, claiming to have seen a picture of Dennis in bed with Melinda's best friend.

Melinda might believe his denials, especially since Molly would support them. But then again, she might not, especially if Jenny were to suddenly produce the photo she'd appropriated on that fateful night five years ago. And in that case, Dennis would be totally screwed. If Melinda were to become convinced that her husband and her best friend had combined to betray her, she would throw him out and file for divorce in a nanosecond. She would take their daughter and her father's fortune and leave Dennis to his just desserts.

Dennis simply couldn't afford to let that happen. Yes, he'd been foolish in lusting after his neighbor's wife, but then again, he was hardly the first man ever to do so. And yes, printing and hiding the photos that Jenny had found had been unbelievably stupid. But that too was hardly a capital offense. And the truth remained that if Jenny had not been rooting around in his private things where she didn't belong, nothing would have ever come of it.

What it all boiled down to was this: Dennis had struggled too long and had worked too hard to save himself from the fate to which life had originally consigned him, and he was not about to meekly sacrifice himself now for the sake of the woman that Jenny McIntyre had become.

27

The ad on the website indicated that "Amber" was available for either incall or outcall sessions. Dennis assumed for any number of reasons that the far better choice would be to make an incall appointment. The last thing he wanted or needed would be any sort of connection between his hotel room and a dead hooker.

After checking into a hotel near the airport, he got back into his rental car and drove to a nearby convenience store where he bought a disposable—and untraceable—cell phone. He called the number listed in Amber's ad and listened to the girl's voice on a recording: She was unable to answer his call at the moment; he should please leave a name and number and she would call him back as quickly as she could. In the meantime, he should have "the best of all possible days."

Dennis left a message asking the girl to return his call. Then he sat in the car for the next twenty minutes with the windows closed and the air conditioner running, listening to the radio in an absent-minded way, and tapping his fingers impatiently on the steering wheel. Around him, the city was in motion on a beautiful spring afternoon, the likes of which no one could have ever imagined in Minnesota at this time of year. But Dennis remained oblivious to it all, waiting for the phone to ring.

When it finally did, a young woman's voice asked if this was Terry. Dennis assured her that it was and explained that he had seen her ad on the web and was hoping to make an incall appointment for later that afternoon or evening.

"Well," the young woman said, "Before I can make an appointment to see you, I'll need a couple of references. What other providers have you seen here locally?"

"Oh, gosh," Dennis said, "I haven't seen anyone else locally. I'm here on business for the first time in years; I don't know anyone here in Phoenix."

"I see. What sort of business are you in, Terry?"

"Plumbing supplies. I'm the sales director for a company in Michigan and we're having a meeting of our southwestern reps here in Phoenix this week."

"Well then, why don't you give me the names of a couple of providers that you've seen in other cities, along with their contact information. If they vouch for you, we could make an appointment for a little later in the week."

"I'd be happy to do that, but the problem is that the only free time I'll have is this afternoon and evening. After that, I'm going to be in meetings until I leave."

The silence hung for several moments, then Dennis said, in what he hoped was his most reassuring voice, "Look, Amber, I was really attracted by the picture on your ad, and I was really looking forward to seeing you. I know that you don't know me from Adam, and I understand your need to be cautious, but I can assure you that you have nothing to fear from me. If it will help, I'd be willing to go an extra hundred over and above your usual fee."

"Well," the girl replied hesitantly, "the only opening I have left today would be at five o'clock. Would that work for you?"

"Five o'clock would be perfect."

"Okay then. But just to let you know, in a case like this, I will need to see at least two forms of photo ID so that I know that you really are who you say you are."

Dennis promised that this would be "no problem," and the girl gave him directions to the apartment complex where she took her appointments. "Once you pull into the complex," she told him, "take the first left. Immediately on your right, you'll see several uncovered parking places. Park in one of those spots and call me. I'll give you the number of the apartment and you can come on up."

Dennis told her that he was looking forward very much to meeting her and promised to be there promptly at five. Then he disconnected from the call and heaved a huge sigh of relief.

28

Two years after her conversation with Traci at Sol y Sambra, Jenny was herself a successful escort, making a much more comfortable living while she finished her degree at Arizona State University. As she'd told Traci that night, she could never have imagined being in the life herself, and yet...

She was tired of scrimping and doing without. As a practical matter, she'd been living from hand to mouth ever since leaving Minnesota. And even though she could see the light at the end of the tunnel, it was a long tunnel, and the light was glowing very dimly. Jenny knew that it would still be a very long time before she'd be able to finish college, find a good job, and finally be able to live a bit more comfortably and securely.

As she'd told Traci, she was not prudish about sex, and the sight of her mother romping with Dennis Anderson had effectively destroyed any naïve, adolescent ideas she once might have harbored about sex being some sort of sacred act. Even the thought of commercial sex no longer bothered her, and she honestly believed that Traci's profession was as legitimate as many others. Traci was providing a useful service for which there was an obvious demand, and she was giving good value in exchange for the money that her clients happily paid.

Traci understood, of course, that Jenny was struggling financially, and on more than one occasion she suggested that Jenny might take a date herself now and then to help ease the financial strain. "You wouldn't have to turn professional," Traci insisted. "But every once in a while, I could line you up with a nice guy whose company you'd enjoy and who'd be very grateful, financially and otherwise, for the privilege of spending a little time with you."

Jenny always declined, telling her friend that, even though she was struggling, and even though she had no girlish illusions about love and sex, she just couldn't imagine herself doing such a thing.

It was the demise of the little Volkswagen that finally changed her mind.

Jenny left work just after ten o'clock one Thursday night, started the car, and began backing out of her parking place. The car moved about ten feet and suddenly stopped dead in its tracks, halfway out of the parking spot.

Jenny cranked the ignition, but the engine refused to turn over and fifteen minutes later, the battery gave up the ghost. She put the car in neutral and pushed it back into the parking spot. Then she retrieved her purse, dug out her phone, and called an Uber to take her home.

The next morning, she had the car towed to the garage. She spent an hour in the customer waiting room, reading her sociology assignment, before the service manager came into the room shaking his head. The engine had seized up completely, he said. Of course, they could repair it, but the cost of the repairs would doubtless exceed the value of the car at this point. Jenny accepted the glum news and arranged to rent a car for a couple of days while she decided what to do.

Even the expense of the rental car represented a serious assault on Jenny's precarious financial situation. And with tuition and the rent both coming due, the thought of having to buy a "new" used car was staggering. Her only choice was to take out a cash advance on her credit card, at usurious interest rates, for the down payment on another car. She would then have to figure out how she could possibly manage to make both the payment on the car loan and the one on the credit card.

Realistically, even working two shifts a day, six days a week, it would barely be possible, and Jenny hated to think what the effect of the extra hours at the restaurant would be on her schoolwork. So, at the end of the shift that night, she swallowed hard and asked Traci if she had some time to talk.

* * *

"I wouldn't want to do it on a regular basis," she told Traci. "And I don't want to advertise on the web or anything like that. But I really do need the money."

"I understand your dilemma, Hon. But are you sure? This is a big step, and I know how much you've resisted the thought of taking it. I don't want you to do something that you're going to regret later. If it would help, I can loan you a little money to tide you over for a while."

Jenny shook her head. "No, Trace. I really appreciate the offer, but I'd be even more reluctant to borrow the money from you than from the credit card company. My only problem is that I'm really nervous, and I wouldn't have the slightest idea what to do with the guy once we were alone. I mean, do you just get undressed and let him do whatever he wants?"

"No, not even remotely," Traci said, smiling. "You want the client to *think* that you're letting him do whatever he wants, but you always want to be in complete control of the situation."

"But how do you manage that?"

"Well," Traci said, still smiling. "I have an idea about that."

Jenny arched her eyebrows and Traci said, "I have a client that I've been seeing for a couple of years. He's a nice guy, mid-forties, a local executive, very good-looking and very well off.

"I'm thinking that I could tell him that I have a very attractive friend who wants to get into the business and that I want to show her the ropes, using one of my clients to practice on. I'm sure that he'd jump at the chance. That way, I'd be there with you and could walk you through the first experience. And we could split what would be a very nice fee for a couple of hours' work."

* * *

The client's name was Tim. And, in fact, he was a pretty nice guy. He understood that, under the circumstances, Jenny was nervous and shy, and he tried to be as sympathetic and accommodating as he could.

Jenny watched first, as Traci went through what was, apparently, a well-practiced routine of welcoming the client, making him comfortable, then moving him into the bedroom and ultimately into bed. Through it all, Traci guided Tim, encouraging him to first undress her, then undressing him and leading him through a variety of sexual positions until he finally came in a shuddering climax.

While he recovered, Tim and the two women shared a glass of wine. Then, after thirty minutes or so, Tim said he was good to go, and they went through the whole process all over again, this time with Traci watching and with Jenny taking her first paying customer.

Tim was obviously very turned on by the situation, but he was gentle and considerate with her. When it was over, he left the women an envelope with a thousand dollars in it and asked Jenny if he could see her again. Jenny said that he could, and since the routine had been such a success, the two women used it again with three of Traci's other clients. Thus, at the end of two weeks, Jenny had the genesis of a client list with the names of four very prosperous and generous men.

Like Traci, Jenny continued to work at the restaurant, although she drastically cut back the number of shifts she was taking. Her "straight" job still provided her with a steady income, but even more important, it provided cover for the much larger amounts of money that she was now making in her other line of work.

29

Two years down the road, Jenny accepted a late afternoon appointment with Terry, an executive in town from Michigan. As she always did, she made a note of his name and number so that she could add it to the client database on her computer. Later, she would add to the file any additional information about Terry that she managed to glean during the appointment. If, after some time had passed, he wanted to schedule a subsequent appointment, Jenny could refer to the database to determine if she wanted to see him again or not. She could also use it to refresh her memory about Terry, about the topics they had discussed and any special requests that he might have made. Finally, the record would come in handy should the client ever use Jenny as a reference with another provider.

Terry had been unable to provide her with any local references, but like most women at her end of the profession, Jenny had a contingency plan to deal with such situations. She never saw clients in her own home, but only in their hotels, in their own homes (if she knew the client well enough), or in the apartment that she and Candee shared for the purpose of taking incall appointments. And in each case, there were various safeguards built into the situation.

As was her practice in such cases, Jenny gave Terry directions to the apartment complex where she and Candee rented their unit and gave him very specific instructions about where to park.

From the living room window, she could see the uncovered parking spots very clearly. When Terry arrived and called for the unit number, she would first write down the license plate number of the vehicle he was driving. She would have him get out of the vehicle before giving him the apartment number, and this would allow her the opportunity to size him up and to make a snap decision about whether or not he looked drunk, too physically unappealing, or otherwise potentially troublesome to invite up.

Assuming that the client passed muster, Jenny would give him the unit number. While he made his way up the stairs, she would call Candee's voice mail and recite his plate number, along with a description of the vehicle he was driving and his phone number. Once the client got to the door, Jenny would open it, leaving the security chain in place, while the guy showed her two photo IDs.

If the name on the IDs matched the name the client had given on the phone, and if he didn't have liquor on his breath, Jenny would then open the door and invite him in. She would explain that, for safety's sake, since he was a new client, she had already called a friend and given her the guy's name, phone number and the plate number of his vehicle. And if the guy had no problem with that, she'd give him a smile and ask him if he'd like to get comfortable.

* * *

When a white Toyota Camry pulled into the parking lot at ten minutes to five that afternoon, Jenny was already waiting at the window, watching and holding her cell phone by her side. The car pulled forward into an uncovered spot directly under Jenny's window, allowing her a very good look at the driver, even before he got out of the car. Thirty seconds later, Jenny was still standing in shock at the window when her cell phone began to ring.

Even after five years, there was no way she would have failed to recognize Dennis Anderson. He might have gained a little weight, but his hair was still the same, and there was no mistaking his face. Her mind spinning, Jenny tried to assess the situation.

"Terry" had said that he'd seen her picture on the web.

The one thing she'd most feared in the two years since she'd posted the ad was that someone from her past might one day stumble across it. But the picture showed a much more mature version of the girl she had once been, with significantly longer hair and in partial profile. She'd also provided a physical description of herself that was considerably at variance with that of Jenny McIntyre. And having done all of that, she earnestly hoped that no one who might have known her back in Minnesota would ever recognize her photo, even if they found the website.

Obviously, her effort had failed. The fact that Dennis Anderson—the one man she hated more than any other on the planet—was now parked below her window, could not possibly be a coincidence. But what was he doing here? Was he going to try to talk her into going back to Minneapolis? Or, having seduced her mother, was he now looking for a shot at Jenny as well?

After ringing four times, the cell phone defaulted to voice mail. Jenny stepped back from the window, telling herself that this was not the time to panic. She took a couple of deep breaths, then punched the button to access her voice mail.

She had one new message, and when it began playing, she heard a voice she now recognized as Dennis' say, "Hi, Amber. It's Terry. It's just now five o'clock and I'm in the parking lot at your apartment complex. Please call me back and let me know where I'm supposed to go. I'm really looking forward to meeting you."

"Terry" recited the number of his cell phone and then disconnected.

Jenny knew damned good and well where she wanted to tell him to go, but she waited for another few seconds, then dialed the number. He answered on the second ring, and Jenny said, "Terry? It's Amber."

When "Terry" confirmed the identification, she said, "Hey, Sweetie, I'm really very sorry, but I'm sitting on the side of the expressway with a blown front tire. I'm waiting for the auto club to get a tow truck out here and take care of me, but there's no way I'm going to be done in time to see you tonight. The good news is that since we talked this afternoon, I've had a cancellation at one o'clock tomorrow afternoon. Would that work for you?"

"Terry" said that he wasn't sure that his schedule would permit that and offered to come out and help Amber with her tire problems. She declined, telling him that the tow truck should be there at any minute and again apologized for being unable to keep the appointment.

145

"Terry" said he would try to free up the time on the following afternoon and promised to stay in touch.

Once off the call, Jenny stood back from the window, watching as the Camry remained parked for another couple of minutes. After what seemed an eternity, it finally backed out of the parking place and rolled slowly through the open gates of the apartment complex.

Jenny watched as the car disappeared. Then she quickly changed into her street clothes, gathered up the few personal possessions that she kept in the apartment and began the process of making herself scarce.

30

Driving out of "Amber's" apartment complex, Dennis Anderson swore and slammed his hand into the steering wheel. The stupid bitch had to pick *tonight* to get a fucking flat tire?

Earlier in the afternoon, when the girl had accepted the appointment, he'd hoped that he could worm his way into her apartment, take care of business, and maybe even be on his way out of Phoenix before the night was over. Now he was stuck here for at least another twenty-four hours.

He knew from talking to Melinda that Molly was not planning to get to Phoenix for at least another couple of days. That meant that he still had a little bit of breathing room, but it did not make him feel any more comfortable about his situation. And he now cursed the day he'd ever gotten a hard-on for the woman.

Dennis had always thought that Molly was a knockout, and she was exactly the sort of woman that he preferred physically. Still, that didn't explain why he had developed such a jones for her. After all, Melinda was still a reasonably attractive woman herself, with a nice body that she was only rarely reluctant to put to good use in bed.

They'd begun sleeping together almost as soon as they met in college, and it was clear early on that they were very compatible in a good many ways, including sexually. In addition, Melinda was the only child of a very wealthy father who doted on his daughter and who seemed to genuinely welcome the idea that Dennis might one day become his son-in-law. And so, a few months after they both graduated, Dennis had happily married her.

The early years of their union had mostly been good ones, clouded only by their disappointment when they had been unable to conceive any children. A series of doctors had never been able to explain why this should be the case, but try as they might, it just hadn't happened, and so in the end, they had reconciled themselves to the notion that they would have to be fulfilled in each other. But then, seemingly out of nowhere, had come the miracle of Mary Ellen.

Both Melinda and Dennis had been ecstatic when the doctor told them that Melinda was pregnant. Melinda's father, by then a widower, was thrilled by the prospect that he would finally have a grandchild, and he was deeply moved when Dennis and Melinda told him that they were naming their baby daughter after Melinda's deceased mother.

Inevitably, the baby's birth put something of a damper on their sex life, but that was only to be expected given that they were both now a lot busier and getting a lot less sleep. After a couple of years had passed, and once Mary Ellen was sleeping through the night, Dennis and Melinda settled into something of a new sexual routine, perhaps not as frequent or as inventive as in the days when they were first together, but still, all in all, one that seemed to satisfy each of them for the most part.

Which meant that there was no logical reason why Dennis should have become so obsessed with Molly McIntyre.

But, of course, as is so often the case, logic didn't have a damned thing to do with it. The sight of Molly simply touched something primal and inexplicable at the core of his being, an urgent, desperate need that thousands of years of evolution and the relatively thin veneer of polite civilization could never begin to extinguish. From the moment Dennis had first caught sight of Molly in a tee shirt and shorts, directing the movers as they unloaded her family's furniture into the house next door, he was hooked. And as the two couples became increasingly close friends over the years, his determination to have her one day grew accordingly.

His desire was exacerbated by his growing unhappiness with his own wife. In the years after they were first married, Melinda had worked as a legal assistant. During that time, the two of them together had enjoyed a fairly healthy income and had developed some rather expensive tastes. Then, three months before Mary Ellen was born, Melinda had quit her job, putting a sizeable dent in the family income just as their expenses were beginning to increase dramatically.

Once Mary Ellen was of an age where she could be going to day care and then kindergarten, Dennis had suggested that Melinda might go back to work, at least part time. She had emphatically rejected the idea, and at the same time had also refused to consider adopting a more modest lifestyle, apparently assuming that somehow, Dennis should magically come up with the money necessary to support their family all by himself.

Melinda's refusal to go back to work had become an increasing irritant and the situation was only aggravated by the fact that every time Dennis looked over at the house next door, he saw Molly McIntyre who not only drove him to distraction physically, but who also had a successful career. Molly was bringing home a very significant paycheck every month and at the same time she and Alan had somehow managed to successfully raise her daughter to near adulthood. Dennis could not begin to understand why Melinda couldn't have done the same thing, and his growing discontent about the situation served simply to amplify his desire for Molly.

Dennis was not a stupid man, and he knew better than to ever make even the slightest move in that direction, at least initially. But that certainly never stopped him from fantasizing about his next-door neighbor or from dreaming that someday, somehow, an opportunity might arise to finally bring those fantasies to life.

.

31

Eighteen hours after "Amber" had abruptly cancelled his appointment claiming tire problems, Dennis Anderson was virtually certain that the girl had somehow found him out and bolted.

Three hours after leaving the apartment complex, he had called "Amber's" cell phone with the good news that he *could* break free for an appointment at one o'clock the following afternoon as she'd suggested. He asked her to please call back and confirm the appointment, but by ten o'clock the next morning the girl had made no reply, and so he called her number again and left the same message. Two hours later he still had heard nothing from her.

Dennis realized, then, that "Amber" had almost certainly not been having car problems and that she had not been seriously interested in rescheduling the appointment. He deduced further, that she must have been watching from some vantage point when he arrived at her apartment complex, that she must have recognized him, and that she had invented the story about the flat tire on the spur of the moment as a device to get rid of him so that she could get safely away from the apartment after he left.

It was possible, of course, that the woman was simply an irresponsible flake or, perhaps, an addict of some sort who was incapable of keeping a schedule. But he sincerely doubted it, which meant that there was both good news and bad: If in fact the girl had recognized him, then certainly "Amber" the escort was indeed the long-lost Jennifer McIntyre. But now she knew he was coming, and obviously, she was determined not to let him find her.

Dennis was acutely aware of the fact that the clock was ticking on two separate fronts. His wife believed that he was in Dallas on business, but she was also expecting him to return home fairly quickly. At the same time, he knew from talking to Melinda that Molly McIntyre had finished making her preparations and that she would be arriving in Phoenix on Tuesday, along with Jason Burke, to begin her own search for Jenny.

Dennis knew that if he had not managed to find and deal with Jenny by the time Molly arrived in town, his options would essentially disappear. He simply could not afford to allow Molly and her daughter to find each other. And if he could not remove Jenny from the picture, that left only one other very unpleasant alternative.

Dennis assumed that once Molly and Jason Burke arrived, he could allow himself a day or two at most before insinuating himself into Molly's search. He would monitor Molly's progress through Melinda, and he knew his wife well enough to understand that it would be relatively easy to plant the thought in her mind that he should fly to Phoenix to assist Molly once his business in Dallas was concluded.

Once Melinda suggested the idea to Molly, Dennis would join Molly and could then track her search for Jenny from the inside. He would have to somehow separate Molly from Jason Burke, but he assumed that he could convince Molly that Burke's assistance would no longer be necessary and that Burke might as well go back to Minneapolis. Once that was accomplished, Dennis could assist Molly in her search for two or three days, and at that point, the question of whether or not they actually found Jenny would become academic. At the end of that time, from one end or the other, Dennis would permanently sever the link between Molly and her daughter.

* * *

Dennis realized that eliminating Jenny from the picture was still the much better option. He assumed that the police would devote much less time and far fewer resources attempting to solve the murder of a common hooker than they would to the killing of a visiting businesswoman. He also knew that it would be much easier for him to cover his own tracks in the event of Jenny's death than that of Molly's. And so, at least until Molly arrived in Phoenix, he would still devote every waking moment to finding Jenny.

151

The night that Molly had come to dinner and broken the news that she had spotted Jenny's photo, Dennis stayed up late, claiming that he had work to do in his study. While Melinda snored softly down the hall, he meticulously worked his way through the FantacieLand website as well as several others, studying the photos and noting every reference to the girl in question.

He had found only three. Either the woman did not do "massages," or she chose not to advertise in that section of the website. Nor was she apparently registered with any of the local escort agencies. The same photo and description that appeared on the "Brunettes" page of the site also appeared on the "All Escorts" page. Dennis found the third listing on the "Double Delights" page.

The photo on that page showed "Amber" alongside a petite blonde with the improbable name of "Candee." The ad promised that they were ready to help a lucky client "fulfill the fantasy of a lifetime."

The joint ad showed the same phone number for "Amber" as in the woman's other two ads. It also gave the contact information for "Candee." Dennis had written "Candee's" information on the same page where he had written "Amber's."

Dennis assumed that Jenny had probably noted the number of his cell phone and that she would be watching for calls from that number. But he had no way of knowing whether she might have had the presence of mind to alert her playing partner to the fact that she was trying to avoid him.

Just to be safe, Dennis dropped by a convenience store, bought another disposable phone with a new number, and then called Candee. Now claiming to be Tom Benson, a lawyer visiting Phoenix from Omaha, Dennis asked if he could book an appointment with Candee and her friend Amber for eight o'clock that evening.

This time he was prepared, and when Candee asked him for two local references, without hesitation he rattled off the names of two of the other women who had posted ads on the website that Candee and Amber were using. "It's been a while since I've seen either one of them, though. I hope that they'll remember me."

What he really hoped, of course, was that the woman would not actually follow through and attempt to check the references. Failing that, he hoped that the two women whose names he had provided would be unable to respond to Candee's request for information before eight o'clock, but that Candee and Amber would be willing to go ahead with the appointment anyway.

Of course, there was always the possibility that one or both of the women had actually entertained a client with the generic name of "Tom Benson," and that one or both of them would give him a glowing recommendation.

Candee apparently made a note of the names he had provided and told him that she'd check the references and would call Amber immediately to set up the appointment. She promised that she would call him back with directions to the incall location as soon as everything was in place.

32

Twenty hours after Jenny had looked down to see Dennis Anderson in the parking lot at the incall apartment, "Amber's" cell phone began ringing. When Jenny saw Candee's number on the phone's screen, she thought for a moment about connecting to the call, but then decided against it. It was possible that Candee was calling simply to gossip, or maybe to suggest that they get together for a drink or a movie or some such thing. It was also possible that someone was looking to do business with the two of them together and that Candee was calling to confirm the appointment.

At the moment, Jenny did not feel like gossiping on the phone, nor did she feel like going out anywhere in public. And she certainly had no interest in booking an appointment. So, she set the phone back down on the counter and let the call go to voice mail. A couple of minutes later, she accessed her messages.

"Hey, Hon," her friend said. "I've got a live one for us at eight o'clock tonight—a lawyer from Omaha who's alone here in the big city and wants an incall appointment so that he can do the nasty with two delicious girls at the same time. Give me a call as soon as you can and let me know if it works for you. Later..."

Jenny had thought about returning the call, but she really didn't want to tell Candee that she was attempting to duck a nightmare from her former life. No one in Arizona knew her story, and she wasn't about to start telling it now. She could have made up some excuse—another appointment, perhaps—but she really didn't want to do that either. She had already decided that, for the time being at least, she was not going to return any of the calls that came in to the "Amber" phone, and she thus decided not to return this one either.

* * *

When Amber failed to return her call by five fifteen that afternoon, Candee dialed the number that "Tom" had given her. Dennis answered the call and Candee said, "Hey, I'm really sorry, Honey. I've left a message for Amber, but I haven't heard back from her yet. I don't know if she's going to be free or not."

"Gee," Dennis said, "I'm sorry to hear that. I was really hoping to be able to see the two of you."

"Well, that still may be possible," Candee said, trying to sound optimistic. "But I can't promise it. Here's what we can do, though. I have another friend who's really hot, and I know that she'd love to play with us tonight. I could give her a call and set that up. Or, if you wanted, I could keep waiting to hear from Amber. She may still get back to me, but if she doesn't, maybe you and I could get together, just the two of us. I can promise that we'd have a really fun time."

"Oh, gosh, Candee, I'm not sure what to say."'

He pretended to think about it for a moment, then said, "I tell you what. I really had my heart set on seeing you and Amber together, so why don't we do this? Let's hold off on the appointment for tonight unless she calls back and says she can make it. If she doesn't, why don't you keep trying her and see if you can set up the appointment for some time tomorrow? My schedule is very flexible, and I could probably be there at whatever time would work for you girls. I'd only need about an hour's notice."

"Okay," Candee said, with a hint of reluctance in her voice. "I'll keep waiting to hear from her and I'll let you know as soon as I can set something up. But if she doesn't get back to me tonight or early tomorrow, think about seeing me with my friend, Laura. I can promise that you'd have a really great time."

"I will. But if you can't get in touch with Amber, I may just wait until I'm back in town next time to see if the two of you would be available then."

* * *

Dennis hung up the phone, growing increasingly nervous, angry and frustrated. There had to be some way to get to the damned woman, and he needed to come up with it in a hurry. But twenty-four hours later, Candee still had not called him back with the good news that she had contacted Amber. So, reluctantly, Dennis called Candee late in the afternoon.

"I'm really sorry," she said. "I've left Amber a couple more messages, but she still hasn't gotten back to me. I can't figure out what's going on here. She *always* returns my calls."

Dennis figured that he had a pretty good idea of what was going on, but said, "Look, Candee, I've been thinking about what you suggested yesterday. I'd still really like to see you and Amber together, but if that doesn't work out, why don't I see you by yourself tonight?"

"That would be great, Hon!" the woman responded. "But are you sure you don't want me to ask Laura to join us?"

"No, that's okay. Why don't we hope that Amber returns your call between now and the time I see you tonight? Then I can still see the two of you together. Otherwise, I think I'd rather just see you by yourself."

"Sure, that's fine. Would eight o'clock work for you?"

Dennis assured her that eight o'clock would be fine and the woman gave him the same directions to the incall location that "Amber" had given him two days earlier. Candee promised that she'd leave another message for Amber but that she was looking forward to seeing him either way.

33

Taking no chances whatsoever, Dennis went back to Hertz and traded his white Camry for a dark blue Avalon. After leaving the rental agency, he dropped into a Wal-Mart and bought a hat with a long bill that would shield his face. In the kitchen department, he found a paring knife; in the hardware aisle, he picked up a roll of duct tape; and in the pharmacy, he got a small box of latex gloves.

While still in the Wal-Mart parking lot, Dennis stripped most of the duct tape off the roll and threw it away. He pressed the remainder of the roll flat and checked to make sure that both the paring knife and the remaining tape would fit into the front pocket of his pants without being too noticeable.

He then found the switch for the Avalon's overhead interior light and switched it off so that the light would not come on when the driver's door was opened. And having thus prepared as best he could, Dennis pulled into the apartment complex at eight o'clock that evening and took the same parking place that he'd used fifty-two hours earlier.

Unlike the occasion of his earlier visit, this time he was somewhat protected by the darkness of night and by the fact that the lighting in the parking lot was mediocre at best. Still, he kept his head low, not looking up at the windows above him, as he dialed Candee's number on his cell phone. The girl answered immediately and gave him the number of the apartment, which was on the second floor. Dennis thanked her, and two minutes later he was at the door, ringing the bell.

Trying not to be too obvious about what he was doing, he turned away from the peephole in the middle of the door, giving anyone looking out only a view of the side and back of his head. Thirty seconds after he rang the bell, someone inside released the deadbolt and opened the door about halfway. A young blonde that Dennis recognized from the website as Candee, leaned around the door and said, "Hi, Tom. Come on in."

Dennis walked through the door, and the young woman closed it behind him, twisting the deadbolt closed. She was wearing only a powder blue negligee with matching panties along with a pair of very high heels. Large firm breasts peeked out over the top of the filmy garment, and in spite of the desperate predicament he was in, Dennis found himself getting aroused.

Candee assured "Tom" that it was very nice to meet him and gave him a quick kiss with just a flash of her tongue. She led him over to the couch and, once they were seated, she said, "So what brings you to town, Honey?"

"I'm here for some meetings," he replied. "Mostly routine stuff, though, that even I don't find interesting. I wouldn't dream of boring you with it."

The girl moved closer, pressing her right breast against his arm. In a low, seductive voice, she said, "But you saved some time to have a little fun, right?"

Dennis nodded. "Yes, and now that I've finally had a chance to meet you, I'm very glad I did."

She pulled his head down and gave him a long lingering kiss, this time using her tongue to very good effect. Dennis' hand found her breast and as he began kneading it, Candee sighed and pressed even closer. Dennis broke the kiss. Still toying with the girl's breast, he said, "Did Amber ever call you back?"

She shook her head. "No, she didn't, which is really very strange."

"When was the last time you saw her?"

"I talked to her on the phone last week, but it's been a couple of weeks since I've actually seen her."

"And you don't have any way of contacting her?" he asked, feigning concern. "What if something's happened to her?"

Again, Candee shook her head. "Amber's one of those girls who guards her privacy very closely. The only contact info I have for her is what she posts on the web. I don't have any other way of getting a hold of her, so when I need to talk to her, all I can do is call her cell. But like I said, usually she always gets back to me right away. She's never not returned my calls like this."

Still pressing against him, the girl began slowly caressing his thigh and then let her fingers trail over the crotch of his pants. "I hope you're not too disappointed that it's just me tonight," she whispered.

Dennis touched the hem of the negligee and then gently lifted it over her head, exposing her upper body. He looked at her breasts for a long moment then lifted his eyes to meet hers. "Well," he said, "to be honest, I really was looking forward to seeing both you and Amber together. But right now, I'm very happy to be seeing you all by yourself."

* * *

Forty minutes later, Dennis *was* very happy that he'd decided to see Candee all by herself, and he sincerely regretted the action that he now felt compelled to take. Lying naked on the bed beside Candee, he propped himself up on an elbow and began tracing his fingers along her leg. "So how long have you and Amber been working together?" he asked.

The girl shifted slightly on the bed opening herself to his touch. "About six months or so. Amber had another friend that she'd worked with for a while, a girl named Traci. But Traci moved to San Diego, and her and Amber gave up the apartment they'd been using for incalls. Amber and I sort of knew each other, and she knew that I was looking for someone to share this place, and so we hooked up."

Still moving his fingers over her leg, Dennis said, "So how often do the two of you work together?"

"It varies," the woman said. "During the winter when the seasonal people are here, all of us girls are pretty busy and Amber and I might do one or two gigs a week together. In the summer, though, it's a lot slower and we might do only one a week or maybe one every other week."

"Do the two of you hang out when you're not working together?"

"Sometimes, but not a lot. We have the occasional drink together, but like I said, she's a private person and she keeps pretty much to herself."

The girl reached over and began stroking him. "But what's with all the questions about Amber?" she asked. "Aren't you having a good time here with me?"

Dennis gave her an earnest smile and cupped her left breast. "I'm having a *very* good time here with you. But like I said on the phone, I saw Amber when I was in town last time and I thought that she was a very nice girl. She also seemed like a very responsible person, so I can't figure out why she wouldn't be returning your calls."

"Well, I don't know. But the funny thing is, you're not the only one looking for her at the moment."

"How's that?"

"Well, a guy called me earlier this afternoon and he wanted to book me and Amber too. I told him I was having trouble getting hold of her and so I went up to his hotel by myself. Then *he* started asking me all sorts of questions about her.

"I'm sitting there on the bed with my top off, trying to figure out why this guy is so friggin' curious about Amber and why he doesn't want to get it on with me, when this lady walks into the room and totally freaks me out."

"What the hell?"

The girl nodded. "That's exactly what I said. Then the lady tells me that she's Amber's freakin' mother and that she's trying to find her."

"So, what did you do?"

Candee shrugged. "I got my top back on and was ready to get the hell out of there, but the lady showed me a couple of pictures—like I guess she really *is* Amber's mom—and I felt sorry for her. I told her that I didn't know how to get in touch with Amber but that Ron, the guy who runs the website might know how to reach her."

Dennis hesitated as if thinking about the situation, then said, "Do you suppose that Amber might have somehow discovered that her mother was looking for her and went into hiding or something so that her mother couldn't find her?"

Again, the girl shrugged, still absent-mindedly stroking him. "Maybe. Like I say, it's more than weird that she wouldn't be returning my calls." Rolling up on her side, she kissed him and began squeezing his erection. "Anyway," she said seductively, "that's enough about her. You feel like you're ready for another round."

Dennis pulled back a bit. "I'm getting there, that's for sure," he said. "But I'm curious. If Amber was trying to hide out, where do you suppose she might go?"

The young woman released him and turned up on her side, showing him her back. Now clearly frustrated, she said, "How the fuck would I know? I'm not her damned keeper, and I really don't want to talk about her anymore. Why the hell is everybody suddenly so damned interested in Amber? Her mom, I can understand. But I just fucked you pretty damned good, if I do say so myself. So why are you so hung up on her?"

Trying to keep the woman in a conciliatory mood as long as possible, Dennis cuddled up behind her, then reached over and cupped her breast again. "Hey, Honey," he said softly, "you were fantastic, and I'm sure as hell not complaining. I'm just curious, that's all."

He waited a moment, then said, "So you told Amber's mom to contact the guy who runs the website?"

Her back still to him, the girl brought her knees up to her chest, curling herself into a ball and saying nothing.

He waited another moment, then said, "Candee?"

Again, she said nothing.

Dennis rolled over to reach his pants, which he had carefully dropped right next to the edge of the bed. He looked back to the girl, who was still sulking in the middle of the bed with her back to him. Reaching into the pocket of the pants, he came out with the duct tape and the knife. He set the tape on the bed beside him. Then in one swift, fluid motion, he rolled over, straddled the girl, and clamped his hand over her mouth.

Candee's eyes flew wide open. Thrashing beneath him, she tried to scream, but Dennis squeezed his left hand firmly over her mouth and barely any sound escaped. He slowly shook his head, then showed her the knife in his right hand. The girl stopped struggling and tried to shake her own head, her eyes pleading with him. Dennis placed the point of the knife under her chin and touched it gently against her skin.

Candee fell completely still, her eyes wide with shock and horror. Tears began spilling down her cheeks. In a soft voice, Dennis said, "You need to listen to me very carefully now, Candee. I really don't want to hurt you, but I will if I have to. Do you understand?"

The girl tried to signal that she did, attempting to nod her head without cutting her chin on the knife. "Okay, then," he said. "I'm going to take my hand away from your mouth now so that we can talk. But if you try to scream, I'll cut your throat before you can even get a sound out."

Again, she gave the slightest nod. Dennis removed the point of the knife from her chin and laid the blade flat against her throat. Then he slowly lifted his other hand away from her mouth.

Candee began sobbing. "Please, please," she begged. "I'll do anything you want. Any way you want it. Just tell me. Only please don't hurt me."

Dennis shook his head. Still using the soft voice, he said, "Believe me, Candee, I really don't want to hurt you. But I have to find your friend Amber, and you've got to tell me how I can."

"But I don't know *how* to find her!"

"What did you tell her mother about the guy who runs the website?"

"I told her that the guy's name was Ron and that she could reach him by calling the number for technical service that's on the page where you sign up to advertise on the site. I told her that he might know how to get in touch with Amber."

"Did you tell her Ron's address?"

"No. I figured that if he wanted to tell her that on the phone, he could. But I didn't want him to be mad at me because I told her."

"What is the address?"

"I'm not for sure. It's a photography studio called Starlite Images. It's in a strip mall on Thunderbird Road."

"And this Ron will have Amber's home address?"

Candee nodded.

"But you don't know it?"

The girl shook her head.

"And you don't know where she might have gone?"

Again, she shook her head.

Dennis touched the point of the knife to her throat again. "And you're sure that you don't know any way of contacting her except for the phone number that she uses on the website."

Starting to cry again, Candee shook her head. "No, please believe me, but I don't."

Dennis nodded. Reaching for the roll of duct tape, he said, "I really wish that I could believe you, Candee. But I've got to know for sure."

34

In the end, Candee gave up the names of a few restaurants and other such places where she and Amber occasionally hung out. Otherwise, irrespective of the encouragement that Dennis provided, the terrified young woman had been unable to tell him anything more than she had before he gagged her, bound her arms and legs, and settled down to work with the knife. She'd been more than willing to do so—of that Dennis was certain. But she simply didn't know anything of value that she hadn't already revealed.

While planning the encounter, Dennis had sincerely dreaded the prospect that he might have to resort to some very brutal tactics in an effort to force Candee to surrender her secrets. He discovered, though, much to his amazement, that once the woman was naked, bound and completely at his mercy, instead of being horrified by the prospect of using the knife on her, he was actually aroused by it—something that he would have thought totally impossible only an hour before entering the apartment.

Confused, but at the same time savoring the sensation, he toyed with the woman longer than was absolutely necessary before finally putting an end to her misery. Sitting astride her, he watched as the light slowly faded from her eyes and he suddenly found himself wondering if he might possibly be able to replicate the extraordinary erotic rush that now enveloped him once he finally caught up with Jennifer McIntyre.

* * *

After dressing again, Dennis wasted another twenty minutes making a complete search of the apartment, but that too told him nothing about Amber that he didn't already know.

On a shelf in the closet of the second bedroom was a carton of matches from a local steakhouse. Dennis noted that about a dozen small boxes of the matches remained in the carton. A bathrobe hung in the closet, along with a few tops and two pairs of jeans that were obviously the wrong size for the woman who lay dead in the master bedroom. Unfortunately, there was nothing to suggest the identity of the woman who did fit the clothes or, more importantly, where she might be found.

His last slim ray of hope was Candee's oversized handbag. Still wearing the latex gloves he had put on before binding Candee's arms and legs, Dennis opened the purse. In it he found a package of tissues, three condoms, a small bottle of Astroglide, a lipstick and several other cosmetic items, along with a set of keys, an address book, a cell phone and the woman's wallet. Zippered into a separate compartment in the bag was a small Toshiba notebook computer.

In the wallet, he discovered a little over six hundred dollars in cash, Molly's business card, a number of credit cards, and Candee's driver's license, which revealed her real name and her home address. Setting the wallet aside, Dennis picked up the address book and turned to the page marked "M". He really didn't expect to find a listing for Jenny McIntyre and so was not surprised when there was none.

He then flipped back to the first page and made his way methodically through the names listed. There were no "Jennifers" and only one "Jenny" in the book. "Jenny's" last name was Kellen and her address and phone numbers were neatly recorded in the spaces provided. Dennis was quite sure that this Jenny was not the one he was looking for; if she had been, Candee would have told him so. But if all else failed, he would somehow find a way to get a look at the woman, just to make sure.

The last two pages of the address book contained a list of female names and phone numbers. The list included first names only, arranged in no particular order. It was written in ink, and four of the names and numbers had been crossed out. One of the names with a line through it was "Samantha," and someone—Candee, he presumed—had written the word, "Bitch!" next to the name.

Halfway down the first page of the list was the name "Amber," and with it was the phone number that Dennis had called to make his failed appointment with the woman. Dennis was now certain that this really was the only number that Candee had had for her friend.

He removed the cash from the girl's wallet and dropped the wallet onto the bed along with her keys. He stuffed Molly's business card, the cash, cell phone and address book into his pockets and hooked the notebook and its power cord under his arm. Then, taking one last look at the carnage he had left in his wake, he pulled the baseball cap low over his eyes, switched off the lights and let the door fall closed behind him.

35

Once back in the safety of his hotel room, Dennis booted Candee's small computer. The machine searched for a moment and then asked Dennis if he would like to connect to the hotel's wireless Internet service. He clicked on "yes", and a few moments later, a Yahoo! Homepage appeared. Unfortunately, Candee had not instructed the program to keep her signed in automatically; instead, it invited him to enter an ID and password. Dennis stared at the page for several minutes, trying to imagine what combination of identifiers the woman might have used to access the account. But he realized that he could never hope to conjure them up out of thin air; he could only hope that he might find it somewhere in the computer itself.

He closed the Yahoo! window, terminated the wireless connection, and clicked on the "MS Outlook" icon, but he saw nothing in the Outlook entries that might lead him to Jenny. He closed Outlook and clicked on the "My Documents" tab. It opened to reveal a number of Word and Excel files. Among the Excel files was one titled "Clients" and he double-clicked the file to open it.

Fortunately, Candee had not protected the file with a password, and when it opened, Dennis found himself looking at a client database. It included fields for the clients' names (last names first), their home addresses, work addresses, phone numbers, email addresses, the dates of their appointments, the location of the appointments, the length of the sessions, and the amount of money that the men had paid.

A field labeled "With" contained the names of other women, and in the records where there was an entry in the "With" field, Dennis assumed that the session had included not only Candee but one, and in a few cases, two other women. Finally, there was a field for "Comments," in which Candee had noted particular fetishes and positions that the client had enjoyed and other information about the session.

Many of the fields in the database were blank, and some of the individual records contained no personal information about the client apart from his name and a single phone number or email address. But some of the individual records were filled out completely. Looking at the screen, Dennis shook his head in amazement at the thought that these idiots would have given what were, apparently, their legitimate home and work addresses and phone numbers to a friggin' hooker, leaving themselves wide open to blackmail, exposure, and perhaps even prosecution.

The database was ordered alphabetically by the last name of the clients, but with a couple of clicks, Dennis re-sorted it alphabetically on the "With" field. When the sort was complete, he counted twenty-three entries where the session had included both Candee and Amber, and one other session, listed as lasting four hours, where the two women and the client had been joined by another girl named Jessie.

Looking more closely he saw that the twenty-four total sessions had involved only thirteen individual clients. One of the repeating clients, listed as "Nelson, David", had seen Candee and Amber together a total of four times, including the session with Jessie.

Dennis noted that the four-hour session with the three women had cost Mr. Nelson a cool five thousand dollars. And in spite of the critical task that now commanded his attention, Dennis' mind wandered for a few moments, speculating about what one man might do with three young, beautiful and willing women over the space of four hours, and whether it might have been worth five thousand dollars.

Returning reluctantly to the task at hand, he studied carefully the information about the thirteen clients who had seen Candee and Amber together. He assumed that at least some of the thirteen had belonged primarily to Amber as opposed to Candee, and that perhaps one of them might be coerced into giving up some information about Amber that Candee had not possessed.

Seeing nothing more that might be relevant, Dennis exited the client database and spent some time prowling through Candee's financial records. Hooking apparently paid fairly well, but the woman's financial records were not nearly as well organized as her client database. It appeared that she was spending her money about as fast as it was coming in, and that she had no savings or investments. But certainly, there was nothing either in the financial records or in any of Candee's Word files that would help him in his search for Amber/Jennifer.

Dennis closed the file and returned to the computer's desktop. From his briefcase, he took a spare flash drive and plugged it into a USB port on Candee's laptop. He then copied the woman's "My Documents" folder to the flash drive. He booted his own computer, plugged in the flash drive, and made sure that the files, especially the client database, had been copied to the flash drive and that he could access them on his own machine.

Satisfied that he now had a copy of Candee's files for future reference, he returned to her computer and deleted the "My Documents" folder and all of its files. When the folder disappeared from the screen, he emptied the Recycle bin and shut down the computer. He realized that a talented computer tech could probably still reconstruct the deleted files. But to the naked eye, there was nothing left to connect the computer to the murdered woman, and thus there was no apparent reason why anyone should bother to reconstruct the files, even if they should find the computer.

In the bathroom, Dennis wet a washcloth and thoroughly scrubbed the computer, eliminating any fingerprints that he might have left on it. Then, careful not to leave any fresh prints, he wrapped the computer in a towel and set it by the door.

He sat on the bed and spent several minutes toying with Candee's cell phone. It too was a cheap disposable "burner," and was not protected by a password. Scrolling through the calls recently dialed and received, though, he saw nothing of any help. He then activated the message function, hoping against hope that there might be a message from "Amber" providing some clue as to where she might be found.

Sadly, all he found were messages from several men who were attempting to schedule sessions with Candee and who hadn't yet discovered that she would not be taking any further appointments. The fifth message from the end was his own call, posing as "Tom," the lawyer from Omaha. He pressed "7" to delete the message, then listened to four more messages before the computer-generated voice informed him that there were no additional messages.

Dennis scrolled through the directory and found the number for "Amber's" phone, ready to be speed-dialed. Unfortunately, there was no listing for Jenny or for any variant of the name. Dennis turned off the phone and leaned back against the headboard, resting for a few moments and turning things over in his mind. He did not want to risk getting caught somehow in possession of Candee's computer or her phone. But thinking about having "Amber's" cell number available on a phone that would come up as Candee's on the receiving phone's caller ID, suggested some interesting possibilities.

He decided that he could not yet afford to surrender Candee's phone and so zipped it into a pocket in his briefcase along with the address book and flash drive. He then picked up the computer, walked out to his rental car and drove north to a strip mall several blocks away from the hotel. At this time of the night, the parking lot was deserted and the lights in most of the stores were dimmed.

In the service area behind the stores were several large dumpsters. Dennis got out of the car carrying Candee's computer, which was still wrapped in the hotel towel. He lifted the lid of one of the dumpsters and then, holding the towel by a corner, he let the computer roll down into the garbage.

36

Early Wednesday morning Jenny was absent-mindedly watching the *Today* show while getting ready to go to class, when the newsreader on the local affiliate announced that a young woman had been brutally murdered the previous night at an apartment complex in the northeast corner of Phoenix. Video rolling behind the newswoman showed the building where the crime had occurred, and Jenny gasped in horror as she watched the ambulance attendants carrying a body on a stretcher down a flight of stairs that she recognized instantly.

The newswoman noted that the victim's name was being withheld, pending notification of relatives, and that the police were anxious to talk with the woman's roommate, who was also not identified. She indicated that no other details about the crime were currently available, then turned to another camera and segued into a story about a fatal accident on the Piestewa Freeway.

Her mind spinning, Jenny picked up the remote and snapped off the television. It was possible of course, that the victim was not Candee, but Jenny knew intuitively that it had to be her and that the girl's carelessness had finally caught up with her.

Like every other working girl, Candee had heard the horror stories about abusive clients. She was also well aware of the basic safeguards that most elite escorts used to protect themselves. But while Jenny took these stories to heart and was extremely cautious in her own approach to the business, Candee sometimes acted carelessly. Although she always asked for references, as often as not she didn't bother to check them. When taking a date at a hotel, she rarely called the hotel desk to verify the registration. And, unlike Jenny, she was lax in the routine that she used when seeing clients at the incall apartment.

Jenny had tried to impress upon Candee the importance of being careful, especially since they were sharing the apartment and occasionally working together. Candee always promised to mend her ways, but her resolve was generally short-lived and before long she would fall back into her usual careless habits. In the end, Jenny gave up the argument, but whenever she and Candee were working together, Jenny always insisted on doing the reference checks herself.

On seeing the newscast then, Jenny concluded that Candee—if, indeed, she was the victim—had finally paid the ultimate price for her carelessness. She shuddered at the thought that she might have been in the apartment when Candee's killer had arrived, but her heart ached for the poor girl. The one fault aside, Candee had been bubbly, energetic, and impossible not to like. Jenny had genuinely cared for her and was devastated by the thought that she might be dead.

Desperately hoping that she was wrong, Jenny logged onto her computer and began checking the websites of local news outlets. Two hours later she burst into tears when an update to the story on azcentral.com confirmed her worst fears.

* * *

Stunned by the news of Candee's death, Jenny would have preferred to lay low in her apartment indefinitely, calling in sick to the restaurant and refusing to answer "Amber's" cell phone. But from a financial standpoint, that was out of the question. And so, after taking Wednesday off, Jenny phoned her boss on Thursday morning, told him that she was feeling much better and that he could schedule her for the dinner shift that night.

Regrettably, though, the wages and tips she earned at the restaurant would not be nearly enough to meet her expenses, and so the day after she went back to work at the restaurant, Jenny reluctantly turned "Amber's" cell phone back on and took a date with a long-time client. She screened her calls very carefully, returning only the calls from men that she knew well. She told the men that she was in the process of moving to a new incall apartment and that, for the time being, she would be able to see them only in their homes or in hotels.

Some of her clients knew of her association with the murdered woman and a few of them had occasionally scheduled appointments with both "Amber" and Candee. Jenny decided that it would be way too difficult emotionally to accept any appointments in the future from men who had also known Candee, and so she also refused to return calls from clients that they had shared.

She knew from the news that the police realized that Candee had been sharing the incall apartment with another provider and that they were looking for her. If Jenny thought that she had any information that might have been relevant to the investigation, she would have come forward of her own volition. But she assumed that the police would fairly quickly gain access to Candee's cell phone records and that they would be tracing the calls made to the phone in an effort to find the last client that Candee had agreed to see. She further assumed that, without needing any help from her, the police would also find Candee's computer and on it her client database.

Beyond that, what could Jenny tell them? Only that Candee had been careless in the matter of checking references and in admitting clients to the incall apartment. But that would not bring the police any closer to finding the man who had killed Candee, and it would almost certainly result in Jenny's exposure, which would have been catastrophic for any number of reasons.

Jenny was especially happy now that her name was not on the lease agreement for the incall apartment and that she had never revealed her real name or any other personal information either to Candee or to the clients they had shared. Neither Candee nor any of the clients even knew the name of the restaurant where she worked. Thus, Jenny was confident that there was nothing, either in the apartment, or among Candee's personal effects, that would enable the police to find her.

Jenny did log onto the FantacieLand website and was relieved to see that Ron had removed Candee's ads and photos from the site, including the ad for the two of them together. She assumed that the police would ultimately find their way to Ron. If nothing else, one of Candee's clients was bound to tell the investigators that he had initially found her on the website, and the police would show up at the studio, demanding whatever information the webmaster/photographer could supply regarding Candee, her clients, and her associates in the business.

But Jenny had been careful in that regard as well. She had used an alias in registering for the service. She had only ever seen Ron—and thus let him see her—on the three occasions when he had taken her pictures for the ads. And she had never allowed him to charge the cost of the ad to a credit card that might be traced back to her.

Ron could give the police the cell phone number that had been listed in "Amber's" ad, but that would be of no help either. The number would lead to a pre-paid cell phone provider who would be able to tell the authorities only that the phone had been purchased from a Target store and that it was kept in service because the purchaser continued to buy additional cards, adding minutes to the phone. And even if such records existed, the people at Target would only be able to tell the police that both the phone and the service cards had been purchased for cash.

Jenny had given "Amber's" email address to a few of her clients to facilitate booking appointments. But should the authorities discover the address, it would lead them only to a Hotmail account in the name of J. Douglas who claimed to be a fifty-seven-year-old male attorney, living in Mesa, Arizona. And tracing all the mail from the account would take the police no further than to the various coffee shops, bookstores and other such hot spots where "J. Douglas" had occasionally borrowed a wireless Internet connection.

* * *

Jenny was still more than a little spooked by the idea that Dennis had been in Phoenix and that he had attempted to see her. Certainly, the fact that he scheduled an appointment with "Amber" could not have been a coincidence. He must have recognized her picture on the website, but what was he doing there in the first place?

Had he come to the Valley on business, decided to see an escort, found the website and seen her photo? Certainly, that was not beyond the realm of possibility. The website was linked to several other sites and was designed so that whenever anyone typed the words "Phoenix" and "escort" into a search engine, "FantacieLand.com" would inevitably rank high on the list of results produced by the search.

If Dennis had simply been looking for an escort, he might have easily come across Jenny's ad quite by accident. And it now occurred to her that he might have thus found the ad and noted the similarity between the woman pictured there and the girl he had known five years earlier in Minnesota. Maybe it had been nothing more than curiosity that had led him to schedule the appointment. Perhaps he simply wanted to know if "Amber" might really be the long-lost daughter of his next-door neighbors, and his intentions had otherwise been innocent.

But Jenny understood that there was nothing remotely innocent about Dennis Anderson. This was the bastard who had seduced her mother and convinced her to betray Jenny's father. In doing so, Dennis had set into motion the events that had destroyed Jenny's life and that had led to the death of her father and to that of William Milovich as well.

And what did her mother know? Were she and Dennis still sleeping together? Having found the photo on the website, had Dennis alerted Molly to the fact that he might have found Jennifer? Or had he planned to wait and make sure that the girl in the ad really was Jenny before he revealed his discovery to her mother?

Most important, where was Dennis now, and what did he plan to do? Certainly, he realized that "Amber" had stood him up and had no intention of seeing her. Was he still in Phoenix attempting to find her, or had he given up the search and returned to Minnesota?

On the afternoon that she returned to work, Jenny logged on to her computer and found Dennis Anderson still listed at the same address in Minneapolis and with the same phone number that he'd had when Jenny had been the Anderson's babysitter.

Just before leaving work that night at a little after ten o'clock, which would have been just after eleven in Minneapolis, Jenny stopped at the hostess station which was now closed, picked up the phone and dialed the Andersons' number. The phone rang five times before a voice that Jenny recognized as Melinda's said a groggy "Hello?" into the receiver.

Jenny listened as Melinda said, "Hello?" a second time. Then she hung up the phone and walked slowly back to her car.

The fact that Dennis hadn't answered the phone did not necessarily mean that he wasn't at home. And it certainly did not mean that he wasn't back in Minneapolis. Perhaps he was out at a meeting, although it seemed doubtful at that time of night. Perhaps he had been somewhere else in the house, unable to get to the phone before Melinda answered it, though that too seemed unlikely, given as long as it had taken her to do so.

Perhaps the Andersons had simply moved the phone in the master bedroom to Melinda's side of the bed. And if so, even as Jenny walked back to her car, Dennis might have been safely back in Minneapolis, asleep in the bed next to his wife.

Or perhaps, Jenny knew, Dennis might not be back in Minneapolis at all.

37

Late Friday night, Molly was sleeping fitfully, drifting in and out of a dream about Jenny's seventh birthday party, when her cell phone began buzzing on the table next to the bed. She snapped awake and reached for the phone, noting that the clock radio behind the phone was glowing 11:37. She pressed the button to connect to the call, and said, "Hello?"

From the other end of the call, a raspy voice said, "Are you the woman who's trying to connect with Amber?"

"Who is this?"

"Who I am doesn't matter. Are you looking for her or not?"

The voice sounded like it belonged to a man who might be anywhere from thirty to fifty. A hard rock song was playing loudly in the background, and Molly had to strain to filter the man's voice out of the surrounding cacophony. She swallowed hard and said, "Yes, I'm looking for Amber. Do you know her? Do you know how to reach her?"

"Yeah," the man answered, "I do. In fact, I'm standing no more than twenty feet away from her right this minute."

Molly bolted upright and swung her feet off the bed. "Where are you?"

The man laughed. "Whoa, lady, not so fast. How bad do you want to see her?"

"What do you mean?"

Over the music in the background, Molly heard him say, "I mean, lady, what's it worth to you—in cash?"

Molly hesitated, trying to calculate how much cash she had left in her purse. "I have a little over three hundred dollars, I think."

Again, the man laughed. "Three hundred? Shit, I guess you don't want to see her all that bad."

"Yes, please, I do. It's just that that's all the cash I have at the moment."

In the background, the song ended. Molly could now hear the sound of voices talking loudly, and she concluded that the man was calling from a bar or a nightclub of some kind. A new song began, as loud as the first, and over the music the man said, "You're in a hotel?"

"Yes."

"There must be a cash machine in the lobby."

"Yes, I think there is."

"What's your daily limit?"

"Four hundred dollars."

"Okay. Go down to the cash machine, get your four hundred and add it to the other three. When you've got it together, get in a cab and have the cab drop you at The Body Shop, 2347 Adams Street."

"Just a minute."

Now fully awake, Molly got up from the bed, went over to the small desk, and wrote the address on a piece of notepaper. "The Body Shop?"

"Yeah, it's a strip club. The cabbie will know where it is. The entrance is in the back off the parking lot. You come alone. I know that the cops are looking for Amber too, and I want nothing to do with them. If I see anybody else within a hundred yards of that cab when you get out of it, I'm history. Once you give me the money, I'll lead you to Amber. And don't get cute. The way she looks tonight, you won't recognize her. So, don't think that you can stiff me, then walk in here and find her yourself."

"I understand. How will I recognize you?"

"You won't. I'll be watching for you to step out of the cab. Once you're out of the cab, don't go into the club. Walk to the edge of the parking lot opposite the door to the club and I'll meet you there. And lady? You'd better hurry. I don't know how long Amber's planning to be here."

* * *

178

The phone went dead and Molly took two quick steps and banged on the door that connected her room to Jason's. Then she raced into the bathroom, turned on the faucet, and splashed some water onto her face. Back in the bedroom, she stripped off the tee shirt she'd been sleeping in and quickly put on a bra. She pulled a fresh tee shirt over the bra and was stepping into a pair of jeans when Jason called her name from the other side of the connecting door.

She opened the door to find Jason barefoot, also dressed in jeans and a tee shirt. He shook his head as if still trying to come fully awake and said, "What's happened?"

Molly retreated to the bed, sat down and pulled on a pair of shoes. She quickly described the conversation and told Jason to call down and have the front desk get her a cab. Instead, he sat down on the bed beside her and said, "Wait a minute. We need to think about this."

"We haven't time, Jason. Just call for the damned cab."

"Molly, Jesus! Who in the hell is this guy, and how does he know that you're looking for Amber?"

"What do you mean?"

"Like you said before, *I'm* the one who's been making calls trying to connect with Amber, not you. So why didn't the guy call me? Ron Newton has your number, but you already told him you'd pay a substantial reward if he could lead you to Jenny. Why would he approach you like this? That leaves the card you gave Candee, and she's dead. If this guy got your number from her, you sure don't want to be going out to meet him. This stinks like hell."

"Maybe Newton told someone else that I was looking for Jenny. Maybe Candee told someone other than the person who killed her. Whatever the case, this is the only lead I have to Jenny. I've got to go."

Molly got up from the bed, grabbed her purse from the dresser, and quickly counted the money she had left. She reserved a hundred dollars for her own use and slipped it into the left front pocket of her jeans. The balance of the money she put into the right pocket.

As she snapped the purse shut again, Jason rose from the bed, put his hands on her shoulders and drew her close. "Please, Molly... I

179

know how desperate you are to find Jenny, but this just makes no sense and it's way too dangerous. Call the police; ask them to stake out the place or something. Then, when the guy approaches you, they can arrest him and make him lead you to Jenny."

Molly dropped her head to his shoulder. "I'm sorry, Jason, but there just isn't enough time. And if I do that, the guy—whoever he is—may bolt, and I'll lose what may be my last opportunity to find Jenny. I'm not stupid; I know there's a good chance this may not be legitimate, but I have to take it."

She gave him a quick hug, then broke the embrace and turned toward the door.

Jason took a step in her direction and said, "At least let me come with you."

"I can't. But I wanted you to know where I was going. When I get back, I promise I'll knock on your door again and let you know what happened."

He was still standing in the center of the room, shaking his head, when Molly closed the door behind her.

38

The Body Shop was a small, squat cinderblock building, badly in need of a paint job, in the middle of a neighborhood that had clearly seen better days.

Across the street, a neon sign flickered in the window of a pawnshop, now closed for the night with a heavy iron gate protecting its imposing front door. At the end of the block a gas station/convenience store was still open for business, and a small group of men congregated in front of the store, standing or sitting on the concrete parking barriers, smoking and drinking beer. Otherwise, the neighborhood appeared to be a mixture of light industrial and commercial enterprises, all of which appeared to be in a sad state of decline.

The cab driver turned into a driveway that ran along the side of the strip club and then emptied into the parking lot behind it. Between ten and fifteen cars were scattered haphazardly through the dimly lighted parking lot, but there was no one in sight. The pulsing beat of a heavy bass leaked through the door of the club, the only sound disturbing the quiet of the night other than the traffic passing on the street in front of the building.

Under the portico of her obviously expensive hotel, the cabdriver had turned in his seat and asked Molly if she was really sure she wanted to be going to this address. Clearly the driver had not been excited about the prospect, and as he braked to a stop at the door of the club, he said again, "Ma'am, are you *really* sure you want me to leave you off here?"

Looking at the scene around the cab, Molly was even less excited about the idea than was the driver, and as she formulated her response, a man, obviously drunk, stumbled out the door of the club. He stuck a hand out, momentarily balancing himself against the cab, then made his way uncertainly across the parking lot to a battered pickup truck. Molly steeled herself, then handed the driver two twenty-dollar bills against a meter that read twenty-four dollars. "Yes, I'm sure," she replied. "But I may not be here all that long. I'd really appreciate it if you would maybe drive around the block and check back for me in ten minutes or so. Once I'm through here, I'll be happy to give you another forty dollars for a ride back to my hotel."

The driver was clearly reluctant to see her get out of the cab, but he sighed and nodded his head. "Okay, Ma'am. And don't you worry. I'll be back. You just be careful in there."

Molly promised that she would, then opened the door and slowly stepped out of the cab. Swallowing hard, she closed the door and stood, rooted to the ground, as she watched the cabbie circle thorough the lot back out into the street. Then alone, with only the sound of the bass thudding behind her, she turned and walked slowly away from the club toward the rear of the parking lot.

Three vehicles were parked in the last row, facing away from the club: a spotless gray BMW sedan that looked oddly out of place in this environment, another pickup truck, and between them an aging white van. Molly stood for a moment behind the BMW and then said a very tentative "Hello?" out into the darkness. "Is anyone here?"

Receiving no response, she waited a moment then took a few hesitant steps to her right, in the direction of the pickup truck at the end of the row. As she drew even with the white van, something bounced off the roof of a car two rows in the direction of the club. Molly turned toward the sound, and as she did, a man who'd been crouching on the other side of the van sprung to his feet and grabbed her from behind. Before Molly could make even the slightest sound, the man clamped his left hand over her mouth and began dragging her back into the darkness between the van and the pickup.

Molly began whimpering and shaking her head, but the man simply increased the pressure over her mouth. He dragged her in front of the van, effectively shielding the two of them from the view of the rest of the parking lot. Leaning back against the van, the man pulled Molly tightly to him, still facing away from him so that she couldn't get a look at his face. With his right hand, he brought a knife to her throat.

The man leaned forward and whispered into Molly's right ear. "I'm going to take my hand off your mouth. If you make any sound at all, I'll cut your fuckin' throat. Understand?"

Terrified, Molly nodded slightly. Her captor dropped his hand away from her mouth and clamped his arm around her throat. He touched the point of the knife to her right breast and said, again in a whisper, "Did you bring the seven hundred?"

Again, Molly nodded, and the man said, "Where is it?"

"In the right front pocket of my jeans."

The man shifted the knife to his left hand and laid the point against Molly's throat. Then his right hand passed down the front of her body, lingering for a moment and pressing roughly into the crotch of her jeans. He reached into Molly's pocket, found the money, and slipped it into his own pocket. Then he shifted the knife back to his right hand and returned it Molly's throat. Again, he whispered. "What the fuck do you think you're doing here, bitch?"

Tears now flowing down both of her cheeks, Molly said, "I'm just trying to find my daughter. I just want to see my daughter."

Behind her, the man shook his head. "Well your daughter isn't here, and you're mixing in things that are none of your fuckin' business. I'm going to tell you nicely this time: Get the hell out of Phoenix and go back home where you belong. If you stay here and keep poking around, you and I are going to meet again. And when we do, I'll make you goddamn sorry that you were ever born, let alone that you came to Phoenix. Understood?"

Without waiting for a response, the man grabbed Molly roughly by the shoulders, stuck a knee in her back, and sent her sprawling into a pile of trash just off the edge of the parking lot. Molly stuck out her hands in an effort to break the fall but succeeded only in severely scraping both of her palms as she slid across the asphalt and into the trash. Her head plowed through the garbage and slammed into the ground.

She lay sprawled in the middle of the trash, momentarily dazed, then she slowly raised up on her hands and knees and shook her head, willing her senses to return. She reached back, grabbed the bumper of the van behind her, and slowly pulled herself to her feet, wincing at the stinging pain in her hand as she gripped the bumper. As she steadied herself, she saw the cab pull back into the parking lot in front of the building ahead of her; her assailant was nowhere in sight.

Desperate not to lose her ride to safety, Molly sprinted across the parking lot as fast as her wobbly legs would allow and grabbed the handle of the rear door of the cab. The cabbie had been looking toward the door of the club, apparently expecting Molly to be in the building, and he jumped, visibly startled, at the sound of someone pulling on the door behind him. The man took one look at Molly and jumped out of the cab. "Ma'am, what in the hell happened to you?"

Molly shook her head in response. "Nothing. Please just take me back to my hotel."

"Nothing? Jesus, lady, you're a mess! Your hands and face are bleeding; it looks like somebody beat you up. You get in the cab, and I'll radio for the dispatcher to send the cops."

Again, Molly shook her head. "No, please. That would only make things worse. Really, I'll be okay. Please just get me out of here and back to my hotel."

Now the cabbie shook his head. Clearly operating against his better judgment, he held the door and helped Molly into the cab. Then he made another circle through the parking lot, headed out to the street, and turned in the direction of Molly's hotel.

39

At seven o'clock the next morning, Molly dropped Jason at the airport for his flight back to Minneapolis. They'd been arguing ever since Molly returned from the strip club, Jason pleading that he could not leave her alone in the wake of the attack and Molly insisting that she would be fine.

As she braked the Nissan to a stop at the curb, Jason turned in the passenger's seat and pleaded, "Damn it, Molly, please let me stay and help you see this through. Obviously, it's just too dangerous for you to stay here, trying to find Jenny alone. Two or three more days won't make that much difference to the things I need to get done at work, and the truth is that I'll be worthless there, worrying about you down here."

She shifted into "Park" and turned to face him. "No, Jason. I really do appreciate the concern, but there's no point. I promise that as soon as I get back to the hotel, I'll call detective Richardson and let him know what happened last night. But otherwise, we've done all that we can here. I need to stay until the police find Jenny. But there's nothing to be gained by you waiting here with me and you *do* need to get back to work."

He shook his head, clearly reluctant to go. Taking her hand, he said, "At least promise me that you'll be careful and that you won't go chasing off by yourself into the middle of the night like that again."

"I promise," she said. "From now on, this search is up to the police. All I can do is sit in my hotel room until they find Jenny, and I'll be perfectly safe there."

She reached across the console and gave him a quick hug, then released him. Conceding defeat, Jason opened the door and grabbed his suitcase from the back seat. Leaning into the front seat again, he said, "Please be careful, Molly." Then he stepped back, closed the door, and watched her drive away.

Once back at the hotel, Molly opened her purse and retrieved the card that Detective Richardson had given her the previous morning. Sitting at the small table in her room, she tapped her cell phone and dialed his extension in the Homicide Unit. Richardson answered the call and Molly apologized for interrupting his morning. "It's no problem, Ms. McIntyre. What can I do for you?"

"Actually, Detective, I'm calling for a couple of reasons. I read in this morning's paper the article on your investigation into Ms. Taylor's death. Can I ask if you're making any progress?"

Richardson hesitated for a moment, then said, "I'm sorry, Ms. McIntyre, but there's really not much I can tell you that wasn't in the paper."

"I understand, and I'm really not asking you to divulge information that you wouldn't want to make public, but I just feel so awful about what happened. I only spoke to the poor girl for a few minutes the other night, but I can't stop thinking about her. I guess I was hoping for some reassurance that at least the person who did this to her would be caught and severely punished."

"On that we're agreed. I can only tell you that it's still very early in the investigation and we have a number of leads that we're following. I'm hopeful that they'll be productive."

"I hope so too, Detective. But, as I hope you can understand, I'm also very concerned about my daughter. The fact that something like this could happen to a woman in her profession makes me all that more anxious to find her. I know that Jenny and Ms. Taylor were apparently sharing the apartment where Ms. Taylor was killed, and I assume that you are now trying to find Jenny so that you can interview her. I also assume that you haven't been able to find her."

"Unfortunately, we haven't. "But we're very anxious to talk with her to see what if anything she might be able to tell us about the killing. As I told you before, the two women apparently only used the apartment to see clients. Neither of them actually lived there.

"It's a two-bedroom unit and Ms. Taylor was using one of the bedrooms. It's obvious that another woman—presumably the woman you think might be your daughter—was using the other bedroom and closet. But there's nothing in the apartment that's given us any clue as to what her real name or address might be."

"Certainly, by now you've talked to the landlord or the rental agent..."

"We have, of course. But the lease to the apartment was in Ms. Taylor's name alone, and the rental agency had no idea that another person was sharing the apartment, so that's a dead end. The neighbors have described the roommate as an attractive brunette in her early to mid-twenties, but they couldn't tell us much more than that. For obvious reasons, the two women kept a pretty low profile around the apartment complex.

"One of the neighbors did tell us that she'd seen the roommate coming and going from the apartment a few times and that she drove a red Ford Mustang that was maybe three or four years old. But the neighbor didn't notice the license plate number, and so that's not much help either."

"Were you able to get any help from Ron Newton?"

"Unfortunately, not. He gave us the contact phone number for "Amber," the woman who was sharing Ms. Taylor's apartment, and I called the number, hoping that I might be able to convince her to talk with us. But I got no answer, not even the opportunity to leave a voice mail message.

"I asked Newton for a picture of 'Amber,' thinking that we might make go public with it and ask anyone who knows or sees her to call us. But Newton claims that he no longer has one. Apparently whenever a woman removes her ad from the site, he deletes all the copies of her photos so that, if and when she decides to advertise again, he can attempt to convince her to let him take new pictures."

The Detective hesitated for a moment, then said, "Assuming that this Amber really is your daughter, would you have a picture that we might use for that purpose, Ms. McIntyre?"

Molly paused a moment herself before replying. "No, Detective, I don't think so. The last picture I have of Jenny is now nearly six years old and really looks nothing like the photo that was on the website. I doubt very much that anyone who knows her now would recognize her from any picture I might have."

"Okay, then," Richardson said. "I'll keep trying the phone number in the hope that 'Amber' eventually answers and we'll issue a public appeal, asking her to come forward. Short of that, we can only hope that we get lucky and find some other way to track her down."

When Richardson offered nothing more, Molly described the phone call she had received and the subsequent encounter with her assailant in the parking lot of the strip club. "And you're sure that the only two people to whom you gave your cell phone number were Ms. Taylor and Newton, the photographer?" Richardson asked.

Molly replied in the affirmative and at the other end of the phone, the detective said, "I certainly wish that you would have called us before you went out there, Ms. McIntyre. It's entirely possible that the man who assaulted you is the same man who tortured and killed Ms. Taylor, and if that is the case, then I would have to say that you were very lucky. More than that, you had to know that we would have wanted a chance to talk to this guy, whoever he was."

"I do understand that, Detective Richardson, and I'm sorry. I can only say that I was so desperate for any news of Jenny that I wasn't thinking clearly. I promise that I won't do anything like that again."

"I hope not, Ms. McIntyre, for your sake as well as for the sake of our investigation."

"I understand, Detective, and I promise that I'll call you immediately if anyone else contacts me like that. But in return, I hope that you'll let me know if you have any news of Ms. Taylor's roommate."

"We will," the detective assured her. "And naturally, if you should somehow connect with your daughter before we find her, it's extremely important that you let us know."

"I understand, and you can be sure that I will."

* * *

Molly disconnected from the call and set the phone down on the table, wondering why she had instinctively decided not to tell the detective that she had a copy of "Amber's" ad from the website, including her photo. But it now seemed clear that "Amber" had not also been a victim of the crime that had been committed against Susan Taylor and certainly by now she would have heard about the murder. She could have come forward of her own volition had she wanted to, but she hadn't.

Despite the claim of the woman who had phoned as she and Jason were leaving the police station, Molly was now firmly convinced of the fact that "Amber" was her daughter and her instinctive reaction was to trust Jenny's judgment in the matter. If she had not come forward voluntarily, she must have had a good reason. Perhaps she believed herself to be in danger from the person or persons who had tortured and murdered her roommate; perhaps she simply believed that she had nothing helpful to offer the detective and did not want to become entangled in the investigation. But whatever the case, Molly was not ready—at least not yet—to force Jenny to come forward publicly if she didn't want to.

Shaking her head and hoping that she'd made the right decision, Molly walked over to the window and stared blankly out into the distance without really seeing anything, wondering who had called her out to the strip club last night—and why.

Could it possibly have been the man responsible for killing Susan Taylor, as Richardson had suggested? And if so, would the man really have put himself at such risk just to extort a few hundred dollars from her?

If it wasn't the killer, was it someone who was linked to Ron Newton, the photographer? She was certain that it was not Newton who had attacked her in the parking lot. As she'd told him, she had a good ear for voices, and the man who had threatened her sounded nothing at all like the photographer. Additionally, although she hadn't seen the man, Molly's sense was that her attacker was several inches taller and considerably bulkier than Newton. But why would Newton have sent someone after her?

Was it possible that, in the short interval between the time she'd left Jason's room and the time she was killed, "Candee" had passed Molly's number to someone else? But if so, who? Could it possibly have been Jenny herself? Was it remotely conceivable that Jenny could have sent the man to warn her off?

Molly couldn't imagine such a scenario. But her gut reaction told her that the incident in the strip club parking lot had not been designed simply for the purpose of robbing her and that the seven hundred dollars had been incidental to some larger purpose. Clearly someone felt threatened enough by her search for Jenny to try to scare her away in such a dramatic fashion. But who could it possibly be? Why would they feel so threatened? And more to the point, what would they do when Molly refused to go home?

40

Ron Newton paced nervously back and forth across the fifteen-foot length of the small office in the front of his studio. Seventy-two hours earlier, he'd had hardly a care in the world, but then Molly McIntyre had come barging through his front door, threatening to sabotage the well-oiled machine he'd so painstakingly constructed.

Three years ago, Newton had been scratching out a fairly meager existence as a photographer, doing family photos, high school graduation pictures, and the occasional wedding shoot. Then one afternoon, a woman named Debbi Cernack called and made an appointment to have some photos taken for the website she was developing. She showed up for the appointment three days later, describing in greater detail her occupation as an escort and the sort of website she was creating.

Cernack was, without question, one of the sexiest women Newton had ever seen. They spent twenty minutes or so discussing the photos she wanted him to take, and then Newton quoted the woman his standard rate. At which point, Debbi flashed him a brilliant smile and asked if he might be interested in exchanging professional courtesies.

He was. And in the end, he not only took Debbi's photos, but wound up creating and administering her website as well. She loved both the pictures and the website and recommended that several of her colleagues avail themselves of Newton's talents. Some of the girls paid in cash; others, like Debbi, were happy to trade services. Either was fine with the photographer, and after taking photos for six different escorts and developing websites for three of them, he conceived the idea of creating a website of his own where the women might advertise their services and link to their individual websites.

Newton's idea was to build an elegant, upscale site that would feature only exclusive and relatively expensive escorts—one that would attract a successful, mostly professional clientele that could afford to pay the rates the women were asking. Unlike Adultsearch, or other such sites that accepted ads from any and all comers no matter how skanky the women might be, the escorts on Newton's site would be carefully screened. The photos, while still sexy of course, would be much more tasteful than most of those on other sites, and the copy would not be nearly as blatant and tasteless.

In order to get the website up and running, Newton offered Debbi and the five of her friends he had photographed three months' worth of free listing on the site. The women readily agreed, and once the site was in operation, they all reported a spike in their bookings. The word spread, both among the women and their clients, and within six months, FantacieLand.com was the premier Phoenix website for upscale escorts and the men who were anxious to meet them.

As the business grew, Newton and Debbi maintained a close association, and after seven months, it had been her idea to create an agency. A number of the girls, she explained, didn't want to hassle with maintaining their own websites, renting their own apartments, doing their own reference checks, and dealing with the other more mundane business aspects of their profession. Debbi suggested that she and Newton might partner to develop an agency that would deal with these sorts of matters for women who would prefer not to.

The agency would rent a couple of apartments that the escorts might use, and Newton would create a separate page on the website, intended to suggest that the agency was an entirely separate entity that was simply advertising on the site. He would take the photographs and post them to the agency section of the website. Debbi would act as the "den mother," schooling the girls in the standards of behavior and safety appropriate to escorts at their end of the profession. Together, they would screen the escorts, check the references of prospective clients, and schedule the appointments. And together, of course, they would also take a healthy percentage of each transaction conducted by one of the agency's "representatives."

Nearly two and a half years into the arrangement, Newton and Debbi were prospering nicely. Debbi had now retired from active duty, save for the occasional date with a long-time and very generous client. Newton still maintained the photography studio, mostly for appearances' sake, but the bulk of his income now came from the website and from the agency profits. And, of course, for Newton at least, the fringe benefits of his new enterprise far exceeded those of his earlier one.

This was the world that Molly McIntyre now threatened to jeopardize.

Newton realized that he'd been skating on thin legal ice ever since the day that FantacieLand.com first went live on the Web. On the opening page of the site, he posted a disclaimer containing a lot of legal mumbo jumbo, the sum of which insisted that the purpose of the website was simply to facilitate the introduction of the women who posted ads on the site and the gentlemen who might like to meet them. Before entering the site, a prospective customer had to click on a button indicating that he (or she) understood that FantacieLand.com was in no way responsible for anything that might happen once these meetings occurred, and that the customer would not hold the website liable for anything that might (or might not) happen at such a meeting.

Newton's attorney, who proved to be one of the website's most enthusiastic customers, assured the photographer/webmaster that he was well within his first amendment rights in creating the site. The lawyer drafted the language in the model's agreement in which the women who posted ads on the site promised that they were operating independently and that they were in no way being coerced or even encouraged by the owner of the website to engage in any illegal activities. The lawyer also encouraged the "models" to include on their own websites language declaring that they were not making an offer of prostitution; that they were charging clients only for the privilege of spending time with them; and that any sexual activity that might occur was simply an act of friendship between consenting adults that had nothing to do with the money exchanged.

Newton's position became even more dicey when he and Debbi created the agency. The lawyer incorporated the new operation and created a number of barriers that would make it extremely difficult for anyone other than the most determined investigator to trace the agency's legal owners. The agency's page on the website claimed that it was a matchmaking service whose sole purpose was to facilitate introductions between the beautiful women who posted their profiles on the agency's website and busy executives who didn't have the time to meet such women in more traditional ways.

The women who availed themselves of the agency's services had to sign an even stricter version of the model's agreement in which they promised that they had joined the agency simply for the purpose of meeting prospective companions and that they were not being encouraged by the agency to perform any illegal actions in return for the money collected from the companions.

Thus far, the fiction had held. Either that, or local law enforcement officials had more pressing concerns that had led them, at least until now, to turn a blind eye to Newton's various activities. Occasionally the local police would announce a "major crackdown" on prostitution, and with news cameras in tow, would sweep up a number of poor, pathetic streetwalkers. More rarely, they would conduct a sting operation that would ensnare a few of the less sophisticated women who were openly and very specifically describing their services and their prices on places like Adultsearch.

Save for their presence on the web, Newton and the women who comprised the heart of his operation had maintained a very low profile and thus far had remained untouched. But the photographer realized that any unwelcome attention drawn to his activities might provide the spark that would finally prompt law enforcement officials to take a closer look at FantacieLand.com.

Molly McIntyre threatened to bring exactly that sort of unwelcome attention. Indeed, she had told Newton very forcefully that she would not be at all reluctant to involve the police and her own attorneys in the search for her daughter. It was that threat, and the knowledge of the consequences that sort of attention could bring, that had led Newton to drop his guard and admit to being the webmaster.

He had tried to convince McIntyre that he had no knowledge of her daughter beyond that which he had shared with her. And, unfortunately, he'd been telling the truth. Newton would have gladly delivered "Amber" or Jennifer or whoever the hell the girl might be, to the McIntyre woman on a silver platter. And in the case of most of the women who advertised on the website, he could have. But "Amber" had guarded her privacy more closely than virtually any other woman who had ever signed up for the service.

On the three occasions he had taken her pictures for the site, Newton had attempted to engage the woman in conversation, but she had refused to be drawn out and would give him no details of her personal life other than those she'd provided on the model's release form.

Newton had probed, gently questioning other women who used the site and who worked for the agency in an effort to learn what they might know about "Amber." But the girl was apparently as guarded with her fellow escorts as she was with the photographer himself. None of Amber's colleagues could tell him anything about the woman that he didn't already know.

Once he and Debbi had created the agency, Newton approached Amber about joining the team. She was one of the most attractive independents on the website, extremely sexy while at the same time projecting an air of youth and vulnerability, and Debbi was convinced that, if handled properly, Amber could be a serious earner.

Newton spoke to Amber, calling the number that she'd listed on the website. He promised that by pooling their efforts, Amber could make a lot more money and probably take fewer dates in the process. In addition, Newton and Debbi would relieve Amber of virtually all of the drudge work involved in meeting clients, checking references, and the like. Amber had listened politely before declining the offer, insisting that she was perfectly happy with her career just as it was. But if she ever changed her mind, she promised that she would get in touch.

Newton had been in the process of recruiting Candee for the agency's roster, and had hoped that by doing so, he still might have a shot at signing Candee's roommate and occasional playmate. But then, in impossibly short order, Molly McIntyre had appeared on the scene, claiming to be the mother of his number one draft pick, and Candee had managed to get herself killed. Either would have been problem enough, but the two incidents together posed the threat of completely upending Ron Newton's FantacieLand.

When the police came calling in the wake of Candee's murder, Newton told them the truth: The woman had arranged her own dates and he knew nothing of them. He had no way of knowing whether the poor girl had actually been killed by a client or by some sick wacko who had forced his way into her apartment without even knowing her occupation.

When the detective—Richardson—had raised the issue of Candee's roommate, again Newton had told him the honest truth. He showed Richardson the same material he had shown to Molly McIntyre and insisted that he knew nothing more about "Amber." He had always assumed, he said, that the woman's real name was Jennifer Douglas. He had no idea how to contact the girl beyond the information she had provided on the website and in the model's release form, and he had no idea whether, in fact, "Amber" might be Molly McIntyre's long-lost daughter.

When Richardson had asked for a photo of "Amber," Newton denied having one, believing that it would be better for him if the police were unable to find the girl and thinking that he might be able to turn her disappearance to his own advantage.

The detective took careful notes and then left, suggesting that he would doubtless be back with additional questions. Newton insisted plaintively that he would cooperate with the investigation in any way that he could and promised that Richardson would discover that all of Newton's activities were strictly within the letter of the law.

* * *

Newton understood that as long as the case went unresolved, he could expect the police to be poking around in his business, which was something he could ill afford. But it now occurred to him that if he could steer the police in the direction of a plausible suspect who had nothing whatsoever to do with Newton's operations, that would deflect attention away from him, at least for the moment and perhaps even permanently.

In his effort to recruit Candee, Newton had suggested that by joining the agency, Candee could give up her incall apartment and use one provided by the agency. He suggested that would save her a considerable sum in rent and maintenance every month. The girl allowed that such an arrangement would save her a little money, but probably not as much as Newton might have anticipated. She went on to explain that she was paying a part of the rent in trade, occasionally screwing the resident manager who was single and without a steady girlfriend.

Mulling over the possibilities, it struck Newton that the manager might make an excellent diversion. If Newton offered up the manager as a viable suspect in the girl's death, perhaps he could get lucky and deflect the attention of the police away from FantacieLand. That would leave only the problem of Molly McIntyre, and Newton was determined that he would not allow the woman' pathetic search to upset the enterprise he had so carefully constructed.

When McIntyre refused to be deterred by his initial argument, Newton had directed Debbi to phone her, pretending to be "Amber" and telling McIntyre that she was not her daughter and that she would not meet with her. When McIntyre returned to the office and challenged him about the call, he lied and told her that Amber had called him, insisting that her mother was dead. Newton hoped that would be enough to discourage the woman, but when that proved not to be the case, he had reluctantly called Carl Collins.

Collins was the friend of a friend whom Newton had used a year or so ago to discourage a client who had become enamored of one of the agency's girls. The client had convinced himself and was attempting to convince the escort that she should belong to him and to him alone. When the girl made it plain that she had no such interest in such an arrangement, and when the client had refused to take "no" for an answer, Carl had convinced the man that he should.

Newton paid Collins three hundred dollars to lure Molly McIntyre into the parking lot at the strip club and impress upon her the wisdom of giving up her search and returning home immediately. He didn't know if the woman would be smart enough—or scared enough—to take the advice. But pacing the floor of his studio, Newton desperately hoped that she would. He was in no way ready to allow Molly McIntyre to threaten either his livelihood or his freedom, even if it did mean making another call to Carl Collins.

41

If the information in Candee's database could be believed (and Dennis fervently hope that it could), Arthur Walsh was the executive vice president of a Phoenix construction company. In studying the database, Dennis observed that Mr. Walsh had never visited Candee alone. He had only done so in the company of Amber, which suggested to Dennis that most likely Walsh had been Amber's client and that Amber had invited her roommate to join them on a few occasions when Walsh was feeling especially frisky.

Dennis wondered if Amber had kept client records as meticulously as Candee's, and if so, how often Arthur Walsh might have appeared in those records. However, even without knowing that, Dennis figured that the material in Candee's database would be enough to give Walsh a few sleepless nights.

Dennis thought it highly unlikely that the police might be trying to track the dead girl's cell phone signal as a means of finding her killer, but he decided not to take any chances. Shortly after nine o'clock on Sunday morning, he pulled into the parking lot of a Village Inn, which was located near a busy freeway interchange. He found a space away from the restaurant and retrieved Candee's phone from his briefcase. For safety's sake, he had removed the battery and SIM card from the phone. He now installed them again, turned on the phone and punched in the number of Walsh's cell phone, which he had copied onto a piece of scratch paper.

Holding Candee's phone, and thinking back to the events of Tuesday night, Dennis shivered slightly as a brief echo of the sensations that had gripped him that evening reverberated through his central nervous system. He squeezed his eyes shut for an instant and then a man with a deep baritone voice interrupted his reverie with a gruff, "Hello?"

Snapping back into the moment, Dennis said, "Good morning, Mr. Walsh. I only have a few moments here, so please listen carefully to what I have to say, and don't interrupt."

"What the hell?" the other man asked.

Ignoring the question, Dennis continued. "Four months ago, you paid eight hundred dollars for two hours of fun and games with your friend Amber and her girlfriend Candee at the girls' incall apartment. You paid another eight hundred for a repeat performance two months later, and last month you paid nine hundred for a session that ran two and a half hours."

"Who the hell is this?"

"I said no interruptions! Now listen to me very carefully. I don't give a shit who you fuck, but I do need to see your girlfriend, Amber, and I need you to help me find her. She's not responding to the phone number she listed in her ad, but I'm figuring that you know her well enough to know her real name and that you have some other way of contacting her. You need to give me that information."

In a distinctly lower and more threatening voice, Walsh said, "Listen, pal. I don't know who the hell you are or what the fuck you think you're doing here, but I have no idea what you're talking about. I don't know anybody by those names; I sure as hell haven't been paying anybody for sex, and I have no idea how to get in touch with this Amber person."

Dennis chuckled, "Well, that's too bad, because they certainly know you. And Candee kept very detailed records that I now have in my possession, including dates, times, the amounts that you paid, and the things that you asked them to do.

"In one hour, I'm going to call you back on this phone, and you're going to tell me how to find Amber. Once you do, you're off the hook. But if you don't, I'll be calling Mrs. Walsh and telling her that she should expect to receive a photocopy of the relevant entries from Candee's database. I'll be sending the same information to the president of your company."

"Now wait just a fucking minute!"

"One hour," Dennis said. Then he turned off the cell phone and again removed the battery and SIM card. That done, he started the car, drove carefully out of the parking lot, and merged into the traffic heading toward the freeway entrance ramp.

* * *

Exactly an hour later, Dennis parked again, this time in the lot of a large shopping mall. Leaving the engine and the air conditioner running, he turned on Candee's cell phone and punched in Walsh's number. Walsh answered on the second ring, his greeting much more tentative than it had been sixty minutes earlier.

"Well," Dennis said, "I'm waiting. How do I find Amber?"

"Listen, you son of a bitch," the man said, again in a low voice. "I have no idea how to find her. I only ever used the phone number that she listed in her ad. If she's not answering her phone, I don't know what to tell you."

"Well, I guess that's just too bad for you. Maybe you should give your wife and your boss a head's up to let them know what's coming."

"But what the hell does that accomplish? I can't tell you something I don't know. There's no point in fucking me over. What do you want with her anyhow?"

"That's no concern of yours, Walsh. The only thing you need to know is that I want to find her and if you don't help me do it, you're going to find yourself in deep shit."

"Then you have to give me more time ... please."

"Time for what?"

"I'm not shitting you. I don't know how to get a hold of Amber other than the phone number that she listed on the ad and the email address that she gave me. But I know somebody who might."

"Who's that?"

"A guy I know who's been seeing her for the last couple of years. He's the one who set me up with her in the first place. He's probably the most regular client that she has, and if anybody knows how to find her, it would be him. I'll call him and see what I can find out, but he doesn't keep a regular schedule and I don't know how soon I'll be able to talk to him."

"Okay. You've got ten hours. Be ready to answer the phone at eight o'clock tonight and tell me what I need to know. Otherwise, the photocopies of Candee's database go into the mail first thing in the morning."

42

After yet another night of very little sleep, Molly dragged herself out of bed shortly after eight o'clock on Sunday morning. She used the bathroom and then, still dressed in the tee shirt and pajama bottoms she had worn to bed, she booted her computer and logged on to FantacieLand.com. She really didn't expect that Jenny would have posted her ad on the site again, and so wasn't all that disappointed when she failed to find it. But she would keep on checking the website periodically, just in case.

She left the website and turned on her cell phone. The device powered up and spent a few seconds searching for a signal. Molly was halfway across the room, headed in the direction of the shower, when the phone beeped at her. Returning to the desk, Molly picked up the phone to discover that someone had sent her a text message at six thirty-two in the morning. She pressed the key to retrieve the message and read:

when i was 12 i tripped in the driveway and sprained my ankle. melinda took me to hospital. now go away & leave me the hell alone!!!

Stunned, Molly stared at the screen for nearly a full minute.

The accident had happened on a Thursday afternoon while she and Alan were both at work. Jenny had come home from school, anxious to get into the house for some reason that Molly could not now recall. She was running up the driveway when she caught her heel on a section of the drive that had heaved up a couple of inches during the spring thaw. Jenny had gone sprawling, scattering her books across the driveway, skinning her arms on the concrete, and badly spraining her ankle.

Crying, Jenny had picked herself up, limped across the lawn and punched the Anderson's doorbell. Melinda made a quick call to Molly, then bundled Jenny into the car and took her to the emergency room.

The X-rays indicated that the ankle was badly sprained but fortunately was not broken, and Molly arrived just as the doctor finished wrapping it. Molly took Jenny home and had spent the next couple of days nursing her until she was back on her feet. And now, ten years after the fact, Molly stared at her cell phone in disbelief as Jenny resurrected the memory of that afternoon to reject her mother for a second time.

This time there could be no mistake. Molly didn't know for sure if the woman who had phoned earlier actually was her daughter, but certainly no one other than Jenny could have been using the incident of the sprained ankle as proof of her identity in an effort to warn Molly away.

Her heart breaking, Molly sat back on the bed and dropped her head into her hands. For a full ten minutes, she wept in despair, crushed by the thought of losing her daughter all over again. Then she took a swipe at the tears with the sleeve of her tee shirt, picked up the cell phone and pressed the sequence of keys that would allow her to identify the caller and respond to the message.

Her spirits sank again as she looked to the phone's screen and read the message, "Caller Unknown." Thoroughly depressed and more frustrated than she had ever been in her life, Molly hurled the phone across the room and watched with a grim sense of satisfaction as it bounced off the wall and settled on the carpet.

Twenty seconds later, the phone began ringing.

Molly bolted from the bed, retrieved the phone and connected to the call, only to find Dennis Anderson on the other end of the line. "Hey, Molly," he said. "I'm finally here and checked into the hotel. Why don't we get together and you can bring me up to date?"

Molly took a moment to collect herself and said, "Good morning, Dennis. Sorry, I just got up a few minutes ago. Have you eaten breakfast yet?"

"No. I just got in and wanted to touch base with you first thing. Would you like to get some breakfast?"

"That would be fine, Dennis. Why don't we meet downstairs in the coffee shop in thirty minutes or so?"

Showered and dressed in a pair of jeans and a polo shirt, Molly walked into the restaurant to find Dennis nursing a cup of coffee and reading the morning paper. He rose from the table and gave Molly a quick hug. "I really appreciate your coming, Denny," she said, "but I'm not sure what good we're going to be able to do at this point."

Dennis motioned in the direction of the chair on the other side of the table. "Well, why don't we sit down, and you can tell me what you've done so far?"

Once they were seated, Molly described the events that had transpired since she and Jason had arrived in Phoenix, culminating with the distressing text message she had received an hour earlier. Dennis shook his head as Molly described how "Amber" had removed her ad from the website so soon after Molly had discovered it, and he expressed his horror at Molly's description of Candee's murder. "The breaks have certainly all been running against you," he said sympathetically. "Are you sure that the guy who runs the website was being completely honest when he said that he had no way of contacting Jenny?"

Molly shrugged. "My sense is that he was telling the truth. I threatened to sue him; I threatened to sic the police on him, and it seemed clear that he didn't want the grief that would result if he didn't level with me. It's possible that he was lying, but I really have no way of knowing, and I also don't have any other leverage that I can use against him. I know that the police have interviewed Newton, and I'm sure that if he did know how to contact Jenny, he would have told them."

Dennis nodded. "That makes sense, certainly. Do you think ..."

Before he could complete the sentence, Molly's cell phone began ringing. She connected to the call and Sean Richardson identified himself and asked if he might drop by the hotel to see her. "Of course, Detective," she replied. "Do you have some news?"

"I do, but I'd prefer to give it to you in person. I can be there in about twenty minutes if that's convenient."

"Yes, certainly Detective. I'll be waiting."

Molly disconnected from the call and explained to Dennis that the detective was coming to see her. Dennis quickly settled the check and the two went back to Molly's room. Molly paced anxiously around the room as the minutes dragged by at a glacial pace until Richardson finally arrived. Molly introduced the detective to Dennis and then she and Richardson took two of the chairs at the table while Dennis sat on the edge of the bed. Getting right to the point, Molly said, "You have some news for me?"

Richardson nodded. "Yes. I wanted to tell you that we've arrested a suspect in the murder of Susan Taylor. I also wanted to tell you that the tip that led us to the suspect came from a woman claiming to be Ms. Taylor's roommate at the apartment where she was killed."

"You've talked to Jenny?"

"No," the detective said. "I'm sorry to disappoint you, but I don't think I did. The woman insists that she is not your daughter. She says that she's from California and has never been anywhere near Minnesota. She also claims that her mother has been dead for years."

Molly shook her head and Dennis said, "Can you tell us the whole story, Detective?"

Richardson shifted in his chair so that he could look from Molly to Dennis. "A woman phoned the department early yesterday afternoon, asking for the detective who was investigating Ms. Taylor's murder. The call was transferred to me and the woman identified herself as Amber, Ms. Taylor's roommate. She told me that she was afraid for her safety and that she had gone into hiding. She said she would not meet me in person, but that she had information about the case.

"She told me that the resident manager at the apartment complex—a guy named Steve Westby—had figured out that Ms. Taylor was using the apartment for prostitution. She said that Westby had been blackmailing Ms. Taylor, forcing her to have sex with him in exchange for him not ratting her out to the owners of the apartment complex and to the authorities. Amber said that after a while Westby became obsessed with Ms. Taylor and insisted that she should not have sex with anyone other than him.

206

"The woman—Amber—claims that Westby struck Ms. Taylor during the course of an argument over the matter and threatened to kill her if she didn't give up her occupation and see him exclusively. She claims that Taylor was terrified of Westby and was planning to give up the apartment in order to get away from him.

"To make a long story short, we brought Westby in and questioned him. We have evidence, principally fingerprints, that puts him in the murdered woman's apartment. Initially he claimed that he was in the apartment for perfectly legitimate reasons in the course of his duties as manager. Under further questioning, he then admitted to having sex with Ms. Taylor, but he insists that the sex was consensual—that she was trading sex for a reduction in the rent.

"We've now interviewed another resident in the complex who says that he saw Westby coming down the stairs from the direction of Ms. Taylor's apartment around ten o'clock the night of the murder. That's about the time the Medical Examiner estimates that Ms. Taylor was killed. The witness can't be certain, but he thought Westby had come out of Ms. Taylor's apartment.

"When we confronted Westby with that, he admitted that he had been in the apartment that night. He claims that he and Ms. Taylor had a date and that when she didn't answer the door, he let himself in and discovered the body. He also admits to making the anonymous 911 call reporting the murder, but he continues to insist that Ms. Taylor was dead when he entered the apartment.

"Obviously, we don't yet have enough evidence to secure a conviction. We're still awaiting the results of DNA and other tests that we hope will bolster the case against Westby, but for the moment at least, we're pretty sure that this is our guy."

Molly nodded. "And you're sure that the woman who called you is actually the woman who shared the apartment?"

"Not a hundred percent. We *are* certain that the woman who called knew Ms. Taylor. She told me some things that only someone reasonably close to her would have known. But we have only her word that she was the woman sharing the place.

"She also described the picture on the website of the woman you thought might be your daughter. She claimed that it was a picture of her, taken by the photographer, Ron Newton, a little over a year ago. She said that Newton had taken the photo of her and Ms. Taylor together a little over eight months ago.

"We've checked with Newton and he confirms the dates. So, I'm afraid we're faced with two unpleasant alternatives here, Ms. McIntyre. Either this woman is not your daughter, which is what she claims, or she is your daughter but refuses to admit it and does not want to see you."

Molly shook her head vigorously. "She *is* my daughter. There's no doubt about that now."

She retrieved the message from her cell phone and handed the phone to Richardson. "There's no one other than Jenny who could have sent that message, Detective."

Richardson nodded and returned the phone to Molly. "But assuming that's the case, she makes it very clear that she doesn't want to see you."

"I understand that, but I still don't know why. And I refuse to accept it until she tells me face-to-face that she wants nothing more to do with me. I assume that you'll keep looking for her?"

Richardson paused a moment then shook his head. "No. I'm sorry, but we won't—not for the time being anyway. I explained to the woman—whoever she is—that if Westby had killed her friend, we would certainly need her testimony in order to convict him. She said she understood that and would come forward before the trial, when she could feel more comfortable. But she refuses to do so now, and we have no way of compelling her to come in. She's not committed any crime that we're aware of—at least not with regard to Ms. Taylor's murder—and so we have no cause to arrest her, even if we were able to identify and find her."

"But," Dennis said, "certainly you could arrest her for prostitution."

"Of course we could, Mr. Anderson. But that would alienate her, and we're not going to jeopardize our case against Westby for something trivial like that. If the evidence against Westby continues to prove out, we'll have plenty of time before we'll need her testimony and we'll hope that well before that she'll surface and we can coax her in."

"We understand. Did you at least trace her phone call?"

"We tried, but we weren't able to do so."

"Well, I'm sorry," Molly said, obviously angered. "But I *don't* understand. You're telling us that you're simply going to drop the search for my daughter?"

"I'm sorry, Ma'am," but as I just explained, we have no reason to pursue her, at least not at the moment."

"Well, I just cannot accept that, Detective Richardson. I know my own daughter. I've seen her picture; I've seen her signature; I've received a text message from her. And I will *not* leave Phoenix until I've had a chance to see her."

Now in a decidedly harder tone of voice, the detective looked directly at Molly. "I'm sorry, Ms. McIntyre, but you don't have a choice in the matter. Even if the woman is your daughter, she's now a material witness in a homicide investigation. We're obviously in a very delicate situation here, and we simply can't afford to have you scaring her off by continuing to try to contact her. I have to ask you not to persist in this search."

Molly shook her head and in a more conciliatory tone Richardson said, "Look, Ms. McIntyre, I can certainly understand how difficult this must be for you. But for the moment at least, our efforts to find and convict the person who murdered Susan Taylor have to take priority over your search for your missing daughter.

"Even you should be able to understand that, Ms. McIntyre. You told me that Ms. Taylor seemed like a nice young woman and that you were horrified by her death. Certainly, you don't want to do something that might jeopardize our ability to convict the man who tortured and murdered her."

A tear dropped out of Molly's eye. "Of course I don't. But I can't abandon my daughter again."

Richardson now rose to his feet and stepped in Molly's direction. "I understand that, and I'm certainly not asking you to abandon her. But if you drive her away, we both lose. If she panics and leaves Phoenix for good, what are the chances that you'll ever see her again? At least this way, if she ultimately comes forward on her own, we'll have a chance to determine once and for all if she is your daughter."

Molly stood quietly. After a few seconds, Richardson asked, "I'm assuming that Jenny's fingerprints are on file from when she disappeared?"

Molly nodded.

"All right, then. I'll contact Minneapolis and have them sent down. We'll compare them to the fingerprints we recovered from Ms. Taylor's apartment, and that should pretty quickly settle the issue of whether Taylor's roommate was your daughter or not. In the meantime though, for both our sakes, please don't spook her into running."

43

With two seconds left on the clock, Steve Ford pulled up just shy of the three-point line and let loose a shot that escaped his fingertips barely an instant ahead of the buzzer signaling the end of the game. With the rest of the capacity crowd in the Footprint Center, Jenny jumped to her feet. Clutching the hand of her date, Matt Stobel, she watched as the ball arced gracefully through the air. It seemed to hang at the peak of the arc for the briefest of moments, as if deliberately tormenting the anxious crowd. Then it dropped through the hoop, touching nothing but net, and giving the Suns a one-point victory over the hated Lakers.

The crowd exploded and the noise in the arena suddenly rose from merely deafening to somewhere in the range of sensory overload. Along with all the other fans, Jenny and Matt remained on their feet, screaming at the top of their lungs, hugging and high fiving everyone within reach.

Twenty minutes later, the stadium was still rocking as they made their way outside into the gathering dusk. Jenny clutched Matt's arm and allowed him to pilot them through the throngs of people clogging the sidewalks around the arena. It took them another ten minutes to finally reach Matt's car in the parking garage, and as he held the door for her, Jenny turned and hugged him close. "Thanks," she said. "I can't tell you how much I needed an evening like that."

Matt, who was a major player in the Valley's real estate business, had been one of "Amber's" first clients, and he remained by far her favorite. At forty-six, he was a genuinely handsome man with a full head of dark brown hair and the deepest blue eyes that Jenny had ever seen. A little over six feet tall, he was in great physical shape at around a hundred and eighty pounds. He'd dressed for the game in a pair of gray slacks that he wore with a crisp white dress shirt over soft black loafers.

Jenny had long ago concluded that Matt was about the last man in Arizona who still had enough pride in himself to dress decently, and this was one of the things that she liked most about him. On one occasion when she had seen him at his home in Paradise Valley, she had insisted that he show her his closet. He did so, even though he seemed somewhat embarrassed by the request, and Jenny was not surprised to find a beautiful and meticulously organized room filled with clothes by Brioni, Armani, and Pal Zileri.

In addition to being a "gentleman" in the best sense of the word, Stobel was also a perfect client. He saw Jenny on a regular basis, at least once every two weeks and occasionally more often than that. He was gentle and considerate and interested only in fairly straightforward sex. He was never crude or rough; he was not interested in acting out kinky fantasies, and he had made it clear from the beginning that he did not expect Jenny to do anything that made her uncomfortable.

Two years past a bitter divorce, Matt was still extremely gun shy with respect to romantic entanglements, and, for the moment at least, he preferred his sexual life to be uncomplicated and free of any emotional overtones. That said, it was obvious that he genuinely liked Jenny and that he enjoyed spending time with her apart from the sex. He sometimes asked her out to dinner or to a ball game, and Jenny happily accepted when Matt occasionally suggested an appointment over a long weekend out of town in some interesting vacation destination.

On a few occasions, Stobel had come to the incall location, and three times he had asked her to come to his home. But generally, he reserved a nice room in one of the Valley's best hotels where both he and Jenny could feel completely comfortable. In and around the sexual play, they almost always enjoyed a nice bottle of wine and good conversation about politics, the arts, and other such topics. Matt was intelligent, very well read, and Jenny enjoyed the discussions and learned a great deal from them.

She'd also come to enjoy the sex.

Jenny's sexual experiences with Brian, her high school boyfriend, had been her first, and perhaps inevitably, they'd been awkward and somewhat embarrassing. Brian too had been a virgin, and as novitiates, they both had a lot to learn. Still, Jenny had been developing a very normal and healthy appreciation for sex right up to the moment when she had discovered the pictures of her mother and Dennis Anderson on that awful night five years earlier.

Jenny had been so repulsed by the images, and by the betrayal that they represented, that in that instant her own sexual development had slammed to a halt. From that moment, every time Jenny experienced a sexual impulse, the image of her mother having sex with Dennis Anderson rose instantly to the forefront of her consciousness, overwhelming and extinguishing any sexual desire that Jenny might have momentarily felt.

After the night she discovered the pictures, Jenny only had sex only one more time before she turned professional. In her first semester at Scottsdale Community College, she'd begun to fill her science requirements by enrolling in Chemistry 101. The instructor had divided the class into teams of four and had given each team an assignment to be completed by the middle of the term.

Jenny had been teamed with a boy named Vincent who was in his third semester at SCC. Vincent was cute and a little shy, but he'd been at the college long enough to know his way around the campus and the college system. And, in addition to doing more than his fair share of work on the assignment they'd been given, Vincent gladly helped Jenny acclimate to the college.

After they'd been working together for three weeks, Vincent screwed up his courage and asked Jenny if she'd like to go to a movie. She accepted and after two more dates, Vincent took her home and she asked him if he'd like to come in for a beer.

She hadn't intended the question to be an invitation to sex, but they wound up sitting on the couch making out, with the beers sitting largely untouched on the table in front of them. Though Jenny remained physically and emotionally unaffected by the activity, Vincent was clearly aroused, and out of curiosity as much as anything else, she allowed the activity to continue right up to the point where Vincent slipped his hand under her sweater, nudged the strap of Jenny's bra off her shoulder, and cupped her naked breast.

At that point, Jenny broke free of Vincent's embrace, pulled his hand from under her sweater, and sat up straight on the couch. Hurt and confused, Vincent asked if he'd done something to offend her.

Jenny assured him that he had done nothing wrong and that the problem lay with her and not with him. But she couldn't explain the problem. Certainly, she was not about to describe for Vincent the images roiling through her mind of her mother screwing the next-door neighbor, and it was clear to Jenny that Vincent remained convinced that her difficulty was with him.

Sitting on the couch, silently cursing both her mother and Dennis Anderson for spoiling such a moment—and for so much else, Jenny held Vincent's hand and attempted to apologize. He insisted that he understood, although clearly, he didn't, and that made Jenny feel even worse. Sitting there, she wondered what difference it would make if she did take Vincent to her bed? Would she experience no physical pleasure at all? And how would she feel emotionally and psychologically during and after the act?

Thinking about it, it struck her that she could not possibly feel any more emotionally bankrupt than she already did, so what was there to lose? Perhaps having sex might even constitute a redemptive act that would exorcise the sexual demons from her psyche and leave her emotionally and psychologically whole once more. The idea, she knew, was scarcely plausible. But then again, what if it did?

Out of the silence that had fallen between them, Jenny reached up, drew Vincent's face down to hers, and gave him a long, soft kiss. Slowly breaking the kiss, she looked up into his eyes and said, "Do you have a condom?"

* * *

Sadly, the act of having sex with Vincent did not magically restore Jenny to sexual health and well-being. Once the two were naked and in Jenny's bed, Vincent had come fairly quickly while Jenny continued to feel nothing either physically or emotionally. A half an hour later, feeling only empty and sad, she gave him a light goodnight kiss and locked her apartment door behind him.

Three days later, Vincent called and asked Jenny for another date. She thanked him and told him that she thought he was a very nice man and that lots of girls would be lucky to have him. But for reasons that she couldn't explain, she said, she was taking a break from dating and did not want to go out with him or with anyone else for the foreseeable future.

After her experience with Vincent, Jenny did not have sex again, or even a close approximation thereof, until her first date with Traci's client, Tim. With Tim, and with all the clients that followed, the sex was purely mechanical, at least on Jenny's part. While her clients clearly enjoyed themselves, Jenny remained detached, going through the physical motions and feigning the reactions that the clients hoped she might experience.

She was not making love. And, as a practical matter, she was not even having sex. The client was having sex, and Jenny was merely facilitating. She imagined herself as a professional woman on the order of a chiropractor, an osteopath, or a physical therapist. She provided an important and valuable service for clients who often had no other recourse. And in her view, the fact that she utilized her sexual organs in her professional capacity, as well as her hands and her brain, rendered the service—and the relief—that she provided, no more demeaning or immoral than the treatments provided by any other honest practitioner.

Matt Stobel had been the third client that Jenny and Traci had seen together during Jenny's initial "training" period. And although Jenny liked Stobel immediately and was grateful for his generosity, she had felt no more for him sexually than she had for any of her other clients. Which was to say, of course, that she felt nothing for him in that way at all.

That had changed, quite unexpectedly, about six months ago. At the height of the summer, with temperatures in Phoenix exceeding one hundred and ten degrees for seven days in a row, Matt had called and asked Jenny if she'd like to escape to Colorado for a long weekend. She readily accepted, and four days later, they flew from Phoenix to Telluride and stepped off the plane into the blessed cool relief of the high mountain air.

They had dinner that night at a small Mexican restaurant, and after a couple of excellent margaritas in the restaurant bar, they walked three blocks back to their hotel through the cool night air, with an infinite galaxy of stars blazing overhead. They undressed slowly and made their way to bed. As often as they had gone to bed together, they were now well practiced in the way that they related and reacted to each other. Jenny knew very well what Matt liked. She knew how to give him the maximum amount of pleasure and was happy to do so. Matt was still a client, certainly, but he was also a friend and Jenny enjoyed making him happy.

With Matt, Jenny no longer had a "routine," and she had long since stopped faking reactions that she didn't feel. He was intelligent enough to know that she was providing a service and nothing more, and he would have been insulted and perhaps even hurt, had she felt compelled to simulate a response that she wasn't honestly experiencing.

Thankfully, Jenny was no longer haunted by the image of her mother and Dennis Anderson in bed together whenever she found herself in a sexual situation. The first few times that she saw clients, with Traci and then by herself, she was so nervous that there was no room in her thought process for anything other than getting through the moment at hand. Then, as she gained experience, her nerves settled somewhat and when seeing clients, she focused intently on her routine and on the clients' reactions and banished any other thoughts from her mind.

As a consequence, when she crawled into bed with Matt that night in Telluride, she fell into his arms without a thought of her mother and Dennis Anderson. With all the time in the world, she and Matt exchanged lingering kisses while gently caressing each other. They spent several minutes playing with each other orally and then, sensing that he was ready, Jenny deftly unrolled a condom onto his penis.

Taking her gently by the shoulders, Matt lay Jenny down on the bed and slowly eased his way into her. Lying beneath him with her eyes looking into his, Jenny began moving in rhythm as Matt's pace gradually intensified. She was thinking of nothing in particular, simply going with the flow and trying to ensure that, especially tonight, his experience would be as pleasurable as possible.

And then, suddenly, as Matt approached his climax, Jenny felt herself reacting. An intense pleasure, the likes of which she had never experienced, suddenly began building and coursing from her center throughout her entire body. Completely unable to control herself, she dug her fingernails into Matt's back—something a competent professional would never have done—and thrust herself up to meet him in a shuddering climax that literally left her breathless.

* * *

In the wake of her first orgasm in five years—and only the third of her life, Jenny apologized to Matt for getting so carried away and for the damage she had inflicted on his back. He responded by smiling gently and telling her that he was very happy if he had finally been able to please her as much as she had always pleased him. The scars on his back, he assured her, were a small price to pay for the privilege.

The shared orgasm deepened their friendship, but it did not alter their professional relationship in any fundamental way. Matt remained a client, and neither he nor Jenny was sufficiently divorced from reality to think that they should ever be anything more to each other than that. Matt continued to see Jenny on a regular basis and occasionally, though not always, she experienced another orgasm which she saw as simply an added bonus to an already enjoyable experience.

She did not, however, suddenly begin to take pleasure from the interactions with her other clients, and she did not feel any strong impulse to jump immediately back into the dating pool. But finally, the potential at least existed. Perhaps at some point, once she had finally graduated from college and left her first profession for her second, she would be able at long last to leave Jenny McIntyre's bitter memories in her wake and forge a lasting, loving, sexual relationship with a player to be designated later. And for that, she was very grateful.

* * *

Following the basketball game that evening, Matt and Jenny picked up Chinese takeout and returned to his home. They were leisurely making their way through the dinner out on the patio, enjoying each other's company and the spectacular view of the city lights sparkling below, when Matt touched her arm. "I didn't want to say anything about this before now," he said, "but something very odd happened this morning."

Jenny arched her eyebrows, inviting him to continue, and he said, "You know, Arthur Walsh, of course."

Jenny shrugged. "Sure I do. You introduced us."

"I know I did. But I got a very strange phone call from him this morning."

Jenny swallowed a bite of Chicken Yaksisoba and set her chopsticks on the plate. "Strange in what way?"

"He told me that he's been trying to get in touch with you over the last couple of days to schedule an appointment. He said that he'd called your phone repeatedly and sent you two or three emails but that he'd gotten no response. He said he was sure that he hadn't done anything that might have upset you or led you to stop taking his calls and that he was concerned about you. Then he asked if I knew your real name and address and if I had another phone number for you so that he could try to contact you that way."

Her heart suddenly racing, Jenny looked across the table, the concern clearly reflected in her face. "What did you tell him?"

Matt set down his chopsticks, reached across the table and laid his hand on her arm. Shaking his head, he said, "Don't worry, Amber. I told him that I didn't know your real name or your address and that the only phone number I've ever had for you is the one that he has."

"What did he say to that?"

"He asked if I'd seen you lately or if I had an upcoming appointment scheduled with you. I wasn't quite sure what he was up to, and there was something in the tone of his voice that bothered me. So, I told him that I hadn't seen you in the last two weeks. I told him that I'd tried to call you a couple of times myself and that I hadn't gotten an answer either."

Jenny swallowed hard and squeezed his hand. "Thank you."

Still touching her arm, Matt looked into Jenny's eyes and said, "Is anything wrong? *Are* you avoiding Arthur?"

Again, Jenny squeezed his hand. She turned away for a moment and when she looked back at Matt a tear rolled slowly down her cheek. She nodded her head and began crying softly. Matt walked around the table, gently drew her up out of the chair and into his arms. Holding her tightly, he said, "What is it, Amber? What's wrong?"

Jenny clung to him for a long moment. Then, as she disengaged a bit, he handed her his handkerchief. Jenny nodded her thanks and Matt led her over to sit down on a couch near the patio wall. He sat with his arm around her as she dried her tears. Kneading the handkerchief in her lap, she said in a soft voice, "You know that I was sharing my incall apartment with another provider?"

"Yes, I know that."

"My roommate—Candee—was murdered in the apartment Tuesday night."

"Oh Jesus, Amber! Murdered by whom?"

Jenny shook her head. "I don't know, and as far as I know, the police haven't arrested anyone yet. Candee ... she was careless. She didn't take the kinds of precautions that a girl in this business needs to take. I'm assuming that she made a date with some asshole that she didn't know, that she didn't ask for references, and that the son of a bitch killed her."

With that, Jenny began crying again and Matt squeezed her close. "I'm so sorry, Honey. I can imagine how scared you must be. What are you going to do?"

Again, she shook her head. "I don't know. Obviously, I'm never going near that incall apartment again, and for the time being, at least,

I'm only seeing clients that I know very well, either in their homes or in hotels."

"Have you talked to the police?"

"No. If I knew anything that would help them find who did it, I would. But I have no idea who she might have been seeing that night, and if I did come forward, I'd only be exposing myself without helping Candee at all."

"You don't think they might find you?"

Jenny sniffled and wiped her nose. "They haven't so far. My name wasn't on the lease—only Candee's was—and so the police have no way of knowing who her roommate was."

"So, what's your problem with Arthur? Certainly, you're not suspicious of him?"

Jenny shook her head.

Looking down into her lap rather than at Matt, she said softly, "No, it isn't that. It's just that ... a few times Arthur asked if he could see me together with a girlfriend, and I brought Candee along. After what happened to her, I just can't bring myself to make a date with a client who used to know her too."

Softly caressing her back, Matt nodded. "I understand that, certainly."

"But there's something I don't understand."

"What's that?"

"Arthur told you that he'd been calling me and that I wasn't returning his calls?"

"Right."

"But he hasn't."

Now looking up into Matt's face, Jenny continued, "I've been watching my phone closely and I have been checking my email. I haven't had a call from Arthur's phone. And I haven't had either a voicemail or an email message from him either."

"Then I don't understand. Why would he call and tell me that? And why would he be asking about your real name and address?"

Jenny shook her head. Looking down again at the handkerchief that lay balled up in her lap, she whispered, "I don't know, Matt. I only know that suddenly I'm scared as hell."

44

Dennis Anderson had met the hooker in Vegas, five years earlier.

He'd come into town a day early for a meeting with a client and checked into the Mirage. At about eleven o'clock that night, he took a break from the tables, sat down at the bar in the Baccarat lounge and ordered a Jack and soda. He'd been sipping at the drink for about five minutes, absent-mindedly watching the action in the casino unfold around him, when the blonde appeared and sat down at the bar, leaving one empty stool between them.

The woman was somewhere in her early thirties, five-four or so, with a trim waist and medium-sized breasts. She was dressed fairly conservatively for Vegas, in an expensive pale silk blouse over a tasteful gray skirt. But she was also sporting a pair of black shoes with fetish heels that screamed sex.

Apparently paying no attention to Dennis, she ordered a ginger ale. The bartender dropped a napkin on the bar in front of her and a minute later returned with the drink. The woman lifted the glass, took a small sip, and carefully set the glass back on the napkin. Only then did she turn to her left and give him the smile. Dennis returned the smile, noting that the girl's eyes seemed slightly dilated, and he wondered if she might be high on something. "Are you in town on business or pleasure?" she asked.

Dennis fluttered his hand. "A little of both. How about you?"

Again, she smiled. "I'm not visiting; I live in Vegas." She offered Dennis her hand and said, "I'm Chrissie."

Dennis took her hand for a moment and then released it. "It's nice to meet you, Chrissie. I'm Ted. So, what do you do here in Vegas?"

"I'm a dancer."

"Are you in one of the shows here in town?"

Shaking her head, the woman leaned over a bit in his direction. In a quiet voice, she said, "No, Honey. I dance privately."

Dennis nodded and closed the distance between them. "And, if I might ask, how much is a dance?"

She gave him a soft smile. "Five hundred dollars an hour. And believe me, Ted, it's worth every last penny."

* * *

It was only as they were walking toward the elevator that Dennis realized how similar in physical appearance the woman was to Molly McIntyre. Her face looked nothing at all like Molly's, but from the neck down, the resemblance was uncanny.

And that's when the idea struck him.

As they walked down the long hallway from the elevator to his room, the girl seemed a bit unsteady on her feet. Perhaps it was just the heels, but Dennis was now even more convinced that she was high. And once she was standing in the room next to him, with the door locked behind them and the five hundred in her hand, she agreed that, for another five hundred, he could take a few pictures of them doing it together.

Dennis pulled the nightstand away from the wall and moved it out into the middle of the room alongside the bed. He set his digital camera on the table, knelt down behind the camera and looked through the view screen at Chrissie who was now lying naked on the bed.

The perspective wasn't quite right, and so he got his briefcase out of the closet, stood it on the table, and then set the camera on the briefcase. Checking again, he saw that the angle of the shot was now much better, and so he set the timer on the camera and let it automatically shoot a picture of Chrissie looking seductively into the lens while she toyed with her right nipple.

Over the next twenty minutes, he posed the girl in a variety of positions, then set the timer on the camera and joined her on the bed. Finally satisfied that he had enough shots to work with, he turned off the camera and went to work on Chrissie for real. Ten minutes later, his eyes tightly shut, and his mind intently focused on a vision of Molly

McIntyre writhing beneath him, he exploded into a mind-blowing orgasm.

* * *

A few nights later, with Melinda long in bed asleep, Dennis closed the door to his study, slipped the memory card from his camera into his computer, and saved his Vegas photos to a new folder. He then spent an hour or so browsing through the digital photographs he had saved to his "My Pictures" folders.

Perhaps three-quarters of the photos he'd taken of Molly McIntyre were saved in a folder labeled "Friends and Neighbors." The rest were stored in the "Family Photos" folder, and were pictures in which Molly, Alan, and Jennifer McIntyre had been posed with members of his own family.

After carefully studying the pictures, he copied about fifteen photos that included Molly to the new folder that he had just created. Over the next two nights, working in Photoshop, Dennis digitally removed the hooker's head from the Vegas photographs and substituted Molly's in its place.

He'd taken fourteen photos of himself posed with the girl, Chrissie. In most of the pictures, his own body obscured at least some portion of hers, which made it that much harder for a person looking at the finished result to realize that Chrissie's body was not an absolutely perfect match for Molly's. Dennis assumed, of course, that no one else would ever see the pictures. But for his own purposes, he wanted nothing to distract even himself from the illusion he was attempting to create.

In the end, he was able to generate four photos in which an existing image of Molly could be digitally manipulated so as to fit seamlessly into one of the photos that he had taken of himself and the girl in his room at the Mirage. His original intent was simply to leave the pictures hidden on his computer where no one else could ever find them. But he was very proud of the job he had done and thus he decided to print out one four-by-six copy of each of the pictures, to see if they looked as good on paper as they did on his computer monitor. Once satisfied that the pictures were as perfect as he could possibly make them, he would destroy the prints.

* * *

If anything, the four prints looked even better than Dennis could have hoped, and he doubted that many professional photographers could have done a better job with the project. He knew that it was insane to keep the prints, even for a brief period of time, but he decided to do so anyhow. His study was off limits to everyone else in the house, including Melinda, Mary Ellen, and Lisa, the cleaning lady. Certainly, the pictures would be safe enough for a while, carefully hidden behind the encyclopedias. And that would allow him the opportunity to enjoy the results of his work at a more intimate level, without all that technology mediating between the images and his imagination.

He'd come home from the club two nights later, angry at Melinda for spending five hundred dollars that afternoon for the shoes she'd worn to dinner. They'd fought about it in the car on the way home, Dennis demanding to know when in the hell she was going to finally demonstrate some self-restraint when it came to spending money on clothes, and Melinda insisting that she wasn't spending any more than most of the other women in their circle of friends.

Once they'd gotten into the house, Dennis had gone directly to his study, claiming that he had an important phone call to make and anxious to spend some quality time, even if only vicariously, with a woman who would have looked sexy as hell no matter the cost of the clothes she might be wearing.

He closed the door, quietly locked it behind him, then walked over to the bookcase and retrieved the envelope in which he had hidden the pictures of himself and "Molly." He sat down in the chair at his desk, opened the envelope, took out the pictures, and suddenly realized that he was holding only three of the four prints he had made.

Dennis carefully lined the pictures up on his desk, making sure that two of the photos had not somehow gotten stuck together. Then he picked up the envelope and checked to be certain that the missing picture was not in it. The panic slowly rising through his system, Dennis turned and looked from the desk back to the bookcase, but the picture was not lying anywhere on the floor.

He knew, rationally, that something had gone terribly wrong. He had looked at the photos just the previous night. He had held all four of the pictures in his hand, and he knew that he had put all four of them back in the envelope at the same time. He had then closed the envelope and hidden it back in its place at the bottom of the bookcase.

The picture had not somehow fallen out of the envelope and landed somewhere among the books, but Dennis looked anyway. And after an hour of going through every drawer in his desk, of searching carefully through the bookcase, of turning over the cushions on the chairs, and of looking under every stick of furniture, Dennis knew what he had known instinctively the moment he had first opened the envelope: Someone had found the pictures.

But who?

Certainly, not Melinda. If so, she would have exploded in fury the instant she saw them. It could not have been the cleaning lady, who was not due again for another two days. And it beggared the imagination to assume that, at six years old, Mary Ellen might have somehow discovered and opened the envelope to find a picture of her father and her "Aunt" Molly, and that she would have taken one of the pictures and then carefully put the others back in their proper place.

Which left Jenny.

In his anger at Melinda and his desire to get into his study, Dennis had paid no attention whatsoever to Jenny when he and Melinda had returned home from the club. He'd simply marched straight down the hall to his study, leaving Melinda to pay the babysitter and to say goodnight for the both of them. Clearly Jenny had said nothing about the picture to Melinda. Was she now next door, showing the photo to her parents?

Dennis walked through the now darkened house into the living room. He parted the curtains and looked across the lawn at the McIntyre's home, but there were no lights showing anywhere in the house. To all appearances, Alan, Molly and Jenny had all gone to bed.

Might Jenny have settled on another plan of action?

Dennis let the curtain fall back into place, then went back up to his study and retrieved the three remaining pictures. In the guest bathroom, he tore the pictures into little pieces and flushed them down the toilet, careful to make sure that every last little piece had disappeared.

He then spent the next hour moving quietly through the house, looking in all the places where the girl might have left the picture for Melinda to find. He was particularly careful in searching the kitchen and Melinda's sewing room. He slipped into Mary Ellen's room, and as the little girl slept softly, Dennis used a small flashlight to look through the room, but he failed to find the picture.

The other possibilities were the master bedroom and Melinda's bathroom. But if Jenny had chosen to leave the picture for Molly to find in one of those rooms, she obviously hadn't left it out in the open or Melinda would have seen it on her way to bed.

The following morning, Dennis waited until Melinda had put on her robe and made her way downstairs to begin making breakfast. Once she had, he closed the door and made a quick search of both the bedroom and Melinda's bathroom. But again, the picture was nowhere in evidence.

On leaving the bedroom to go down to breakfast himself, Dennis had absolutely no idea what Jenny might be planning to do with the picture. But, as a practical matter, he knew that the situation was now out of his control, and all he could do was brace himself for the inevitable explosion.

45

Molly and Dennis both had work to do for their respective employers on Monday morning, and so they agreed to remain in their rooms, get their work out of the way, and then meet for lunch. A little before noon, Dennis knocked on Molly's door. Once in the room, he looked at her and shook his head. Then he reached out and touched her arm. "You look beat," he said.

"I am. I feel like we're just spinning our wheels here. I wish that I could think of something more constructive we could do."

Without removing his hand from her arm, Dennis said, "I know, Molly. And I understand how frustrating this must be for you. But you need to have confidence in the police. Obviously, they have resources that we don't, and certainly they know the situation here much better than we do."

Molly finally broke the contact, moving away and walking over to stand by the window. Looking out at the mountains in the distance rather than at Dennis, she said, "I understand that, and I know you're right. It's just that I feel so helpless, and I'm so scared for Jenny."

"Of course you are—you're her mother. But you won't do her or yourself any good if you run yourself ragged fretting over things that you can't control."

Dennis hesitated for a moment and then, still talking to Molly's back, he said, "Are you really certain that staying here in Phoenix is the best thing to do at this point? I know how desperate you are to see Jenny in person, but she's made it very clear that she has no intention of meeting with you, at least not now."

Molly finally turned back to look at him. "You think I should just give up and abandon her?"

"No, I'm not suggesting that at all. But I thought that Detective Richardson made a couple of very good points. It seems to me that if you stay here and continue to press your search you might run the risk of driving Jenny out of Phoenix for good. She might go to another city, change her name again, and make it impossible for you to ever find her."

"But what other choice do I have?"

"Well, maybe the best thing to do for the moment would be to go back to Minneapolis for a bit. Let the police compare the fingerprints like Richardson suggested, and if it turns out that it was Jenny who was sharing the apartment with the murdered girl, you could wait for the police to establish contact with her. Perhaps they could then convince her to meet with you. Failing that, you could come back once the trial begins and when Jenny appears to testify, you could see her then."

Molly shook her head. "I'm sorry, Denny, but I just don't think I could do that. There's no way I could sit in Minneapolis, biding my time, knowing that Jenny is still here in Phoenix and perhaps still in danger. I'd never be able to focus on anything else; I'd simply go crazy."

Dennis nodded. "I understand, and it was only a suggestion. But we aren't doing Jenny or anyone any good just sitting in this hotel room, getting cabin fever. Why don't we get out of here and try to find a restaurant with a patio, where we can sit outside, have a nice lunch, and get some fresh air? That would help us both feel better and think more clearly."

"Actually, that sounds like an excellent idea. Give me ten minutes to freshen up, and I'll meet you in the lobby."

* * *

Fifteen minutes later, Molly stepped out of the elevator into the lobby and found Dennis in conversation with the hotel concierge. Dennis waved at Molly, wrapped up his conversation, and joined her at the door. As they waited for the parking lot attendant to bring up his rental car, Dennis said, "The concierge says that there are a number of good restaurants with outdoor seating in the Kierland Commons shopping mall on Scottsdale Road. Why don't we drive over there, scope it out, and see if we find a place that looks good?"

The attendant delivered the car and Dennis held the door as Molly got into the passenger's seat. Dennis then walked around, got into car, and slipped it car into gear.

Once heading north away from the hotel, he looked briefly to Molly and said, "I'm afraid that the GPS system crapped out yesterday, so we're going to have to navigate the old-fashioned way. There's a map with the rental agreement in the glove compartment. Would you take a quick look and see if this street goes through all the way through to Greenway?"

Molly nodded and opened the glove compartment where she found a folder containing Dennis's copy of the rental car agreement and a map. She unfolded the map, found the hotel's location, and used her finger to trace along the street they were currently traveling. Nodding again, she said, "You're fine. This street does go through all the way. You can turn right on Greenway, and it should be about a mile from there to Scottsdale Road."

"Great," Dennis said. "Given that we had hardly any breakfast this morning, I'm suddenly feeling famished."

Molly folded the map and slipped it back into the folder. Only as she was putting the folder back into the glove compartment did she notice the date on the front of the folder. She hesitated for a moment, thinking that there had to be a mistake. Then she set the folder back in her lap and again pulled out the map, this time slipping the rental contract out with it. She set the contract on top of the folder in her lap, and as she unfolded the map for the second time, Dennis glanced briefly in her direction. "What's wrong?"

"Oh, nothing," Molly replied, as if dismissing the thought. "I was just trying to get straight in my head how all of the cities in this valley relate to each other geographically."

While Dennis again focused on the traffic around them, Molly made a pretense of studying the relative arrangement of Phoenix, Scottsdale, Glendale, Mesa, Tempe, and the other cities and towns that together comprised the greater metro area. After a couple of minutes, she began folding the map again, and for a brief moment, she used the map to shield her face from Dennis's view as she glanced down at the front page of the rental car contract that was lying on her lap. But there had been no mistake: The date on the contract itself agreed with the date printed on the front of the folder. Dennis had rented the car on March eleventh, not on the fourteenth.

Trying to appear nonchalant, Molly finished folding the map, set it on top of the contract, and then put the map and the contract back into the folder. She returned the folder to the glove compartment and then sat back in her seat, trying to imagine what Dennis Anderson might have been doing in Phoenix for three days while claiming that he had been in Dallas.

* * *

Kierland Commons in no way resembled a traditional shopping mall. It turned out instead to be an upscale shopping, dining, and residential area, laid out along a grid of streets designed to recall the downtown of some small but obviously very prosperous town. Dennis spent several minutes looking for an empty parking place, and Molly noticed a number of high-end clothing, jewelry, and home furnishing stores, as well as several restaurants.

Watching the shoppers strolling in and out of the stores, Molly flashed back to a time when she would have reveled in the idea of losing a day, just enjoying herself in a place like this. She could easily imagine the family vacation that the three of them might have had in Phoenix at this time of year, with Alan playing golf somewhere while she and Jenny shopped or maybe spent the day at a luxurious spa. But the fates had conspired to rip that opportunity, and so many others, away from her, and it appeared that they were now poised to tear from her grasp this one last and totally unexpected chance to be reunited with her daughter.

Finally, as they were driving down Main Street, a woman in an SUV backed out of a parking place directly in front of a restaurant called the Zinc Bistro and Dennis pulled into the spot. A railing separated the outdoor dining area in front of the restaurant from the sidewalk proper, and Molly and Dennis walked up to the hostess station and spent a few minutes looking at the menu that was lying there. Finally, Dennis turned to her and said, "What do you think?"

Molly shrugged. "It looks fine to me, and there are a couple of open tables outside. Maybe we should ask for one while we still have the chance."

As Dennis nodded his agreement, an attractive young hostess returned to the station. Dennis asked for one of the two remaining tables outside, and once they were seated, the hostess left them with menus, promising that their server would be with them shortly.

Twenty minutes later, their lunches were served. Molly, who was clearly depressed, quietly picked at a chicken Caesar salad without actually consuming very much of it, while Dennis ate a hamburger and wondered how he was ever going to get his hands on Jenny before either Molly or the police were able to find her. At the moment, he had only the slimmest hope of doing so, but he was increasingly certain that his life depended on it.

* * *

Five years earlier, when Dennis had first discovered that the picture of him and "Molly" was missing, he'd been prepared for the worst. He assumed, of course, that upon seeing the photo, Molly would be completely baffled. Naturally, she would indignantly insist that she had never gone to bed with Dennis. But would Alan believe his wife, or would he trust instead the "evidence" in front of his eyes?

Whichever the case, Dennis was absolutely certain that upon seeing the picture, Alan McIntyre would come charging across the strip of lawn that separated their two houses and beat him within an inch of his life. For three days and for three virtually sleepless nights, Dennis had waited for the explosion. But surprisingly, nothing happened. And then, late on the fourth night, came the news that Jenny was missing.

Leaving Melinda to stay with Mary Ellen, Dennis had gone next door and stayed with Molly and Alan into the early hours of the next morning, waiting for news of Jenny. But there was no news until the police arrested William Milovich. And in the wake of the arrest, and upon learning of the evidence that the detectives had discovered in

Milovich's room, Dennis concluded, along with everyone else, that poor Jenny had somehow fallen victim to a sexual pervert, and that she would never be seen alive again.

The fact that Milovich would grab the girl so closely on the heels of her discovery of the picture seemed to be one of life's more amazing coincidences, but it did not occur to Dennis that it was anything more than that. He still had no idea what Jenny might have done with the photo, and for the next several weeks, he lived in mortal fear that the Molly or Alan might find it among their daughter's possessions. But then Alan was killed by the police and almost immediately thereafter, Molly sold the house and moved into her new condominium.

Dennis and Melinda had helped Molly pack up the things she was moving to the condo and to dispose of the furniture and other possessions that she was not taking with her. Not surprisingly, Molly had reserved for herself the task of packing up the things in Jenny's room, but through it all, the picture never surfaced.

In the end, Dennis decided that he would never know what Jenny might have been thinking when she took the one photo and left the other three. But he concluded that, whatever her intentions might have been, she had ultimately destroyed the picture sometime in the three days before she had tragically fallen into the hands of William Milovich.

On one level, it bothered Dennis to think that the poor girl had died believing that her mother had betrayed her father in such a fashion. But at the same time, he was very happy to have dodged the bullet. And he rationalized the guilt he felt by reminding himself that poor little Jenny should never have been snooping around in his study in the first place. To discover now, at this late date, that Jenny was still alive was the shock of Dennis's life. And, given his increasingly precarious financial situation, it could not have come at a worse possible time.

Dennis sincerely regretted the fact that he'd had to kill poor Candee. And he regretted even more the fact that he would now have to eliminate either Jenny or her mother as well. In the hope of convincing Molly to give up the search and go home, he had used his disposable cell phone to send Molly the text message purportedly from Jenny. Dennis remembered well the incident of the sprained ankle, and he fervently hoped that invoking that memory would be enough to convince Molly that she was hearing from Jenny herself and that Jenny was rejecting her.

If, as a result, Molly abandoned the field and returned to Minnesota, Dennis was confident that he could return to Phoenix in a couple of weeks and resolve his problem from that end of the equation. But he also understood that should Molly refuse to return to Minneapolis in the very near future, his options were rapidly playing out.

46

Figuring that checkout time would be somewhere around ten o'clock, Ron Newton waited until noon on Monday before calling the hotel using a burner phone. The switchboard operator asked how she might direct his call, and he responded by asking for Ms. Molly McIntyre's room. Fifteen seconds later, the operator returned to the line. "I'm sorry, Sir, but there's no answer. Would you like her voicemail?"

"No, thank you. Ms. McIntyre is still in the hotel, though, right? She hasn't checked out or anything like that?"

"No, Sir. She's still with us."

Newton thanked the woman, hung up the phone, and cursed his luck.

His efforts to deflect the police away from any further investigation of Candee's murder had succeeded brilliantly, at least for the time being. After Debbi had called, pretending to be "Amber" and offering up Steve Westby, the cops had swooped down on the poor mope in no time at all. The morning paper had reported Westby's arrest on suspicion of the murder and indicated further that a witness had seen Westby leaving the apartment at around the time of the killing. Newton had no idea how in the hell that might have happened, but he was grateful for the good fortune, nonetheless.

Thankfully, the paper made no mention of the tip that had led the detectives to Westby in the first place. Sooner or later, Newton realized, the police would have to see "Amber" in person or their case against the manager would almost certainly go up in smoke. For the time being, though, they seemed to be willing to give her some space.

On his instructions, Debbi had told the detective that she was too frightened to come forward in person, at least for the moment. But she promised she would do so soon. Newton hoped that by the time the police realized that was never going to happen, the trail to "Amber" would have gone stone cold.

In the alternative, the cops might actually track down Jennifer Douglas, whoever the hell she really was. Naturally she would deny making the call tipping the police to Westby, and that would muddy the waters thoroughly. But no matter how it played out, Newton felt confident that the attention of the police would now be successfully diverted away from FantacieLand.

That further assumed, of course, that Molly McIntyre could be convinced to drag her sorry ass back to Minnesota and give up the search for her long-lost daughter. But two and a half days after her visit with Carl Collins, the bitch was still stubbornly refusing to leave. And as long as she remained, roiling the water, Newton could not feel safe.

Newton sat at his desk for another three minutes, thinking about the situation. Then, reluctantly, he picked up the phone, and called Carl Collins.

47

Molly and Dennis returned to the hotel and spent the late afternoon and early evening looking at websites where Phoenix-area escorts advertised their services. Molly did not really expect to discover that Jenny had posted a new ad and returned to work, but if there was even the slimmest chance that she had, Molly did not want to miss it.

Reading the ads and looking at the photos left Molly thoroughly depressed. She would still vigorously defend the right of consenting adults to engage privately in whatever form of sexual activity they might choose. But the sheer number of the ads, and the blatant commercialization of what she had always considered to be such a sacred and intimate act, left her shaken and sick at heart.

Still, she read the ads carefully, looking at the photos and reading the women's physical descriptions in the event that Jenny might have returned to work using a name other than Amber. But after going through dozens of ads, neither she nor Dennis found anyone resembling Jenny.

Throughout the afternoon, as they sat opposite each other at the small table in her hotel room, looking at websites on their respective computers, Molly continued trying to puzzle out the reason why Dennis would have rented a car in Phoenix a full three days ago when he claimed to have arrived in the city only yesterday. What had he been doing, and why had he not contacted her immediately upon his arrival? And why had he told Melinda that he was still in Dallas as recently as thirty-six hours ago?

Molly could think of no logical answer to those questions or to any of the others that were now suddenly buzzing through her mind. But she knew instinctively that something was badly amiss. Dennis obviously had a private agenda, and Molly could only assume that it related to her search for Jenny. If Dennis had legitimate business in

Phoenix that demanded his attention before he could come to Molly's assistance, he certainly could have said so. There would have been no reason for him to lie, either to her or to Melinda. Clearly, though, he *had* lied, and Molly realized that she would have to figure out why as quickly as she possibly could.

* * *

A little before eight o'clock that evening, Dennis excused himself, saying that he had to go back to his own room and do some work. Molly thanked him for his help in looking through the ads and told him that she was going to order some dinner from room service and read for a while before going to bed. "I'm really beat," she said. "After I order the dinner, I'm going to call the front desk and tell them that I'm not to be disturbed again until tomorrow morning. Then I'm going to crawl into bed and try to get about ten or eleven hours of uninterrupted sleep."

"That sounds like an excellent idea," Dennis said. "I've probably got a couple of hours of work to get out of the way and then I'm going to do the same thing. Why don't we meet in the coffee shop for breakfast, say around eight thirty?"

"That would be fine, Denny," Molly replied. "Perhaps by then one of us will have had a brilliant idea that we can work on tomorrow."

Dennis gave her a quick hug at the door and then left. Molly locked the door behind him but remained in the room only long enough to grab her purse, along with a scarf that she stuffed into the purse and the valet's ticket for her own rental car.

Molly was now very thankful that Dennis had not seen her car. She had no idea what he might be up to, but if he did leave the hotel rather than remaining in his room to work, she was determined to find out where he might go.

Molly hurried down the hall to the bank of elevators and was grateful when a car appeared within seconds of the time she had pressed the "Down" button. Once down on the ground floor, she walked quickly through the lobby and out to the kiosk at the front of the hotel where the parking valet was stationed. Again, her luck held, and no one was waiting ahead of her. The attendant took her claim check and quickly bought her Nissan rental to the door.

She slipped the car into gear and pulled out into the street. Looking back at the front of the hotel in the rearview mirror, she watched the attendant return to his station. Traffic was light, and after driving half a block down the street, she waited for a truck to pass in the opposite direction. Then she made an illegal U-turn and headed back to the hotel.

Rather than turning left and pulling under the portico where the attendant would take the car, she turned right and found a parking place twenty-five yards away from the portico that would give her a good view of the front of the building. She turned off the engine, killed the headlights, then pulled the scarf from her purse and tied it over her head, concealing her hair. Then she settled in to wait.

* * *

After leaving Molly, Dennis returned to his own room only long enough to pick up his computer and Candee's cell phone. Then he went downstairs and retrieved his rental car from the parking valet. Still determined not to take the slightest chance that the police might be attempting to track Candee's cell phone, he drove a couple of miles to a nearby shopping complex. He parked in front of an OfficeMax store and then used the phone to call Arthur Walsh.

The phone rang three times before Walsh answered and offered a very tentative "Hello?" His tone of voice clearly suggested that this was a call he really didn't want to take. Wasting no time, Dennis said, "Do you have a name and address for me?"

"No, I don't," Walsh said, the level of panic evident in his shaky voice. "I talked to my friend who introduced me to Amber, but he told me that he hadn't seen her himself for the last few weeks. He has no idea what her real name might be or where she lives. He's only seen her in hotels and in the incall apartment that she uses."

Dennis sighed heavily into the phone. "Well, Arthur, I guess that's just too damned bad. Tell Mrs. Walsh that she should be expecting a package in the mail."

"No, wait a minute, goddammit! If I had the information, I'd give it to you. But there's no sense fucking me over when I can't do what you want. I don't know how to get a hold of the girl except for the number in her ad, and neither does my friend. What do you expect me to do?"

Dennis watched as a mall security SUV rolled slowly through the aisle directly in front of him. The rent-a-cop driving the vehicle glanced briefly in Dennis's direction but continued on through the rows of parked cars without stopping.

"What I expected, Arthur, was that you'd appreciate the seriousness of your situation and do a better job for me."

"But I'm telling you that I can't do that. My friend is the only other person I know who uses Amber. He can't tell me something that he doesn't know, and I can't tell you."

"How long has your friend been seeing Amber?"

"I dunno know.... Two years, maybe."

"And what's your friend's name?"

"I can't tell you that."

In an exasperated tone of voice Dennis said, "You can and you will, Arthur. I'm giving you a chance to get off the hook here."

"But only by putting my friend *on* the hook. I can't do that."

"Well," Dennis said slowly, "It's your choice, Arthur. I won't tell your friend where I got his name and number. But if you don't give him up, I'm going to use Candee's client database to fuck you over good."

For several long seconds, only silence came from the other end of the line. Finally, in a voice so quiet that Dennis could barely hear him, Walsh said, "His name is Matt Stobel."

Dennis dug a pen and a scrap of paper out of his shirt pocket and wrote down Stobel's name and phone number. Returning the pen to his pocket, he said, "Okay, Arthur, keep your fingers crossed. If your buddy tells me how to get in touch with Amber, you're off the hook. Otherwise, you're fucked."

Without waiting for the other man to respond, Dennis disconnected. He set the phone into the pocket of the driver's side door then picked up his computer from the passenger's seat and powered it on.

While he waited for the machine to come to life, he carefully surveyed the scene around him. A few people were walking through the parking lot, headed toward their vehicles, and the lot was thinning out as the stores in the complex began to close. But no one was walking near his car, and nobody appeared to be taking any interest in his activities.

A stand-alone building across the parking lot from the OfficeMax housed a small restaurant and bar and as Dennis glanced in that direction, a woman walked tentatively out the door. She stood in front of the building for a moment, perhaps attempting to clear her head, perhaps trying to remember where she might have left her car, or maybe a little of both. Finally, she turned and began walking slowly and very deliberately in Dennis's direction.

She could have been anywhere from thirty-five to fifty, overweight and cheaply dressed—a woman looking like she'd been used hard, with hair that had been cut to require a minimum amount of maintenance. She made her way to a beat-up Chevy three spots down from Dennis and began fumbling through her purse.

The purse finally surrendered a set of keys and the woman unlocked the door. She braced herself against the roof of the car for a couple of seconds, and then settled into the driver's seat. After another minute or so, she finally pulled away, remembering to turn on her headlights only once she was halfway across the parking lot.

Dennis closed his eyes and shook his head, suddenly nine years old again, cowering in his bedroom while his parents raged through another whiskey-fueled battle out in the living room of their dilapidated house in Akron, Ohio.

There'd been very little love lost in what passed for Dennis's childhood home. His parents were both products of lower middle-class families and neither his mother nor his father had possessed either the intelligence or the drive to rise above their humble origins. Their second biggest mistake, they each insisted—often in the presence of their son—was to have ever become involved with each other. Their biggest mistake, they often reminded each other when they believed that Dennis was out of earshot, was conceiving a child out of wedlock, which had bound them to each other and to that child for the rest of their miserable lives.

Dennis's ultimate defense had been to withdraw into a world of his own, a place where no one else mattered and in which his own survival trumped every other concern. Inexplicably, given his home environment, he was a bright child and a very good student. And at an early age he was smart enough to realize that a good education was his only ticket out of the life to which his parents had doomed themselves and, almost certainly, their son as well.

What his parents might have lacked in ambition, Dennis made up for several times over. During his high school career, he wasted no time whatsoever on extra-curricular activities. He did not date and he did not make a single friend of any consequence with whom he might have wasted time, just hanging out. Rather, he focused obsessively on maintaining his grades and on building up the savings he was accumulating by working a series of part-time jobs.

He turned eighteen three days before his high school graduation and four days after that, he packed his few possessions into a rusty old van and said goodbye to Akron, Ohio. He wasted precious little time with fond farewells to his parents, who made virtually no effort to conceal their relief at the departure of a son they had never wanted in the first place and whom they had certainly never understood.

Blessedly on his own at the University of Michigan, Dennis maintained the discipline and the focus that had served him so well in high school. He enrolled in the School of Business where he concentrated on Finance and Marketing. Practical to the core, he fulfilled his basic degree requirements but otherwise steered clear of any course that did not seem directly applicable to his chosen path.

Once securely settled on that path, Dennis allowed himself to let up and enjoy life at least a bit. He began dating occasionally, and early in his senior year he met Melinda Robertson, the daughter of a successful

Minneapolis industrialist who seemed, for any number of reasons, to be an ideal catch. And thus, four years after arriving in Ann Arbor, Dennis left Michigan with an excellent job offer and with a fiancé. Against seemingly impossible odds, he had saved himself, and the bedrock conviction of his still-young life was that no one would ever be allowed to take away from him the success he had earned at such a dear expense.

* * *

The computer beeped, signaling that it was ready to go, and Dennis snapped back into the present. He opened Candee's database, sorted the client list alphabetically and checked for Matt Stobel's name without finding it. He quickly read down the list of names from "Adams, Rick" to "Tillman, Edward." But there was no Matt and no Stobel anywhere on Candee's list, and Dennis reluctantly concluded that Stobel had not been seeing Candee as well as Amber.

He shut down the computer and sat in the car for another couple of minutes, collecting his thoughts. Then he opened Candee's phone again, looked down at the paper in his lap, and dialed Stobel's number. The phone rang twice before a very confident masculine voice answered the call, saying, "This is Matt."

"Mr. Stobel," Dennis said, "you don't know me, but we have a friend in common named Amber."

"Who is this?"

"Who I am is unimportant," Dennis replied. "What's important is our common friend."

In a voice that continued to sound just as confident as his initial greeting, Stobel said, "Well, I'm afraid you're mistaken about that. I don't know anyone by that name."

"Look, Matt," Dennis said in a smooth voice. "We're both men of the world so let's not waste time bullshitting each other. I know Amber; you know Amber, and I need you to put me in touch with her."

"Well, if you and this 'Amber' are such good friends, I don't see why you'd need me. Why don't you just call her yourself?"

"I would and I have. But for some reason, she's refusing to return my calls. I understand that someone told her a story about me that's completely untrue and now she's refusing to see me or return my calls. All I'm looking for is a chance to sit down with her so that we can talk this out and I can correct any misimpressions she might have been given."

"Well, that's your problem pal, not mine. Even if I did know this person, why should I help you?"

"You're right, Matt It *is* my problem, at least for the moment. But if you don't help me, it will become *your* problem. And it'll be a big one, I can promise you."

"And just how do you think that might happen?"

"Well, it strikes me that it would certainly be unfortunate if Mrs. Stobel, not to mention your boss, were to find out about your relationship with Amber. I'm sure that Mrs. Stobel would be particularly unhappy to learn that you've been carrying on with a common prostitute for the last two years."

"Well," Matt said slowly, "*If* that were true, I'm sure that Mrs. Stobel *would* be very upset. But since it isn't, and since you therefore couldn't possibly have any evidence to support such a wild story, why should Mrs. Stobel believe you?"

Dennis chuckled. "I'm sorry to disappoint you, Matt, but in fact I *do* have evidence to support my story. As a matter of fact, I have a very entertaining piece of audio tape that I'm sure the missus would find very intriguing. I'd be happy to mail her a copy if you'd like. Believe me, she'd have no difficulty recognizing your voice, and there'd be no mistaking what you were doing on the tape."

For a few long moments, Dennis heard only silence from the other end of the phone. Then Stobel said, "And what is it you want me to do, exactly?"

"I only want an opportunity to talk to Amber in person so that I can try to straighten out this problem that's apparently developed between us. So, what I want you to do is call her and make an appointment to see her tomorrow. Mid-afternoon would be best.

"I want you to pick a motel somewhere in northeast Phoenix or north Scottsdale. Get over there and register in the morning. I'll call you a little after noon. You can give me the name of the motel and the room number. I'll tell you where to leave the key, and once you do, you'll have done your job. You'll be free and clear with nothing to worry about."

"And what will you do?"

"I'll pick up the key and I'll be waiting for Amber when she comes to keep your appointment. That will give the two of us a chance to get the air cleared between us and then we'll all be happy again."

"But what if she's not available?"

"I'm sure she'll be available for you, Matt, especially when you tell her how anxious you are to see her. And even if she has to break another appointment, I'm sure you'll be able to convince her that she should do it, especially given how much you have on the line here."

Again, there was a long pause at the other end of the line. Finally, Dennis heard Stobel exhale heavily into the phone. "Okay, asshole. You've put me in a position where I really don't have a choice. I'll do the best I can."

"See that you do, and then we can put all of this unpleasantness behind us."

48

Molly had been sitting in her rental car, watching the front door of the hotel, for only about five minutes when she saw Dennis walk out through the doors, carrying his computer under his arm. He presented his claim check to the parking lot attendant who returned with the car almost immediately. Molly watched as Dennis got into the car and pulled out into the street. Only then did she start her car and slip out into the street behind him.

Fortunately, traffic had picked up a bit, and Molly was able to keep one or two cars between herself and Dennis as he drove north up the street. She had a brief moment of panic when Dennis got through an intersection just as the light was changing. But Molly had now been in Phoenix long enough to observe that a good many valley drivers apparently interpreted the yellow caution light simply as an invitation to speed up and shoot through an intersection anytime within a couple of seconds of the time that the light might actually turn red.

Luckily, the driver in front of her did exactly that. Molly sped through the intersection behind him, thankful for the fact that there was no policeman watching, and even more so for the fact that the drivers at the cross street had possessed enough good sense to wait until the road had cleared ahead of them. A few blocks later, Dennis signaled a right turn into a shopping mall. Molly slowed, creating some distance between their two cars, and then turned into the mall behind him.

Dennis's abrupt departure from the hotel had seemed to confirm Molly's suspicion that something was seriously amiss, and following him, she'd been gripping the steering wheel so tightly that the tension had spread all the way into her shoulders and neck. But now, watching him pull into a parking place, it suddenly occurred to her that maybe there was nothing sinister about this trip at all. Perhaps Dennis had returned to his room and suddenly discovered that he was missing something that he needed before he settled down to work. He'd taken his computer with him and he had now parked in front of an OfficeMax store. Was he perhaps looking for a spare battery or some other accessory for the computer?

Molly took a parking place a row behind and several cars down from Dennis. She shut off the engine, killed the headlights, then slumped down behind the steering wheel and watched him. She realized that once Dennis got out of the car, there was nothing that she would be able to do. Hardly anyone else was walking through the parking lot and there was no way that she could follow him through the lot without running the strong risk that he might turn around and see her.

But then, to her surprise, Dennis did not get out of his car at all. Instead, Molly watched him sit there for a moment and then bring his left hand up to his ear and begin talking, obviously having made or received a call on his cell phone.

The call ended after a couple of minutes and again Molly watched Dennis fumble around in his seat without being able to tell what he was doing. But after a few moments, his face was slightly illuminated by what Molly realized must have been the light from the screen of his computer. She watched as Dennis apparently worked on the computer for a few minutes. Then the light disappeared and Dennis leaned over toward the passenger's seat, apparently setting down the computer.

For another few minutes he sat in the car, occasionally looking around him, and Molly wondered if he might be expecting to meet someone. But then his left hand returned to his ear again, and she realized that he was on another call.

This time the conversation lasted for four or five minutes, then Dennis set down the phone again and started his car. Molly waited a few seconds before starting her own and followed Dennis toward the exit that would take him out of the mall. He was about a hundred yards from the exit when the brake lights suddenly flashed and the car came to an abrupt halt as Dennis stopped and looked into his rearview mirror.

Molly was barely thirty feet behind him and there was no other car between them. Ten feet short of Dennis's car, Molly lowered her head, quickly flipped the signal indicating a right turn, and veered down an aisle leading to a Lowe's home improvement store.

In the rearview mirror, she watched Dennis's car, which remained stationary for perhaps thirty seconds. Then, as she pulled into a parking spot in front of the Lowe's, she watched as Dennis backed up a few feet and then pulled into the drive-through lane of an In-N-Out restaurant. As his car disappeared behind the building, Molly backed out of her parking place, drove up the aisle and took a spot with a better view of the burger place.

After a few minutes, Dennis's car appeared at the drive-up window. He passed some money to the person at the window and received his food in exchange. He then pulled into a parking place in front of the restaurant and sat there for several minutes eating his dinner.

Molly watched Dennis get out of the car long enough to deposit his trash in the appropriate container. He then returned to the car and she followed him directly back to the hotel. Molly drove slowly around the block, giving Dennis time to surrender his car to the valet and get back up to his room, then she pulled into the hotel driveway and exchanged her own car for a claim check. In the event that Dennis might have detoured into the hotel bar or something, once Molly walked through the doors, she moved as quickly as she could to the elevators and rode up to her own floor.

49

At twenty after one in the morning, Molly was lying in bed, still tossing and turning, trying to figure out what Dennis Anderson might be up to, when her cell phone began ringing. She snatched the phone from the nightstand and saw that the caller was "unknown." She connected to the call and said, "Hello, this is Molly."

From the other end of the line a female voice said, "I told you to go home and leave it alone! But you just wouldn't listen, would you?"

Molly bolted up to a sitting position. "Jenny? Is that you?"

Now a male voice that she recognized immediately from their encounter in the strip club parking lot laughed into her ear. "I told you to leave it alone too, Mommy. But you didn't listen to me either, did you?"

Molly swung her legs off the bed and dropped them to the floor. With her free hand, she turned on the bedside lamp. Into the phone she said, "Who is this, and where's my daughter?"

Again, the man responded with a harsh laugh. "You don't need to know who I am. As for Jenny, she's standing right here beside me and it's time for the three of us to sit down together and have a little chat."

"Let me speak to her now."

"No, Lady. Not now. But very soon. And only if you do *exactly* what I tell you to do."

Molly hesitated for only a second before saying, "I will."

"Good. Now the first and most important thing you need to do is not to break this connection. You need to keep talking to me from now until the moment the three of us are face-to-face. If you lose the call, you lose your daughter. Forever. Understood?"

"Yes. But what if we get a dropped call?"

"Lose me, lose her. Period. No excuses."

"I understand. But please believe me. I will do exactly as you ask. If something happens to the call, it will not be me. If something does happen, please don't think I'm trying to trick you or anything. Just call me back immediately and reestablish the connection."

"Lady, are you fucking retarded? Don't lose the call! It's all on you. Now get dressed. And keep talking to me while you're doing it."

Molly got up from the bed, stepped to the closet, and pulled a pair of jeans off the hanger. "I'm getting my clothes together," she said, grabbing a pair of tennis shoes from the closet floor.

She moved back toward the bed and carefully set the phone down on the nightstand. Then she pulled the jeans on over the panties she had been wearing in bed. Bending over toward the phone, she said, "I'm almost ready; I'm just putting on my shoes."

Leaving on the tee shirt she had been wearing in bed, she quickly slipped into the tennis shoes, then picked up the phone again. "I'm ready," she said.

"You have a rental car?"

"Yes."

"Describe it."

"It's a white Nissan Sentra. I don't know the plate number."

"Okay, go get the car and keep talking to me while you do. Once you're in the car, I'll tell you where to go."

Molly grabbed her purse and the key card for her room and made her way downstairs, describing her movements into the phone as she did. The lobby was completely deserted, but fortunately someone was staffing the valet booth, even at this hour. The boy set down the magazine he'd been reading and retrieved Molly's Sentra. The phone still at her ear, she handed the valet two dollars and settled in behind the steering wheel. "I'm in the car," she announced into the phone.

"Which hotel are you staying at and what's the address?"

Molly recited the name of the hotel and the cross streets. "Okay," the voice said. "Make your way from the hotel to Scottsdale Road. Once you're there, go north. And until you get there, give me a running commentary on the streets and buildings you're passing."

"I understand. I'm at the street now, waiting for traffic to clear."

Her heart racing, Molly stopped the car for a moment before turning right from the parking lot into the street. Holding her personal cell phone to her left ear, she reached into her purse and fumbled around until she found the phone that her company issued her for business. She turned the instrument on and muted the volume. Then she said into her personal phone, "I'm out in the street and headed toward Scottsdale Road. It should take me five minutes or so to get there."

On the other end of the call, the voice from the strip club said, "Just keep talking, Molly."

Thankfully the streets were relatively empty at this time of night. Molly set the cruise control for five miles under the posted limit. Still holding her personal phone into her left ear, she set the business phone on the console and pressed 911. Then she set the volume to the lowest level, leaned to her right and listened for the response. A moment later, a faint voice said, "Nine-One-One. What is the nature of your emergency?"

With the cruise control commanding the accelerator, Molly brought her knees up under the steering wheel to keep the car on course. With her right hand, she picked up the business phone, carefully placing her thumb over the small speaker. Now talking into both phones, she said, "Where are you taking me?" Then she quickly straightened her right arm, holding the business phone as far away as she could, praying that the man directing her movements would not hear the response from the nine-one-one operator.

Into her left ear, the man said, "You'll know soon enough. Just keep giving me a travelogue."

Molly brought the business phone back closer to her mouth. Into both instruments she said, "I want to know where you're holding my daughter. I want to talk to her so that I know you haven't harmed her."

Again, she moved the business phone away. Into her left ear, the man said, "All in due time, Molly. All in due time."

Molly brought the business phone back closer to her mouth. "Please," she said. "I'll do anything you want. I'll *pay* anything you want. Just please don't hurt her. I'm about to turn north onto Scottsdale Road and I'm coming to you exactly as you want. I'm not going to give you any trouble."

Approaching Scottsdale Road, and figuring that she had risked enough, Molly muted the business phone and set it into the console beside her without disconnecting from the call. Slowing as she reached the intersection, she said a silent prayer that the operator would be alert enough to understand her dilemma, that the police would be able to use the GPS locater from the business phone as well as her running commentary to track her movements, and that they'd be smart enough not to move in until she had reached her destination, wherever that might be.

50

Parked a block and a half up the street from Molly's hotel, Carl Collins
and Debbi Cernack watched the Sentra pause at the exit from the hotel
and wait for a couple of cars to pass. Then the Sentra pulled slowly out
into the street, headed in the direction that would take Molly to
Scottsdale Road. In the passenger's seat of the giant Chevy Suburban,
Debbi turned to Collins and mouthed the words, "Thanks, Carl. We
owe you." Then she slipped out the door, walked back to her own car
and headed home. In the Suburban's rearview mirror, Collins watched
Cernack get into her car, then he pulled out to follow Molly McIntyre
from a discreet distance.

He figured that the woman would be smart enough—and desperate
enough—to follow his instructions to the letter. If she wasn't—if she
headed straight to the cops, for example—Collins would see it in plenty
of time to veer off and regroup. Let McIntyre think that he was drawing
her to his position rather than shadowing her movements from behind
and watching to see how she responded.

Collins enjoyed toying with the woman. His reward from Newton
and Debbi would be sweet, no doubt, both in cash and in prime pussy.
But he found that McIntyre—desperate, alone, and obviously scared
half to death—gave him an entirely different sort of rush.

Newton had been very explicit in his instructions and wanted Molly
only roughed up enough to be scared out of town, but Collins
remembered how it had felt, her trembling and pressed back against
him in the parking lot at the strip club. Just thinking about it made him
hard, and he settled back into the seat, listening to her recite the names
of the streets as she crossed through each intersection, her voice
trembling as she did. And he began to think about improvising a bit,
maybe taking a little extra time and adding a fringe benefit to the job.

* * *

Ten minutes later, Collins was still fantasizing about what he might do with Molly when he glanced in the rearview mirror and saw a police patrol car moving up on his left flank. Collins was shadowing Molly at a steady forty miles per hour in a forty-five MPH zone, so he knew that neither of them should have attracted any attention from the cops. Both he and Molly were in the right-hand lane, and he continued to watch as the patrol car steadily approached in the middle lane on his left.

Collins estimated that the police car was doing somewhere between fifty and fifty-five, and as it drew alongside, he dropped the cell phone away from his left ear and chanced a quick glance toward the middle lane before quickly redirecting his eyes back straight down the road ahead of him.

Two bored-looking cops who didn't even glance in his direction. Probably in hot pursuit of a Krispy Kreme shop.

Collins watched as the car approached and then passed Molly McIntyre's Sentra two blocks ahead. A block after that, the cops turned left on Mayo, and Collins brought the phone back to his mouth.

51

At this hour of the morning, the six-lane expanse of Scottsdale Road was nearly deserted. Streetlights weakly illuminated the roadway, supplemented by the lights of the commercial establishments and office buildings that lined this stretch of the thoroughfare. Molly was intent on reciting the names of the streets she was passing and didn't even notice the police car behind her until it was practically on her left rear fender. Instinctively, she moved to touch the brake, but then she remembered that the cruise control was set for five miles under the speed limit and moved her foot away. As the patrol car pulled even, Molly looked to her left.

A young patrolman was sitting in the passenger's seat. He turned his head just enough to make eye contact with Molly and touched his hand to the brim of his cap. The policeman gave her the slightest of nods, then turned back to look straight ahead as the car pulled away from her. At the next intersection, the patrol car turned left and disappeared down the street.

A few seconds later, Molly announced into the cell phone, "I'm just crossing Mayo Boulevard."

In her left ear, the man said, "You're approaching the 101 Freeway. Move into the left lane and go west on the 101. Once you're on the freeway, stay in the right-hand lane and keep talking to me."

Molly signaled and moved into the left turn lane just as the light turned red ahead of her. She announced that she was stopped at the light and described the cars that she saw around her. When the light turned green, Molly made the left turn, accelerated up the ramp and pulled onto the freeway.

Six hours from now, the traffic would be bumper-to-bumper and barely moving at all. But at this time of the morning, the 101 was pretty much deserted. Molly remained in the right lane as instructed and set the cruise control at sixty—again running five miles per hour below the posted limit.

Her mind racing, Molly focused on the image of the young policeman who had nodded at her a few minutes ago. Was he simply acknowledging her, or was he attempting to signal that the police understood her plight and were on the case? For nearly a full minute she drove silently, letting the situation tumble around in her mind, wondering if she even dared to hope that the police might rescue her and Jenny. Then suddenly the man yelled into her left ear, "Where the fuck are you? Talk to me!"

Startled, Molly snapped back into the moment. "Sorry. I'm a little tired and I was concentrating on my driving. I just passed the exit for Tatum. There's a large shopping mall on my right."

"Yeah, well, if you want to talk to Jenny, you'd better pay attention and keep your fuckin' head in the game."

"I will."

* * *

For the next couple of miles, Molly kept up a running commentary, describing the exits she was passing and the traffic around her, wondering where the man was leading her and how much longer the journey would last. Finally, the man said, "You'll be approaching the Seventh Street exit. Take the exit and go north on Seventh."

A minute later, Molly signaled the right turn and took the exit, braking slightly to disengage the cruise control. At the bottom of the ramp she rolled to a stop and then turned right onto Seventh Street. Into the phone she said, "There's a large apartment complex on my right. I can't see anything to the left. It's completely dark in that direction."

A mile north of the freeway, Molly was stopped by a red light at the intersection with Deer Valley Road. Off to the left, blue runway lights and a tower in the distance marked the location of a small airport. The land to the right was vacant.

Even though there were no cars to be seen in any direction, the stoplight held Molly in place for a full minute before releasing her.

When it finally did, she accelerated through the intersection and at that point, Seventh Street squeezed down from six lanes to four and then immediately to two.

The moon was only a tiny sliver in the night sky and a hundred yards past the intersection, the road was plunged into darkness, illuminated only by the beam cast by Molly's headlights as she drove along the narrow, twisting road. The land to her left appeared to consist of scattered industrial sites; on her right the flat desert gave way to a series of small hills, some of which had towers with blinking red lights on their peaks, apparently to serve as a warning for the aircraft headed to or from the airfield to the west. The land was fenced, and Molly's headlights picked out some small bushes and a few cacti, along with all the litter and other debris that had been trapped against the fence.

Less than two miles to the south, a metropolitan area of four million people was hunkered down for the night. But Molly suddenly found herself out in the middle of nowhere as though she'd somehow been transported to the dark side of the moon, miles from civilization or from any sort of assistance. Into the phone she said, "I'm still driving north on Seventh Street, but I'm seeing only a few scattered lights on my left."

"Before long, you should see a sign for the Central Arizona Project water control plant. It's on your left, and the sign looks like a large tombstone. You'll see the lights of the plant beyond the sign. Start slowing down when you see it. On your right, across from the plant and just before you cross the canal itself, is a gravel road that leads to a gate in the fence that protects the canal. Pull up to the gate, turn off your ignition and your lights, then stay in your car and wait. I'll be watching, and when I'm sure that nobody's followed you, your daughter and I will come out and join you."

"I see the sign," Molly replied.

Her heart sinking, the hopelessness of her situation suddenly settled down around her like a dense heavy fog. She was out in the middle of nowhere, in the middle of the night, under the direction and at the mercy of a vicious man who had assaulted her only three nights earlier.

She was convinced now that the patrolman had not been signaling her and that the police were not tracking her movements. Even if they were, Molly realized that there was no way they could sneak up and monitor the situation that was unfolding. The man who was directing her had obviously selected this spot very carefully, and if he were up on one of the surrounding hills, he would easily be able to see the police approaching and make good his escape.

The CAP plant loomed ahead of her in the darkness, and into the phone Molly announced that she could see it. As she did, her headlights illuminated the gravel road on the right that must lead to the canal. Without signaling the turn, Molly slowed the Sentra and turned onto the road.

To Molly's left, a chain link fence guarded the concrete canal, and about a hundred yards away from Seventh Street, the fence jogged out across the road, enclosing both the canal and the service road from that point on. As the man had predicted, a gate in fence blocked further access to the road. Molly braked to a stop in front of the gate and turned off her headlights and the ignition as instructed. Into the phone she said, "I'm here."

As she did, she realized that her position was completely defenseless. She was effectively pinned in position between the gate ahead of her and anyone who might approach in a vehicle from behind. Assuming that the man who had directed her to this spot would be driving and not walking to meet her, once he arrived and parked behind her, she would be boxed in with nowhere to go.

She now understood that she'd made a stupid, terrible, and possibly fatal mistake, ignoring both the advice of and the promise she had made to Detective Richardson not forty hours earlier. The sound of Jenny's voice on the phone had overridden everything else, and in her desperation to see Jenny, Molly had placed both herself and her daughter in a hopeless situation.

Shaking her head at her own stupidity, Molly reached up with her right hand and switched off the dome light so that it would not come on when the car door was opened. Into the phone, she said, "Where's my daughter?"

In her left ear the man chuckled, "Just hold tight, Molly. Little Jenny will be there in only a couple of minutes."

As soon as he'd completed the sentence, Molly switched the phone to her right hand and placed her thumb over the mouthpiece. With her left hand she gently opened the driver's door. She stepped out of the car and carefully closed the door. Then she removed her thumb from the mouthpiece and said into the phone, "I'm waiting."

"Patience, patience," the voice replied.

Molly stepped up to the gate, which was about six feet high and secured by a heavy chain and paddle lock. The adjoining fence was the same height, and both the fence and the gate were protected by three strands of barbed wire that extended the protective barrier another eighteen inches or so. Molly slipped the phone into the back pocket of her jeans and, stretching as high as she could reach, grabbed the bar at the top of the gate.

She wedged the toe of her right tennis shoe into the chain link about two feet off the ground and pulled herself up. Wasting no time, she slammed the toe of her left shoe into the fence, stepped up another couple of feet and threw her right leg to the top of the gate. Her foot caught the top strand of the barbed wire and pressed it down toward the top of the gate itself. She reached to her left and grabbed the top of the post to which the barbed wire was secured. She held her place for a couple of seconds, then drew a deep breath. Using her hands for leverage off the post, she pushed off her right foot, swung her left leg over the top of the gate and dropped to her feet on the ground. She pulled the phone from her pocket and brought it back to her ear just in time to hear the man say "... to me, dammit!"

"Enough of your goddamn games," Molly thundered into the phone. "I'll talk to you when I see my daughter."

"Give me any more of that attitude, bitch, and the next time you see your precious little Jenny, she'll be lying on a goddamn slab."

As the man completed his threat, Molly saw a set of headlights flash around the curve in the road off to her left. She quickly backed about thirty feet down the gravel road away from the gate and dropped to the ground. The headlights reached the road and turned in her direction. The vehicle rolled to a stop right behind Molly's Sentra and the lights snapped off. Now in the almost total darkness, Molly could barely make out the shape of a huge, dark SUV. From her phone the man's voice said, "Where are you? I told you to wait in the car."

"I'm here," Molly replied. "I decided not to wait in the car. Show me my daughter."

"Not a fuckin' chance until you show yourself first. Step out by the car."

"Not until I see Jenny. When the two of you are standing in front of your truck, then I'll come out."

"You'll come out now, you cunt, or you'll wish to hell you had."

"You lying bastard. You don't even have Jenny, do you?"

"You want to take that chance, Mommy? I meant what I said before."

"I don't believe you. Make all the threats you want, but I'm not coming out until I see my daughter."

"Fuck this," the man said. "We're through playing games."

52

Forty feet ahead of Molly's position, the dome light in the SUV flashed on as the man opened the door. She saw no one else in the vehicle and caught only a brief glimpse of a man who appeared to be tall and stocky. He stepped out of the SUV, slammed the door behind him, and the dome light went out.

From the roadbed, Molly watched as the man approached her Sentra and pulled the door open. A beam of light played over the car's interior and Molly realized that he must be holding a very powerful flashlight.

After a few moments, the car door slammed shut and the light circled the area around the car. Without even needing the phone, Molly heard the man say, "Where in the fuck are you, Molly? Come out now and make it easy on yourself. If you make me come after you, you're really going to regret it."

Without responding, Molly broke the connection and slipped the phone back into her pocket. She could see almost nothing other than the beam of the flashlight as it played over the ground near the car. Then suddenly the man turned and pointed the light straight down the road, pinning Molly in position.

Cursing, the man stepped up to the gate, pointed the flashlight at the lock and chain, and aimed a heavy kick at the lock. For a brief instant Molly could see the man's boot as it slammed into the gate. The gate shuddered violently, and the chain clanked loudly against the silence of the night, but the lock held.

The man jammed the flashlight into his back pocket. Then he reached up, grabbed the top of the gate, threw his foot into the chain link, and attempted to pull himself up and over. But the toe of his boot was apparently too wide to gain any purchase in the chain link, and he slipped to the ground again.

Swearing more profusely now, he stepped back and took a short run at the gate, simultaneously kicking his left foot into the chain link while his arms stretched for the top of the gate. This time the maneuver worked, and he managed to pull himself into an awkward position, lying across the top of the gate and the barbed wire. He hovered there for a couple of seconds, then fell over the gate, landing hard on his butt. As he hit the ground, Molly pulled herself to her feet and began racing as fast as she could, down the road and into the night.

* * *

Carl Collins was beyond furious. It never occurred to him that at the last minute the damned bitch would suddenly decide to stop following orders. And as carefully as he had planned the attack, he never would have dreamed that she'd be able to get over the fence. He'd expected to have her totally boxed in with nowhere to go and completely at his mercy. He'd been looking forward very much to the latter prospect, and now his carefully constructed plan had turned to shit.

Completely pissed, he got to his feet, pulled out the flashlight and hit the switch, but nothing happened. He slammed the fuckin' thing into his left hand a couple of times and hit the switch again. Nothing. Ahead, he could hear the woman's footsteps fading away as she raced down the road ahead of him. Shaking his head, he hurled the flashlight into the night and heard it splash into the canal on his left. The bitch was really going to pay now.

Collins started trotting down the road, straining to hear Molly ahead of him and trying to ignore the fact that his ass hurt like hell from landing so hard on the flashlight. The woman thought she was so fucking clever, but she was still trapped, just as effectively as if she'd stayed in her car like he'd told her to do. To her left was the canal—a concrete ditch, nearly a hundred feet wide with flat walls that sloped down sharply five or six feet to the water, which was in turn about sixteen feet deep. On her right was the chain link fence that protected the canal, six feet high and topped by three strands of taut barbed wire.

Between the canal and the fence was the gravel service road that bordered the canal and that would be blocked by another locked gate less than a mile down the road. Collins laughed grimly to himself. The woman had sealed herself into a goddamn cage; she was just too stupid to know it yet.

A hundred yards down the road, Collins stopped again to listen. An owl hooted somewhere behind him, and ahead he heard the faint footfalls of Molly's tennis shoes slapping against the gravel road. Nodding to himself, he picked up the pursuit again. Half a mile from the gate behind him, the road curved around a bend in the canal and in the darkness ahead of him, Collins saw a CAP service truck parked off on the right side of the road.

Again, he paused to listen, but now heard nothing but silence. He didn't know exactly how far down the road the next gate would block McIntyre's progress, but he did know that he couldn't allow the woman time enough to get over the gate before he reached her. Collins took a deep breath, set his jaw, and began running again, faster now.

He drew abreast of the service truck and was just racing past its left front fender when something slammed into his midsection, throwing him off balance to his left. Collins staggered back, grabbing his abdomen, and turned to see Molly McIntyre clutching a long piece of two-by-four in both hands.

Totally defenseless, he could do nothing watch in amazement and horror as the woman lunged forward and rammed the two-by-four directly into his stomach again. Collins reeled back further and suddenly found himself teetering on the edge of the canal. He threw his hands out and began whirling his arms in a desperate effort to correct his balance. Molly watched his pathetic attempt for only a few brief seconds before slamming the two-by-four at him a third time, driving Carl Collins over the edge and into the canal.

* * *

Molly watched with a grim sense of satisfaction as the man slipped down the concrete bank and splashed into the canal. She heard him thrashing around in the water and make one plaintive cry for help, and then she heard nothing at all.

She pitched the length of two-by-four back to the roadside where she'd found it, then slowly made her way back up the road. It took her two tries to get over the gate in front of her car, and once on the other side, she walked slowly and carefully around the Sentra to the SUV that was parked five feet behind it. Sensing no movement in the vehicle, she tentatively opened the passenger's door and then jumped back. But the SUV was empty. If Jenny had ever been in the vehicle, she wasn't there now, and Molly was no closer to finding her daughter than she'd been five days earlier.

She returned to the Sentra, retrieved the business phone, and noted that there was no signal registering. Even if the police had been trying to track her, they would have lost her somewhere after she'd left the freeway. She turned off the phone and pulled her personal phone from her pocket, noting that she still had a very weak signal on that one. She began to dial 911 and then suddenly stopped.

The man in the canal, whoever the hell he was, had gotten her no closer to Jenny than she'd been before, and bringing the police into it at this point would only serve to complicate matters enormously. Much more important at this point was the question of Dennis Anderson. What was he up to, and was there even the slightest chance that he somehow might lead her to Jenny?

Alone in the dark desert night, Molly stood for several minutes thinking through her options. Then she jammed the cell phone back into her pocket, got back into the Nissan and drove slowly back to the hotel, leaving the police to sort out the abandoned SUV and its missing driver.

53

At eight thirty the next morning, Molly walked into the hotel coffee shop, wearing a light blue polo shirt over a pair of jeans and comfortable black shoes with low heels. She found Dennis, who was also casually dressed, sitting at a table with a cup of coffee and the morning's *Arizona Republic.* He stood, gave her a quick hug and said, "Good morning." Then he pulled out a chair for her and waited until she was seated before returning to his own chair. "How'd you sleep?" he asked.

"Better than I have in ages," Molly said. "In fact, I feel like I'm still asleep. I could use a cup of that coffee myself."

No sooner had she spoken the words than a waitress materialized with a pot of fresh coffee. Grateful for the caffeine, Molly savored the first sip. "So, did you get all of your work done last night?"

"Yes, happily. That's the good news."

"And the bad?" Molly asked.

Dennis shook his head. "I hate to do this to you, but it looks like I'm going to have to spend the bulk of the afternoon working. I have a client who retired to Scottsdale from Minneapolis, and he called the office yesterday looking for me. My secretary foolishly told him that I was here in Phoenix, and so now the old coot wants a face-to-face. He's one of my bigger clients, and I really couldn't say no. I told him that I'd meet him for lunch but hopefully I'll be able to get away from him by the middle of the afternoon. Then I can come back here and join you."

Molly swallowed another sip of her coffee and said, "Well, don't worry about it, Denny. I'm not sure what we might do at this point anyhow, except to wait and hope that the police are able to find Jenny for us. And, as it happens, I'm probably going to spend most of the day working myself. I have a number of calls to make and emails to answer. I've got several reports to review, and I promised Jason that I'd participate in a conference call this afternoon. So even if you didn't have a commitment, you'd be on your own for much of the day anyhow."

Dennis nodded. "Okay," he said. "But I'll get back as quickly as possible this afternoon so that if there is any news, or if you think of anything constructive that we might do, I'll be there for you."

They finished breakfast and walked together back to the lobby. Dennis said, "Unless you want to spend some time looking at websites again, I think I'll go back up to my room and get ready for my client meeting."

"No, that's fine, Denny. I don't think there's anything to be gained by looking at more ads, at least not this soon. I'm going to go up and do some work myself, so why don't we just plan to get together this afternoon? You can call me when you get back from your meeting."

"Okay. And again, I'll try to get back as quickly as I can."

Molly told Dennis that she was going to detour into the hotel gift shop for a moment before going back up to her room and watched as he walked off toward the elevators. Once he stepped into an elevator, she hurried into the shop where she spent thirty-seven dollars for a cowboy hat with a wide purple band that she'd noticed in the window, and another eighty-nine dollars for a dark blue lightweight sweater.

The clerk happily cut the tags off the sweater, and Molly made a quick stop in the restroom just off the hotel lobby to use the facilities. She put the sweater on over her polo shirt and used the restroom mirror to pat her hair back in order. Then she went out to the valet stand and asked for her car.

When the Nissan appeared, Molly tipped the attendant and then repeated her maneuver of the previous evening, again parking where she could have a clear view of the hotel's front doors. Then she put on the cowboy hat and pulled it low down over her forehead, tucking her hair neatly under. It was possible, Molly realized, that she might sit in the car for the entire morning only to watch Dennis emerge at noon and go to a lunch meeting with his elderly client. But every instinct in her body screamed otherwise.

She had no idea what Dennis might have been doing last night, but she could think of no earthly reason why he should drive four miles round trip simply to make and/or receive two phone calls and spend a few minutes working on his computer. Certainly, he could have done both without leaving his hotel room.

The sudden "client meeting" also seemed more than a little odd. Dennis had said nothing about any such meeting until breakfast this morning. For that matter, he had never even mentioned the fact that he had a client living in the Phoenix area. Perhaps all of his behavior was innocent and could be easily explained. But ever since she'd noticed the date on Dennis's rental car contract, Molly's senses had been on high alert, and she was convinced that something was seriously out of whack.

* * *

About five minutes after noon, Dennis retrieved his car from the attendant and drove back to the shopping complex. Again, he parked in front of the OfficeMax store and called Matt Stobel on Candee's cell phone. Stobel answered in the middle of the third ring, saying "Hello" in a distinctly flat voice.

"Did you make the appointment like I told you?" Dennis asked.

"Yes, I did," Stobel said. "But before I tell you when and where, you need to tell me exactly what you plan to do when you see Amber."

Dennis watched an attractive young blonde struggle out of the Office Max, carrying a large box in the direction of a small Mini Cooper. Into the phone, he said, "Look, Matt. You're really not in a position to be making any demands here, but you can rest assured that nothing's going to happen to Amber. I only want a chance to talk to her and clear the air. Now when and where is the appointment?"

"It's at three o'clock in room 227 of the Watermark Hotel on Scottsdale Road."

"You have the key card?"

"Of course."

"Okay, then, here's what you do. You know the Promenade shopping mall at the corner of Scottsdale Road and Frank Lloyd Wright?"

"Yes."

"About halfway through the mall from east to west, there's an In-N-Out burger place just south of Frank Lloyd Wright. I want you to go there and order lunch. Once you've got your burger, eat it outside, sitting at one of the tables on the east side of the building.

"When you've finished, deposit your trash in the container by the front door and put the little red tray they give you on top of the stack above the trash container. As you do, slip the key card under your tray so that it's sandwiched between your tray and the one beneath it. Then get in your car immediately and drive away. Don't spend any time whatsoever waiting to see who might pick up the key card. Do you understand?"

"Yes."

"How long will it take you to get there?"

"Thirty minutes. Forty, maybe, depending on traffic."

"Okay, tell me what you're wearing this morning."

"A pair of gray dress slacks, a white shirt and a red tie."

Dennis chuckled into the phone. "Well, Matt, you might be a tad overdressed for the In-N-Out, but I'll be watching for you. And again, don't do anything cute. Just follow instructions and you'll be off the hook."

"Right," Stobel replied, disconnecting before Dennis could say anything more.

* * *

Dennis set the phone on the seat beside him, started the car, and drove directly through the shopping complex to the restaurant. He found a parking spot in the second row back from the building with a good view of the front of the store. Several people were eating lunch at the tables outside, taking advantage of a lovely day with clear blue skies and temperatures in the seventies.

It suddenly occurred to Dennis that he hadn't given Stobel alternate instructions in case there was no open table when he came outside to eat his lunch. But he figured that the guy was bright enough to realize that the whole object of the exercise was to see that the key card was left in the right spot and that he'd figure out how to get it there.

Dennis locked the rental car behind him, walked into the restaurant and made a quick stop in the rest room. Then he stood in line and ordered a burger, fries, and a Coke.

It was now half past noon, and the place was jammed with a crowd of people, some of whom were eating their lunches and others who were waiting to be served. Outside of the building, a long line of cars snaked from the drive-up window around the back of the store and well out into the mall parking lot. Dennis took his drink cup to the self-serve dispenser, poured himself a Diet Coke, and stood off to the side, waiting for his order to be filled.

Ten minutes later, he was back in his car, eating his lunch with the tray balanced in his lap. He finished the fries and ate about half of the burger. Then he put the unfinished burger on the serving tray, set the tray on the passenger's seat beside him, and slouched down behind the steering wheel, sipping at his Diet Coke and watching for a guy in a white shirt and red tie to go walking through the front door of the restaurant.

Finally, just before one o'clock, a dark gray, late model BMW took a parking spot four places down from Dennis's rental, and Dennis watched as a tall thin man with dark hair got out of the car. The guy wore a white shirt and a red tie over a pair of expensive-looking gray slacks, and he walked directly toward the restaurant with his eyes riveted on the front door ahead of him.

Ten minutes later Mr. Red Tie walked out again, carrying his lunch on a tray. Just as he did, a couple got up from a table almost directly in front of Dennis's car and the man that Dennis assumed to be Matt Stobel took the spot. For a couple of minutes, the guy sat there with his eyes glued to the table. He took two or three bites out of the hamburger he had carried out with him and ate a couple of fries. Then he stood up from the table, carried his tray over to the trash container and dumped what was left of his lunch into the garbage.

Dennis remained in his car, holding the second half of his own burger in one hand and his drink in the other, as if he were just another guy lunching in his car. He watched as Stobel held the red serving tray in his left hand while reaching into his shirt pocket with his right. With his back to Dennis, Stobel apparently took something out of his pocket. He then transferred the tray from his left hand to his right and added the tray to the stack that had already accumulated on top of the trash bin.

Dennis turned his head away and took a bite of the cold hamburger as the man marched back to his BMW and drove out of the lot. Once the car had disappeared from view, Dennis gathered up the detritus of his lunch and walked in a leisurely fashion over to the trashcan. He dumped the contents of his tray into the garbage and set the tray on top of the others in the stack. After doing so, he lifted the tray immediately below his own and removed the key card that was sitting on top of the third tray down. Then he strolled back to his car and drove directly to the Watermark Hotel.

54

Molly had been sitting in the hotel parking lot for a little over two hours when Dennis finally walked through the front doors and retrieved his car from the valet. As he had the previous evening, he drove straight to the shopping center and parked in front of the OfficeMax store.

Molly followed him to the mall and parked her own car one row behind and several spaces to the south of Dennis. Now in the bright sunlight, as opposed to the near darkness of last night, she was able to see clearly as Dennis made a call on his cell phone. The call lasted for a couple of minutes and when it was over, Dennis started his car and pulled away.

Molly followed, giving him a little room, and was surprised to see him drive directly back to the In-N-Out. He parked in the second row facing the building, and Molly found a place two rows behind him and four spaces to the north. As she shifted into "Park" and killed the engine, she watched Dennis get out of the car, lock it behind him, and walk into the restaurant.

About fifteen minutes later, Dennis came back out of the building, carrying a tray of food, which obviously put the lie to his claim that he was having lunch with a client. But what in the world *was* he doing?

Molly watched Dennis eat his lunch at a leisurely pace. She had slipped down as low as she could in the seat of the Nissan, hoping that if for some reason Dennis should turn to look at the scene behind him, he'd see nothing more than a short woman in a cowboy hat and a dark blue sweater. But he kept his attention focused intently on the restaurant in front of him and seemed to have no interest at all in anything that might be happening behind him.

After several minutes, Molly saw Dennis wipe his mouth with a napkin and move as though he were setting the remains of his lunch off to his right. She assumed that, having apparently finished his lunch, he would now leave the restaurant parking lot and move on to his next destination, whatever it might be. But then, as if he had all the time in the world, he continued simply to sit in the car, occasionally taking a sip from a soft drink cup, and watching the scene unfold in front of him.

Molly couldn't imagine what Dennis might be looking at or what he might be waiting for. Looking through her own windshield, she saw nothing more than a good-sized luncheon crowd moving in and out of the busy restaurant. At the tables in front of the building, those customers who could find space were taking advantage of the nice day and eating outside. It seemed that the actual consumption of lunch lasted, on average, about fifteen minutes, and the tables turned over fairly regularly as one party finished its lunch and vacated a table which was then immediately taken by another group.

At long last, Dennis finally got out of his car and took the refuse from his lunch over to the garbage can near the front door of the restaurant. Molly watched as he dumped his trash and then set his service tray on top of the stack that occupied the rack above the refuse container. He seemed to hesitate, fiddling with the trays for a moment, then he returned to his car, started the engine, and drove out of the parking lot.

* * *

Dennis calculated that the Watermark Hotel was about three miles south of Frank Lloyd Wright on Scottsdale Road. Traffic was not too bad for the middle of the day, and the streetlights generally cooperated. He made good time and pulled into the hotel parking lot about ten minutes after leaving the restaurant.

The Watermark was a square two-story red brick building constructed around a large open space with a swimming pool in the middle. The place could have been anywhere from ten to twenty years old but looked like it had been well maintained. Half of the rooms faced out into the parking area and Dennis was relieved to see that the doors to the rooms opened directly to the outside rather than to an interior hallway. The rest of the rooms faced the pool and were accessed by open walkways that led through the building to an interior sidewalk that skirted the pool area.

Room 227 was on the second floor on the north side of the building, facing out to the parking lot. Dennis drove slowly around the building checking the lay of the land, then backed into a parking spot on the north side facing the building, several doors down from the stairs that led up to the second level.

The day had gotten considerably warmer, and the sun was pouring in through the windows of the rental car. Dennis left the engine running to keep the air conditioner working and sat in the car for several minutes surveying the scene. To his left at the end of the building, an Hispanic maid was working her way along the first floor rooms, and Dennis watched as the woman dumped a load of dirty sheets onto the cart and picked up a fresh set before disappearing back into the room she was currently cleaning.

Otherwise, there wasn't much to see. The parking lot was about half full and, other than the maid, no one was in evidence. Dennis reached into the back seat, found his baseball cap, and pulled it on. Then he killed the engine, stepped out of the car, and popped the trunk lid. He lifted the mat covering the well that housed the spare tire, then fumbled around under the tire for a moment until his fingers found the box cutter he had purchased to replace the knife he had disposed of after dealing with Candee.

He slipped the box cutter into his pocket, closed the trunk, and walked slowly but deliberately toward the stairs that led up to the second level. He climbed the stairs, walked twenty-five feet down the exposed walkway and stood in front of room 227. He listened for a moment and, hearing no sound coming from inside the room, took the key card from his pocket and unlocked the door.

Inside, he found a standard motel room with two double beds and one upholstered chair that didn't look like it would be particularly comfortable. On the wall opposite the beds was a long piece of furniture that had been designed for the room—and for the countless other rooms exactly like it—and which was subdivided into a small desk area, a television stand, and a lower section upon which one might set a suitcase.

Dennis walked across the room and into the bathroom at the back of the room. He pulled the shower curtain aside to make sure that no one might be hiding there, and then, confident of the fact that he was alone in the room, he stepped quickly back across the room to the door, locked the deadbolt, and slipped the security chain into place.

To his left was a door that connected to the next room and Dennis checked to make sure that door was locked as well. He then stepped over to the window next to the door and parted the curtains slightly so that he could look out into the parking lot below. But again, he saw no one moving about outside.

Dennis let the curtain fall back into place and glanced at his watch. It was now one thirty-seven in the afternoon. If his luck held, Jennifer/Amber would step into the room in less than ninety minutes, and all his troubles would be over.

55

Molly had little difficulty trailing Dennis south down Scottsdale Road. There was sufficient traffic so that she could stay one or two cars behind him but not enough traffic to jeopardize her chances of keeping up with him. About ten minutes after leaving the shopping complex, Dennis turned left into a motel parking lot and Molly followed.

Upon entering the lot, Dennis veered to the left, away from the motel office. Molly didn't want to lose him, but she thought that following him directly through the lot would be way too obvious and would surely draw his attention. Not certain what to do, she made a split-second decision and turned right, pulling her Nissan under the canopy in front of the office.

Her pulse racing for fear that she might be losing Dennis, Molly waited for about thirty seconds then pulled forward and followed his route around the north side of the building. She drove slowly, looking at the vehicles parked in the lot around her, the panic rising in her system when she did not see Dennis's car among them. She was just about to turn south around the rear of the building when she looked in the rearview mirror and saw Dennis's blue Toyota pulling around the northwest corner of the motel again.

Molly turned into a parking spot at the far end of the building. She pulled the cowboy hat even lower over her forehead and turned to watch Dennis drive slowly to a point near the middle of the motel and then park facing the building.

The bright sun was now shining directly onto the windows of Dennis's car and Molly could not see what, if anything, he might be doing inside the car. She sat stock-still, slumped down in her own car, hoping that if Dennis should look in her direction, the glare off the windows would prevent him from seeing her as well.

Finally, after perhaps four or five minutes had passed, Molly watched as Dennis got out, walked around to the back of the car, and opened the trunk. He fooled around for a minute or so before putting something into the right-front pocket of his pants and closing the trunk. Then, apparently paying no attention at all to his surroundings, he walked across the parking lot, climbed the stairs to the second level and stopped in front of the door to one of the guest rooms. After a moment, he pulled out a key card, walked into the room, and closed the door behind him.

Molly waited for a couple of minutes, and when Dennis did not reappear, she backed out of her parking spot at the end of the building and took another closer to the stairs and facing the room that Dennis had just entered. She lowered the back windows a bit, in the hope of getting some fresh air into the car, then shut off the engine and settled in to wait.

* * *

At five minutes after three, Molly was still watching the motel room door when a red Ford Mustang pulled into a parking spot directly in front of the stairs leading up to the motel's second level. A few moments later, an attractive young woman with long, dark hair stepped out of the car.

The woman was wearing a pale gray blouse over a skirt and heels and carrying a small purse. The clothes were well cut, conservative and yet very fashionable, and Molly's first impression was that the outfit was fairly expensive. As the young woman reached the front of the car, she turned back for a moment and pressed a button on the key fob in her hand to lock the car remotely. And in that instant, Molly recognized her as Jenny.

For a long moment, Molly sat glued to the seat in her car, paralyzed and unable to move. She watched as Jenny walked confidently up the stairs and knocked on the door of the room that Dennis had entered an hour and fifteen minutes earlier. A moment later, Molly watched as the door to the room opened about halfway. She saw her daughter hesitate for a second and then a man's hand grabbed Jenny by the wrist and

276

jerked her into the room. An instant later, the door slammed shut again.

Her heart pounding, Molly bolted out of her car and sprinted across the asphalt parking lot, leaving the door of the Nissan open behind her. She raced up the stairs, tossing the cowboy hat aside, and a moment later she was beating on the door of the room where Jenny had just disappeared. "Open the goddamned door, Dennis," she yelled. "I'll have the cops on your ass in an instant!"

After a few seconds, someone pulled the door open and Molly dashed into the room. The door slammed shut behind her, and she turned to see Dennis squeezing Jenny tightly against his body and holding a box cutter to her throat. "Shut the fuck up, Molly," he warned. "Another sound out of you and I'll cut her throat, I swear to God."

Tears flooding down her cheeks, Molly instinctively stepped forward, reaching a hand out toward her daughter. "Jenny, honey ..."

"No, no," Dennis said, squeezing Jenny tighter and taking a step back away from Molly. "Just sit on the bed and shut up."

Reluctantly, Molly took three steps back and sat down on the bed as instructed. "Jenny ..." she said again.

Tears were flowing down Jenny's cheeks as well, but she appeared to be more angry than scared. Looking at Molly with sheer hatred in her eyes, Jennifer McIntyre spoke to her mother for the first time in over five years. "So, what's this, Mommy—another one of your fucking games?"

Crying harder now, Molly shook her head in disbelief. "Jenny..."

Jenny jerked her head back in Dennis's direction. "What? You think I don't know that the two of you were screwing each other behind Daddy's back? Did it never occur to you that I might have found out about it and that I ran the hell away from you because of it?"

Afraid to move, Molly remained rooted to the bed. But again she raised her arm, reaching out in Jenny's direction. Shaking her head, she said, "Jenny, my God, what are you saying?"

Through her own tears, Jenny said, "Don't try to deny it. I saw the goddamn pictures!"

"Honey ... what pictures?"

"The pictures of you and this asshole fucking each other. *Those* pictures. Or did you forget that you'd decided to preserve the glorious moment for the permanent record? I loved you with all my heart and then you disgusted me. I've hated you since the moment I saw the pictures, and no matter what happens here, I want you to know that I always will."

Too stunned to respond, Molly sat on the bed, sobbing and shaking her head. Finally, she said, "Jenny, I don't know what you're talking about. Dennis and I? We never ..."

"Bullshit! And to hell with the both of you." Turning her head slightly in Dennis's direction, she said, "I saw you at the incall. You killed Candee, didn't you, you sick bastard?"

"If it means anything," Dennis said, "I really didn't want to. But I needed to get to you, and when you ducked out of our appointment, Candee was all I had left. But she couldn't tell me how to find you, and so I had to do what I had to do."

"Dennis," Molly said, horrified. "What are you saying? What's all this about?"

"Well, it's a long story, five years in the making, you might say. One night when she was babysitting Mary Ellen, poor little Jenny here went snooping around where she didn't belong, and she found some pictures of you and me in bed together. I gather that she was a bit upset about the idea and so, instead of falling into the hands of that slob, William Milovich, she ran away to Phoenix and went into the whoring business."

Totally confused, Molly wiped at her tears. "What in the world are you talking about? What pictures? You and I never went to bed together..."

"Well, you know that, and I know that, but unfortunately for all of us, Jenny here got a different perspective on the matter."

Jenny squirmed slightly against Dennis's embrace. Again she said, "Screw the both of you. I *saw* the pictures! And whatever pathetic game you're playing at now, the two of you can just go straight to hell."

His left arm around Jenny's waist, Denny squeezed her harder to him but lowered the box cutter a few inches away from her throat. "I hate to say it, Honey, but in this case your mother is right. We never went to bed together. I know you found the pictures, and even though you won't believe me, I'm sorry as hell that you did. But that wasn't her in the pictures."

"What—like you think I wouldn't recognize my own mother?"

"Of course you would. But what you actually saw was your mother's face superimposed on the body of another woman. I had a jones for your mother back then, but I wasn't stupid enough to actually make a play for her. So, I paid a woman in your current profession to let me take some pictures of the two of us doing it together. Later I photoshopped the pictures, substituting your mother's face for the hooker's. Then, for whatever reason I will never understand, you went snooping around in my study and found them. If you'd simply spent the evening tending to Mary Ellen as you were being paid to do, none of this would have ever happened."

Jenny shook her head and closed her eyes tightly for a moment, as if to block the unthinkable from burrowing its way into her mind and putting the lie to everything that she'd believed—everything that she had built her life on—for the last five and a half years. Then she opened her eyes again, looked into the face of her mother who was sobbing on the bed in front of her, and realized that the unthinkable was, in fact, true.

Now crying herself again, Jenny looked down at Molly sitting on the bed and said, "Mommy ... I'm so sorry."

With that, Molly could no longer contain herself. She stood from the bed and stepped in Jenny's direction. "No!" Dennis shouted. Then, in a soft but firm voice, he said, "Back on the bed, Molly. Otherwise, I *will* kill her."

Although every fiber of her being resisted, Molly again sat down on the bed. "But why, Dennis? I don't understand. Why are you doing this?"

Dennis sighed heavily, the regret apparent in his voice. "I'm sorry, Molly, I really am. I never wanted any of this to happen. But when you came over to the house and showed me Jenny's picture on the website ... well, for reasons that are just too complicated to explain, I couldn't afford to have Jenny suddenly coming back to life with what appears to be a picture of you and me in bed together. It would destroy me."

"And so you killed that poor girl?"

Dennis shrugged, saying nothing.

"And you were going to kill Jenny too?"

Again, Dennis made no response.

"And what do you think you're going to do now?" Molly asked. "Kill *both* Jenny and me? And do you really imagine that somehow you might get away with it? Are you really that sick?"

"To tell you the truth, I'm not sure what I'm going to do at this point. I don't know how in the world you wound up here, and I wish to hell that you hadn't. But you've really left me without much choice in the matter."

Shaking her head, Molly said, "You'll never get away with it, Denny. The police know that you were helping me look for Jenny. Do you really think that they won't come after you in a heartbeat?"

"They might. But then again, they might not. There's really nothing I can do other than to run the risk."

"Look, I don't care about myself, only Jenny. You said that all of this started because you were obsessed with me. Well, okay, you can have me. I'll do anything that you want. Just let her go. Please, Denny..."

Holding Jenny tighter, Dennis said, "I'm sorry, I really am. But I'm afraid that ship has sailed. I've got no other choice."

"Well, you bastard" Jenny said, "here's something else you'd better consider. Take a real good look at that alarm clock that's staring straight at you from next to the television set over there."

"What about it?"

"It's a nanny cam, and it's recorded everything you've said and done since I walked into this room. When Matt called me last night and told me that someone was trying to blackmail him into making this appointment, I figured it might be you. He agreed to help me, and we came over this morning and set up the camera before he dropped off the key card. He's monitoring the feed in the connecting room and we set it up so that the signal is going to a computer in his house. By now, he will already have called the cops."

Trying to look closely at the clock, Dennis said, "Nice try, Jenny, but I don't believe you."

"Well, believe this, asshole." Nodding in the direction of the connecting door, Jenny said, "If you've already called the cops, Matt, knock twice on the connecting door."

For a moment, nothing happened, and then the lock on the outer door to the room clicked open. Dennis took three steps deeper into the room, dragging Jenny with him as Matt Stobel stepped through the door. Showing Dennis the cell phone in his hand, he said, "Let her go. The cops are on their way. I've given them the plate number on your car and told them you were in the process of assaulting two women. You need to give it up."

"Bullshit." But Dennis was now clearly unsettled and, as if on cue, the faint sound of a wailing siren materialized in the distance, clearly drawing rapidly closer to the motel.

Molly rose to her feet and reached her hand out to Jenny. In a soft voice she said, "It's over, Dennis.... Think of Melinda.... Think about Mary Ellen.... Please don't make this any worse than it already is."

Dennis hesitated a moment, chanced a glance at the door, then looked back to Molly and to Stobel. Still holding Jenny tightly against his own body, he said, "Sit back on the bed, Molly." Nodding at Matt, he said, "Move on into the room and sit on the bed next to her. And be quick about it!"

Stobel nodded, and giving Dennis as much room as he could, he stepped over to the bed and sat down next to Molly. For the longest ten seconds of her life, Molly watched as the two men stared each other down. Then Dennis looked over at her, shook his head sadly and said, "Here, Molly. Take your daughter."

In one fluid motion, Dennis dropped the box cutter away from Jenny's throat and, using his other hand, he shoved the girl in Molly's direction. Then he turned and sprinted for the door as the wail of the police siren died in the parking lot below. As Jenny fell into her mother's arms, Stobel pushed himself up off the bed and ran to the door.

Standing in the doorway, he saw Dennis practically flying down the stairs, still gripping the box cutter in his right hand as two policemen stepped out of a squad car at the base of the stairs. Dennis reached the ground and raised the box cutter. Without hesitating for even a second, he threw himself in the direction of the policeman closest to him as the second officer frantically reached for his weapon.

The sound of the gunshot exploded through the silence of the midafternoon, and Dennis was propelled backward by the force of the bullet that slammed into his chest an instant before he reached the policeman. The box cutter went flying from his hand and Dennis slumped to ground, moments from drawing his last breath.

The patrolman who had fired the shot moved cautiously in Dennis's direction, using both hands to keep his gun trained on the fallen man. Reaching Dennis, he kicked the box cutter further out of reach, then holstered his weapon and called for backup and an ambulance as he waved his partner up the stairs.

Matt Stobel stood immobile at the top of the stairs, showing the palms of his hands to the second officer and assuring him that there was no further threat. The patrolman reached the top of the stairs and instructed Stobel to remain in front of him and to move back toward the open door. Stobel nodded his understanding and moved back along the concrete walkway, continuing to face the patrolman and being careful to keep plenty of distance between them.

His weapon still drawn, the policeman moved slowly along the walkway until he reached the open door of room 227. Finally glancing away from Stobel, the officer turned to look into the room where he saw two women sitting on the bed, sobbing and clinging to each other as if their very lives depended on it.

Epilogue

On a bright sunny morning early in April, Jenny McIntyre stood at the side of her father's grave, holding tightly to her mother's hand. In the distance, gardeners were working to clean up the leaves and other debris that had accumulated over the long winter. It was an unseasonably warm morning, and the promise of spring was in the air. Within a few weeks, the flowers would be starting to bloom.

For ten minutes the two women stood there, each alone with her thoughts. Then Jenny knelt down and laid a bouquet of flowers at the front of her father's headstone. Tears running freely down her cheeks, she said in a soft, choking voice, "I'm so sorry, Daddy."

Unable to control her own tears, Molly drew her daughter to her feet and hugged her tightly. "It was not your fault, Jenny. There is only one person to blame for all of this, and it is not you."

With one arm around her mother's neck Jenny sniffled and used the other hand to swipe at her tears. "You know that I will never believe that. If I hadn't gone poking around in Dennis's study ... If only I'd been smarter ... If only I'd had more faith in you, none of this would have ever happened."

Squeezing Jenny tighter, Molly shook her head. "No, Honey, no. If Dennis hadn't created those horrid pictures, none of this would have ever happened. But once he did, this whole tragedy was set into motion. And the rest of us—me, your father, and you most of all—were caught up in it."

Shaking her head, Jenny turned to look again at her father's grave. "But Daddy ..." she said.

Molly stepped back and cradled her daughter's face in her hands. Looking into Jenny's eyes she said, "Your father loved you, Jenny, more than anything or anyone in the world. And if he could, he'd be the first to agree with me. More important, your father would tell you that you've already punished yourself way beyond anything that you might have deserved for the sin of simply giving in to your natural curiosity. And I know with all my heart that what he would say—that what he would want—would be for you to put this behind you and get on with your life."

Tears shimmering in her eyes, Molly held her daughter tightly. "Your father and I both loved you so much, and we were both always so proud of you. That hasn't changed, and it never will. It's time to put the past behind you, Jenny, and to honor your father's memory by continuing to be the daughter he adored so much."

Molly clung to Jenny, wishing desperately that the moment would never have to end. Then she leaned back a bit and, using her thumbs, tenderly wiped away Jenny's tears.

The two women turned back to look at the gravesite for another long moment. And then Molly McIntyre took her daughter's hand. "Come on, Jenny," she said softly. "It's time to go home."

Acknowledgments

This book has been a long time coming to fruition and I'm grateful to several people who helped to move it across the finish line.

Andrew Gharibian of German Motor Works in Scottsdale offered excellent counsel regarding the mechanics of Molly's classic BMW. Thanks also to Alana Ramirez for her advice and support. I'm especially indebted to Jacque Ben-Zekry, an extremely talented editor, who read the manuscript several times and offered valuable suggestions for its improvement. The opportunity to have worked with Jacque has been one of the great pleasures of my writing career.

Thanks also to the members of the Hard-Boiled Discussion Group at the Poisoned Pen Bookstore in Scottsdale, Arizona; to the members of the West Shore Community Library Book Club in Lakeside, Montana; and to the members of the Crime Fiction Book Club in Tempe, Arizona. The opportunity to meet regularly with these well-read and always-entertaining men and women is a great pleasure and is always a source of inspiration.

Thanks again to Gene Robinson and the team at Moonshine Cove for their efforts with this novel. As always, it was a pleasure working with them.

Again, I'd like to thank the readers who have supported my books, and I'm especially grateful to those who have posted reviews of the books to sites like Amazon, Goodreads and others. On-line reviews, even if they only amount to a couple of sentences or so, are especially important to a book's chances of success, and I'm grateful to those who have taken the time to do so.

And, as always, thanks to my wife Victoria and to my cat, Zane Grey, who, sadly, remains much more popular on social media than I am.

Lightning Source UK Ltd.
Milton Keynes UK
UKHW040629071122
411784UK00003B/213